Éilís Ní Dhuibhne was born in Dublin. She has written plays, collections of short stories and novels, including *The Bray House*, *The Inland Ice*, *Dúnmharú sa Daingean* and *The Dancers Dancing*. She has also written novels for children. She has a doctorate in Folklore and Medieval Literiture from Universily College, Dublin.

She has been the recipient of many awards for her work, including the Stewart Parker Award, The Bisto Book of the Year Award, the Butler Award for Prose, and the Oireachtas Award for a novel in Irish. *The Dancers Dancing* was short-listed for The Orange Prize for Fiction 2000.

GW00401349

Also by Éilís Ní Dhuibhne

Blood and Water
The Bray House
Eating Women is Not Recommended
The Inland Ice
The Dancers Dancing*
Dúnmharú sa Daingean

*(also available in Review)

The Pale Gold of Alaska

and other stories

Éilís Ní Dhuibhne

First published in 2000
by Blackstaff Press, Belfast

First published in this edition in 2001
by REVIEW

An imprint of Headline Book Publishing

10 9 8 7 6 5 4 3 2 1

ISBN 0 7472 7081 3

Typeset by
Letterpart Limited, Reigate, Surrey

Printed and bound in Great Britain by
Clays Ltd, St Ives plc.

Headline Book Publishing
A division of Hodder Headline
338 Euston Road
London NW1 3BH

www.reviewbooks.co.uk
www.hodderheadline.com

The story 'The pale gold of Alaska' was inspired by a line in
Micí Mac Gabhann's
Rotha Mór an tSaoil.

CONTENTS

The pale gold of Alaska   1

The day Elvis Presley died   35

Nomads seek the pavilions of bliss on the slopes
   of middle age   75

Sex in the context of Ireland   93

The makers   115

At Sally Gap   129

The truth about married love   147

Oleander   167

The banana boat   195

THE PALE GOLD OF ALASKA

S oon after her eighteenth birthday, Sophie left Dunegal and went
to America with her sister Sheila. They embarked at the port of
Liverpool, and sailed as steerage passengers on a White Star liner
called *Maid of Erin* to New York. The idea was that they would join
their older sister, Winnie, who had provided the money for their
fares, in Philedelphia as soon as they arrived. They were planning to
get jobs as housemaids. Winnie, who was twelve years older than
Sophie and eight years older than Sheila, had friends in Germantown
where she had been working for six years. She would be able to fix
them up in good situations without difficulty.

The plan was scuppered before the *Maid of Erin* was a hundred
miles west of the Irish coast. On their second night at sea a storm
blew up, whipping the sea into raging mountains and fathomless
valleys: dark, terrifying – above all nauseating. Sheila, whose body
was thick as a ploughman's, succumbed to seasickness, while
delicate Sophie by some miracle remained unscathed. The ship was
full of moaning, tortured people; it was sour with the smell of
vomit, and jagged with the howls of bewildered children. Although
the storm abated after a few hours, and for the rest of the voyage
the ship glided over a buttermilk ocean between silvery blue skies,
the illness lasted nearly as long in Sheila's case. She was not an easy
patient, being both demanding and self-pitying. As often as Sophie
could she abandoned her sister and sought the comfort of the lower
deck to which steerage passengers had access at certain, limited
times.

There, on her third day at sea, she met a weaver called Ned

Burns, one of the few passengers besides herself who had escaped sickness. Lighting his pipe in the shelter of his palm, he had spotted her over the ridge of his broad weaver's hand as she strolled slowly along the narrow gangway; he had smiled and asked her for the time of day. (A quarter past three – they were allowed to walk on the deck between three and four o'clock every afternoon.) By the time Sheila had got her sea legs Ned had shown Sophie how to elude the stewards and walk on deck whenever she felt like it. And by then it was too late to nip the relationship in the bud. Before the *Maid of Erin* had reached its destination, Ned had asked Sophie to marry him.

He was four years older than her, a tall, fair-skinned, curly-haired man, with a boyish face, and a thin mouth which in his case succeeded in looking vulnerable rather than mean. His manner was quiet, and this, coupled with the lips and his surprised-looking eyes, conveyed the impression that he was lacking in self-confidence, or weak. But he was neither of these things, as Sophie discovered very soon after meeting him. His eyes did not evade, but stared steadily into hers, as if pleading with her – for what she was unsure, but she believed she could give it to him, whatever it might be. Also, although he was not talkative in company, when alone with Sophie he had plenty to say, unlike any man or boy she had ever known before. What he said was often very amusing, usually in an acerbic way; he was always willing to be unkind or even cruel if that served his wit. He came from a village in south County Derry.

'Sure they're all like that in Derry,' Sheila had said, when Sophie had offered Ned's sense of humour as an excuse for her engagement to him. Why she had to offer excuses she did not know. But his good looks, his apparently trustworthy personality, would not seem sufficient motivation to Sheila. Probably nothing would.

'Well,' Sophie said as firmly as she could, 'I've said yes.'

'You'd never have got away with this sort of carry-on at home.' Sheila began to cry. Tears of frustration or annoyance, or jealousy or anger, rolled down her face, which was a round potato face, pocked with bumps and shadowy mistakes, not at all like Sophie's. Sophie's face reminded people of a glass of new milk, or a spray of thyme, or other things of that kind, redolent of nature at its most beguiling and benign. 'It's ridiculous, getting married at your age.'

It seemed no more ridiculous to Sophie than going to work as a maid in the house of a complete stranger in a foreign country. She said this, somewhat tactlessly, shouting it over the noise of the engines, which accompanied them all the time on board, a constant roar like that of an infuriated bull. They were watching the New York skyline as they conducted this final, decisive conversation. Night had fallen and some of the buildings of the city were lit, creating spots and pools of light, scattered haphazardly on an inky background like saffron-coloured flowers, flaming orange lilies in the sky.

Sheila paused before replying, to stare at the skyline and to allow her mind to flirt with the exoticism of her present situation.

Soon she would be in America.

'America'. It was a word she had carried in her head for a long time. A word, a dream and a hope, shining in her eyes, encouraging her heart.

But it was not something her mind could encompass, now that the moment of landing was drawing so close. America. The word becoming land and lights and buildings in front of her eyes. Too abruptly it had appeared, in the end, after all the voyaging and imagining. She felt as if she had awoken suddenly from a vivid dream. She tried, briefly, to cling on to it before it vanished completely, before reality rushed in and blotted out the picture she had carried in her head for most of her life. But she was not the sort to linger unnecessarily in the confusing borderlands of consciousness.

Turning her back on the land of the free she gave herself to the sisterly spat. 'At least you'd get paid for it by a complete stranger,' she snapped. The dream was gone already. Petty details rushed into her head to replace what had borne her across the Atlantic on waves of nausea. Now all she could imagine was the lonely time ahead, the interviews with strange foreign rich women, women who might well be impatient and unkind; the days full of new, bewildering work. The shine was dulled, the hope inverted, all the sport drained out of the future by this new turn of events. Loneliness loomed, instead of promise. Everything, even her own body, seemed terrifying. The realisation of her homeliness hit her like a punch in the belly; no man would ever make an impulsive proposal to her. Probably no man would propose to her at all, even after long and careful consideration. No widower or fat old bachelor, no country bumpkin that better women would reject. She would live out her days in the kitchen of a stranger's house, slaving until she died, alone in this new hostile continent.

They were met in Philadelphia by their sister Winnie, who had jobs lined up and waiting for the two of them, for Sheila and Sophie. She was not pleased when she found out that Sophie's plans had changed. Now Sophie was not interested in working as a maid. She was going to be a married woman; she was going to live in a rented room with Ned.

'And how will you pay back your passage, may I ask?' Winnie twisted her long mouth and raised her thick black eyebrows.

'Never you fear, you'll get your money back,' Ned retorted. 'Sophie will be making more dollars than the pair of yez.'

How? wondered Sophie.

She would be working in a textile mill, that was how. It was not the future she had foreseen for herself, when she had agreed to marry Ned. But it would be her destiny, for a while, all the same.

Sophie and Ned got married almost immediately in St Patrick's Chapel. Sheila and Winnie as well as several neighbours from their home in Donegal came to the wedding, and afterwards to a saloon owned by somebody from home. Lynch's was the name of the establishment. Ned drank quite a lot, the day of his wedding, but Sophie, Winnie and Sheila did not drink a thing. There was nothing available in Lynch's Saloon that wasn't alcoholic. They had never touched a drop of any kind of alcoholic drink in Ireland, and they were not about to start now.

Afterwards Ned and Sophie went to live in a room they would

share with two cousins of Ned at the back of a row house in Moyamensing. The men worked in the cloth mills at Southwark where Ned and Sophie had been taken on. Ned drove a loom and she worked in the finishing room, where a machine rolled the interminable lengths of cloth on to giant spools, ready to go out to the shops. Her job was to check the cloth for broken threads, stains, bits of fluff, to remove what could be removed, and to stop the machine if the cloth needed to be cut. She had to keep her eyes on the cloth as it rolled through on the machine, never stopping, all the time. White, black, blue, grey, were the colours that came through, mainly. Occasionally red, green, yellow – the cloth was dyed every colour under the sun, with strong aniline dyes, brilliant colours she had never seen before. (Where she came from, cloth was blackish-brown, cream, or a rust colour obtained from lichens that grew on the rocks.) Sophie liked the colours. She continued to like them all the time she worked in the factory, even when her back was breaking and her eyes were itchy and red from looking at glaring colours for twelve hours at a stretch.

Ned called her 'Síoda na mBó', which means something like 'silken cow', when they were in the alcove that contained their bed, and which was concealed from the main part of the room by an old cream-coloured woollen blanket with faded blue stripes at one end, the end that touched the floor. They had to speak in soft voices there, so the cousins in their bed out in the room would not hear. 'Silky cow, silky little frisky heifer,' he whispered in her ear as they snuggled under the blankets in their corner – it was April, still quite cold, especially inside the damp old house. He pulled her blouse off and buried his face in her breasts. 'Silk blouse, silk skin, silk breast,' he whispered. She stroked his curls, which were not silky at all, but wiry and dry, completely different from her own smooth hair. She half listened to him, pleased at his compliments, if that is what they were. At the same time she got used to them. Soon it was as if they hardly applied to her at all, as if they were just words he said, the way women in Donegal say prayers. The same words over and over again, uttered in a sleepy singsong voice, uttered so often that the speakers do not even know what they are saying.

Maybe that was how Ned had learned to repeat himself, to chant an incantation over and over again? He liked to pray. Before he got into bed he knelt on the floor and buried his head in his hands, chanted five decades of the Rosary. Sophie had to join in although she had always found the Rosary dull and slightly repulsive. She did not like the sight of broad bottoms sticking out in the air above the bowed heads of their owners, the embarrassingly intimate smell of praying people, the monotonous sad sleepiness of their voices as they repeated the pious, superior words over and over and over and over again. Hail Mary full of grace. Fifty times a night. Holy Mary Mother of God. Pray for us sinners. Until she was half-dead from boredom.

Followed, maybe, by silken blouse, silken skin. Silken sinner. Not fifty times. Just as often as he felt like it.

Sophie, accustomed anyway to the admiration of men, took his laudatory litanies as her due. Kisses and words of admiration were what she mainly got from Ned, in bed, and that was not so different from what she had always received from other men, in the street and at dances, outside the chapel on Sunday – admiration, expressed or tacit, but reliable and regular as the Rosary.

Soon, however, she began to learn that there were limits to Ned's admiration.

Ned wanted her to be neat, well-turned-out, pretty. Also he wanted her to work well and be popular at the mill. But it was important that none of this be taken too far. She should be a credit to him, but only up to a point. At first Sophie did not understand what was expected of her. She did not know that she could easily, without knowing it, step out of the field of Ned's admiration and into another area where he would despise her.

For a few months after they were married, he encouraged her, in every way, to do what she was good at: being attractive and sociable, working well. She made friends in the neighbourhood; she worked as conscientiously as she could; and, with her own money, she bought a new outfit for the summer in one of the big stores in town.

She wore this outfit, a tight black skirt, a white high-necked blouse, a small black and red hat, to Mass the first Sunday after buying it. As usual, it was clear to Sophie and to Ned that many people looked at her with pleasure. Kathleen Gallagher, a middle-aged woman who lived around the corner from them, said, 'That girl is the belle of Philadelphia', and her husband, Dan, nodded and said, 'Some folks have all the luck.' Ned stared at Sophie with his wide blue eyes, and said nothing whatsoever. On Sunday evenings they usually went for a walk together with her sisters, but that evening he said he was going to Lynch's.

'Can I come with you?' she asked.

'You wouldn't want to spoil your expensive rig-out,' he said. It was said in a voice she had not heard before, a dry, jealous voice, full of censure. He ate some bread and continued, in a gentler tone, 'Women don't come to Lynch's, anyway. You didn't like it at our wedding.' So now he was joking again. That was something he could do: move from complaining to joking in a few sentences. It was as if he had to complain, express his annoyance or anger or whatever it was that Sophie's success aroused in him, but that he regretted it almost before the words were out of his mouth.

After that, he took to going to the saloon every Sunday night. Sophie continued the custom of meeting Winnie and Sheila, on her own instead of with Ned. In a way it was easier like that and the sisters, who did not seem to like Ned much, certainly preferred it.

'Nothing stirring?' Winnie asked in September, when Sophie had been married for six months. Sophie was still slender and girlish. She had taken to doing her hair in a new style, pinning it up and letting some fair, wispy curls fall down over her forehead and around her small ears, neat as oyster shells. She tossed her head, dislodging a few more wisps, and did not answer the question.

'You'll have to get out of that factory soon,' Sheila said, with some satisfaction. She had become a parlour maid for an old couple in Germantown, and her life was considerably easier and more luxurious than Sophie's. 'You should get a baby for yourself and then Ned would have to find you a proper place to live.'

Two young men whistled after the sisters, saving Sophie the trouble of thinking of a response. Sheila raised her eyebrows disapprovingly at Winnie. Two old maids already, thought Sophie. That is what they were. Buxom, with their dense hair pinned to the backs of their heads in hard black balls, her sisters looked like women whose fate was sealed. Sealed by themselves: they lived in a city that was full of men, men from all over Ireland and Germany and Poland and Italy and other countries, looking desperately for women. But Sheila and Winnie never met any of them, any man at all, it seemed, except for old fellows who did the gardening or worked in the kitchen in their prim-and-proper houses. Men who were as old-maidish as themselves. They had shut themselves away from the world of men, the world Sophie inhabited. And by now they were afraid of them. If a young man whistled, they assumed the next thing was that he would do something unspeakable to them: the thing Sophie did several nights a week with Ned, the thing they could not – it seemed to her – even imagine. They equated that with being strangled or stabbed to death. Pleasure for Sheila and Winnie, Sophie thought, was having a cream waffle and a strong cup of tea in some rich woman's kitchen, their substantial bottoms positioned to catch the heat of the fire. Beyond that their desires did not seem to stretch. Could this be true?

The young men had been whistling at Sophie, of course, it was assumed by all. Sophie was wearing her Sunday rig-out, her belle-of-Philadelphia hat on top of her distracting hairstyle. She walked daintily, proud of herself, happy to flaunt her fine clothes when Ned was not around to put a damper on her tendency to show off.

Not that it was a question of clothes, or demeanour. Men whistled at her all the time, even when she was wearing her old patched factory dress. If Ned was not with her, they whistled. Maybe they whistled at all young women? Maybe it was the custom of the town?

'She's time enough,' Sheila responded on Sophie's behalf. 'Sure she's only a child herself.'

'People will be talking all the same,' Winnie said.

This was the sort of thing Sophie had to put up with. She was so used to listening to her sisters complaining about her that she hardly even heard it. She knew why she was not expecting, but was pleased with the situation. Time enough for all that. Walking along the dry, summer street under the shade trees, dressed in a snow-white blouse, seeing the crowds of people, was all she wanted. She did not want a baby to expand her waistline and limit her freedom. How could she have a baby in that room, anyhow, with nothing but a curtain dividing her bed from the two cousins?

The cousins were both in love with her. Sophie had known this might happen from the minute she heard about the arrangement from Ned, and she knew it would happen the minute she saw the cousins: they were Ned's age, but genuinely shy and awkward, unlike him. One of them had a girlfriend, a little girl with a sharp, pointed face who had come from Tipperary and who was not very good-humoured. She seemed to spend half her time not talking to the cousin, punishing him for various misdemeanours. He accepted this as normal. Chief among his many flaws was that he was in no hurry to get married. Sophie knew that in the end he would have to capitulate. He would marry this girl – her name was Agnes – whom he did not love, who was not beautiful, and who did not seem to like him very much. He would have to, if he did not find a replacement for her. At least he would know what his wife was like, before the wedding.

In the meantime he permitted himself the marginal amusement of being in love with Sophie. The mixed pleasure of this experience was enhanced, and even more confused, by the fact that his brother was also in love with her, and of course by the secret, silent nature of the emotion. It was never mentioned, by anyone. But anyone could sense it in the room, in the looks that the brothers gave to Sophie, lingering tender looks at her back, shy yearning looks at her face, amused looks or desperate looks at one another. It was obvious to Sophie, and she thought it must be so to everybody. She did not take it too seriously. Men and boys had been in love with her before, and had said nothing about it. As long as you said nothing you didn't need to do anything. It never seemed to do them much harm. They did not die of unrequited love, not at all. They got over it, they went away or they became involved with some other woman. In a way she thought they might enjoy it, this secret, silent passion. It gave them something to think about when they were working – digging fields or footing turf, or standing all day at the huge loom, pushing the heavy shuttle to and fro, to and fro.

The rooming arrangement gave rise to plenty of comment in the factory and in the saloon, some of it ribald. People were careful not to pass remarks in Ned's hearing. He had already got a reputation for being belligerent.

But inevitably he heard something. A reference to Sophie's good looks, followed by a reference to Sophie's band of admirers, followed by a reference to Sophie's husbands. 'Sure she's got three husbands to look after her' was the comment. 'That should do her, with her blondie curls and her black hat' was what was said. It was considerably less offensive than remarks that had been going the rounds for months behind Ned's back.

But it turned out that Ned had not had the slightest suspicion of the emotion that filled the high, dark room. He had not even suspected that the arrangement would look odd, or scandalous, to neighbours. So innocent, or so wilfully blind, was he.

Sophie was to blame for the unfortunate state of affairs, in his opinion. He stopped talking to her. The same punishment that the girl from Tipperary gave to his cousin.

This went on for a week. It went into a second week. It seemed he would never open his mouth again. She could see he had it in him, was the sort of man who could close up inside his shell and never emerge again. Reluctantly, and with some trepidation, she asked him what was going on.

He found it hard to speak. But he did.

He told her she gave herself airs. 'What are you but a factory girl?' he said. 'You're making a fool of yourself, dressing up in fine rags and feathers.' He looked her up and down. 'It's not as if you're all that good-looking.' Then he laughed. So that last bit was a joke, not a criticism. He was back to being his normal fault-finding, joking self.

Not quite.

He led her to the alcove and did not bother drawing the curtain, even though it was broad daylight and the cousins might walk in at any moment. He pulled off all her clothes, the first time he had ever done this. She stood, naked, in the sunlight which fell in a narrow dusty bar across the wooden floor. Then he raised his hand and hit her.

She had never understood the expression 'he saw stars' before. Now she saw them, a galaxy flashing brilliantly in her head. She sat down on the bed, her face numb. He hit her again. Her nose bled a little. She did not scream or say anything. But she began to punch him – on the face, on the chest. Her hands pummelled him, hard, but it was like hitting a stone.

'Stop,' he cried. 'Stop.'

She didn't stop. Her hands flailed out, raining blows on him. He didn't reciprocate them and soon he started to laugh.

Sophie continued to hit him. But after a while she started to laugh too, although she did not know what she was laughing at. They both became infected with giggles, and rolled on the bed, unable to stop laughing.

Then he made love to her, and it was the first time the lovemaking worked, for Sophie. But afterwards he pulled away.

'I'm sorry,' he said, his voice so dry she could hardly hear.

She pulled a blanket around herself. He found her nightgown and threw it to her, drew on his own clothes and dropped to his knees at the side of the bed.

Soon after this, before winter set in, Ned suggested they move. Not to a new room, but to a new place. The west. Montana. There was copper mining going on there, silver and gold mining as well, and more money to be made than in the factories of the east. Also, more fresh air and more space for living. He and Sophie would have a house of their own immediately, instead of having to save in the building society and wait for years, as would happen in Philadelphia. Their pale skins would get pink and healthy; their lungs would breathe freely.

Sophie was unsure. Now that she knew Ned better, going off with him alone, into the wilderness as it were, seemed more dangerous than it had when she had first met him. She knew he would not harm her seriously – the beating had not been repeated, yet, and anyway it was not a beating in the usual sense, the sense in which that word was used in Ireland, and Philadelphia. She heard women shouting and screaming sometimes, on Sunday nights, she saw black eyes and bruises, sad shamed faces, which were not to be commented upon. She did not think that Ned would do that to her again – he was not a drunkard, he was not the sort of man who loses his temper and lets fly. Maybe she could handle him, his attitude which was after all a simple enough matter, of jealousy. She knew she must not go too far. She must not expect too much praise, for anything, from anyone, and above all she must not reveal to him if she got it. That was all that was required, really, to keep him happy. He loved her because she was beautiful, and clever, and sensible, and neat. But she must never carry any of these desirable attributes to what he considered to be excess. That was all. It should be easy enough. She would have to do that anyway, even if she stayed in Philadelphia. She would have to do that as long as she stayed with Ned.

There was the matter of leaving her sisters, and her friends. But she had made friends easily in the factory. There was no reason to suppose that she would not make new ones in Montana. Leaving her job would not be a sacrifice. It was enjoyable to work with other people – ready-made friends, in their scores – but the hours were too long. Having Sunday free no longer seemed like enough when you worked for eleven hours every other day. In Montana, she would not have to have a job. Ned would make enough money for the two of them, or more of them if necessary. She would be a real wife, and mother she hoped, at home in her own house, doing whatever she liked, while he was off in the mines digging for silver, for money, for the two of them.

They travelled to Butte by train, a journey of three days. Sophie sat alone on a wooden seat in a third-class carriage, as a concession to her femininity. Ned went in the luggage van, in the coal van, in the cattle truck, as necessity obliged, thus saving the price of one fare. It was the way the Irish did things. Any man would have considered it madness to waste money on a railway ticket. Tickets for transatlantic ships had to be bought. Stowing away on board ship was too risky. But once you landed in America you never paid for travel again, if you could possibly help it. 'The land of the free,' Ned said, climbing on to the roof of the guard's van.

Missoula, where they ended up, was a town of dirt streets and low wooden buildings. A boardwalk, constructed from two planks laid side by side, provided a footpath. High pine trees grew everywhere, on lots between the houses, on the side of the street. There were general stores, hardware stores, draperies. Several saloons, a hotel. Also three churches, Catholic, Presbyterian and Anglican, the Catholic being the biggest.

The mines were to the north of the town, and Sophie and Ned went there, to a smaller village higher in the Rockies, called Greenough. Ned staked out about a half-acre of land just outside the village, close to a settlement of people who had converged on this place from half the countries in Europe. He did not sign for the land – it wasn't necessary to do that, according to some Irishmen who lived there. First come first served. Did it belong to nobody? Sophie asked, surprised. They laughed and pointed to the high, rugged silver peaks behind them. *Na Fir Dearga*. The red men. They've moved up the mountains. It belongs to us now.

Ned's land was on the edge of a forest, mainly fir and pine. Sophie walked into it between the tall, bare trunks of the fir trees. The sun came slanting through them in thin gold lines and the trunks stretched like telegraph poles towards the sky. The passages between them were like the aisle of the big church in Philadelphia.

Not for long. Ned, with help from two of the other Irishmen, chopped down dozens of the tall trees, a lot more than he needed.

With some of the logs thus gained he built a cabin, and the rest they stockpiled for firewood. The cabin consisted of two big rooms plus a porch (this was Ned's personal addition, his poetic touch). He furnished the rooms with a bed, a table, two chairs. The fire was an open fire, on a stone hearth at one side of the kitchen. Later they would get a stove, and other luxuries.

Ned started work in the silver mines as soon as he had finished the cabin; he apprenticed himself to an experienced miner, who would pay him well while teaching him the miner's trade. Ned worked deep in the earth, all day and sometimes long into the night. Sophie was left alone in the cabin for very long periods. She had never in her life spent so much time on her own. In fact she had never spent any time alone – her parents' house in Ireland was always full of people. Then all there had been was the ship, and the room in Philadelphia.

She got to know some of the other women in the hamlet. There were very few of them – most of the men who came to the mines were single. During the day, the village was inhabited only by these few women and their children. There was no school for the children so their noise was to be heard all day as they played around the cabins, or ran in and out of the forest.

There was work to be done. Getting food, preparing it. They ate meat mostly: venison and wild mutton. There were elk, goats, and sheep in the mountains – also bears and mountain lions. Ned learned how to set traps; he hunted when he had free time, bagging easily what they needed. She had to skin animals, peeling the pelts from their cold bodies with a sharp knife. Then they had to be butchered, hacked into pieces, dried or cooked over the fire. Flour they could buy in Greenough, and transport on a cart to the cabin. She had a big sack in the corner of the room, and every day she baked loaves of bread. In the summer, berries grew richly on the floor of the forest. She gathered perfumed raspberries, bloody blueberries, honey-coloured huckleberries, bitter cranberries. She made three varieties of jam, spending hours tending the pots of viciously bubbling, stickily smelling, viscous messes, watching the chemical colour change: she poured berries of pink or yellow or green or blue from her bowl into the pot. But by the time they were boiled and set they were all a dark, carmine red.

When they had been a few months in the area they bought a cow. Then there was milking to do all summer, morning and evening, the hot flank of the beast on her cheek, the teats tough and testing between her fingers, the heavy odour of the cow dung, cow body, churning through her body night and morning, morning and night. Churning once a week in a barrel made by Ned. Come butter come butter come butter come, the rhythmical turning of the handle like a fast violent reel, her back breaking with the effort of it, her complexion pink as a hot summer rose, her wrist thickening. Butter in golden pats lined up on the table. A neighbour, a Swedish woman, taught her how to sour the milk and make a thick, creamy liquid which tasted sweet and sour at once, which enhanced the flavour of huckleberries, even of bread. She showed her how to make cheese.

Sophie loved the cabin. It was different from the house in Donegal, which she had found stuffy and crowded, and from the room in the city. The wooden walls emitted a pungent, resinous smell. The fire burned wood all the time, adding to the spicy atmosphere. On the walls, she hung animal skins: a thick brown bear skin which they had got for a few dollars in Greenough, beaver skins, a rough buffalo skin. On the floor were deer skins, red and silver, snowy white. She loved the various textures of the furs – the fine silky deer skins, the thick shag of the bear like scutch grass, the dense velvet of the beaver. The shapes of the skins too she liked; they were like flat maps of animals. Alone in the cabin she felt the company of the creatures who had once inhabited the skins.

In September, before winter came, Ned bought her a coat made of sealskin which someone who had come down the river from Canada sold him for a few dollars. The sealskin was thick but flat, silvery grey and silvery white, shimmering like ice or seawater, gleaming like the animal from which it had come. When she wrapped herself in it she felt she was a different person. She did not feel human at all, but part of the huge animal world which surrounded her now on all sides, which was with her inside and outside her cabin. She felt like the animals she did not see but heard in the depth of the night, barking or screaming in the forest and the mountain.

Outside her cabin, close to her front door, was the forest. The high dark green trees, secreting a world of animals, of berries, of strangely shaped fungal growths, some of which they learned to eat, fascinated her. Behind the forest the great mountains loomed, purple or silver, golden or flame-coloured, black or stone, depending on the light. Never had she lived among such high mountains, so close to a vast forest. A clear sweet river – they called it a creek – ran at the end of their clearing, forming a border between it and the forest. In this creek she washed her clothes. In this creek she washed herself, when Ned was away and nobody was looking.

They were not always alone. On Sundays, there was Mass in the morning, and then the saloon. The mores of Philadelphia did not apply here. Women went to the saloon as well as men. They even drank alcohol. Stout was the drink, or whiskey, both from Ireland, with Irish names on the labels. Tullamore Dew. Black Bush. Also a light beer which the Germans liked.

Sophie took to drinking port wine. She sat at a table with a woman called Kathleen Sullivan, drinking this and chatting. The men drank whiskey and played cards. Twenty-one, forty-four, poker. One man had a fiddle. He held it straight under his chin, the way they do in Donegal, and played Irish tunes. Jigs and reels. Old slow songs that brought tears to Sophie's eyes, although she did not know why. Not because they reminded her of home. She was glad to be here, glad to be away. It was much better than Ireland.

There were not enough women.

Men stared at her constantly, even when Ned was present. He didn't like it but did nothing about it, attributing it to the shortage of women rather than to any intrinsic worth of Sophie's. She was careful to maintain her distance with all of them, which was easy enough. They were rough diamonds, not the kind who knew how to talk to a woman. Except on Sundays, when the whiskey and music softened them, their minds were focused on one thing only: money.

Ned was preoccupied with money as well. He spent so much of his time underground, in the dark cold earth, chipping away at the rocks for silver. His pay was good, but he experienced danger for it, as well as backbreaking work. None of the silver he retrieved was his: it belonged to the owner of the mine, who paid him by the hour. He began to work longer and longer hours, greedy for the dollars which were mounting up, slowly, in a bag he kept under the bed in the cabin.

Burglary was a threat.

Anyone was a potential robber. Everyone knew who was earning, who was likely to have money stashed away, who used the bank. Your best friend might rob you. In this community, assembled of people from all over Europe, none of whom intended to stay there permanently, nobody was entirely trustworthy. But you had to hope for the best, trust some sort of moral bond or sense of interdependence that would prevent your workmate or neighbour from breaking into your house and relieving you of every penny you'd got.

You could not hope for that as far as the Indians were concerned.

Sophie was warned to stay indoors as much as possible, both to keep an eye on the house and to protect herself from being snatched away by one of the red men who sometimes roamed around Greenough, looking curiously at the people who had so recently relieved them of their territory. Some of these men were known in the town. They sold skins to the store, they bought whiskey at Clancy's. None of them worked in the mine, however. 'How do they live?' Sophie asked. 'Them fellas?' said Ned. 'Hunting. Fishing. They grow maize.' They used to grow maize in the valley at the foot of the Bitterroot Hills, on the plains. They would settle in a place and cultivate the rough, dry land until it yielded the maize, beans, and the peyote they used as a medicine and a drug. Their women knew how to make the roughest land fertile. But as soon as they succeeded in transforming scrubland to fertile soil, the army moved them on. Now they were pushed into the hills, higher even than the silver mines. They were often starving: the women came down to

Greenough carrying their babies in baskets strapped to their backs, and scavenged in the bins for leftovers, scraps of meat or bread the miners had thrown out. 'They'd eat anything,' Mrs Sullivan said disdainfully. 'They're not like us. They have no sense of cleanliness. Ugh.' All the women in Greenough hated the Indians.

One day, Sophie walked up from the river, carrying a bucket of ice. It was November. The ground was covered with snow and the air was so cold that it seemed to freeze in her nostrils as she breathed. At the mine, the men had to melt the seams with fires and blowtorches before they could begin to dig. Sophie had to put ice in a pot on the fire to get water.

From the eaves of the cabin, hunks of venison and mutton, legs and shoulders, hung, coated with white ice crystals. Whole rabbits, half a deer. Trapping was easy in the winter. And you could take all the meat you could get. There was no danger of it going off, so you could kill more than you needed. All you had to do was skin it and hang it outside the house in the cold, to freeze. When Sophie needed some, she brought it inside and let it thaw out before cooking it.

She was wearing her sealskin coat, which almost kept her warm and which had a huge hood. The hood gave her blinkered vision: she could only see what was in front of her eyes: the river, the spiky trees weighted with snow, the path back to the cabin.

She went into the cabin and put the bucket on the floor, near the fire. She stretched her numb hands to the flames, to thaw the fingers before taking off her coat.

A cold hand, heavy as a falling tree, clamped her mouth.

Another hand gripped her stomach.

So this was it.

What she felt was – nothing. Not fright, not terror. Nothing. It was as if every smidgin of herself, even her capacity to be afraid, had vanished.

Not for long.

She had heard stories. Terrible stories. They seeped into her consciousness. What they would do to you. First all the men of the tribe would rape you. Then you might undergo unspeakable tortures. Not so unspeakable that every child in Greenough did not know what they were – that Sophie did not know what they were. Hadn't Mrs Sullivan regaled her with accounts, whispered over a glass in the saloon, as part of the Sunday night entertainment? Stories to make your hair stand on end. Burnings, in the worst places. Cuts at the most female, intimate parts of you. Finally you would be scalped – after your death if you were lucky.

Now the burden of stories flooded Sophie's head. A deluge of imaginings annihilated her, blacked her out.

When she came to, she was lying on her own bed. The Indian was standing beside her. He had a mug of water in his hand. He handed it to her and she drank a few drops of the ice-cold liquid.

He smiled.

Sophie did not return the smile. But she felt less afraid now. Instead she felt limp and helpless, as if her body had been squeezed in a mangle and all the feeling had been wrung out of it. Or as if her mind and her eyes were outside her body, hovering somewhere over her head like a dragonfly staring down at herself. It was not an unpleasant sensation.

'I need some meat,' he said. His English was slow and all his words were spoken with exactly the same emphasis, like a row of stiff pegs on a clothesline. In this his English was not so different from the English of most people in Greenough. Sophie and Ned spoke Irish usually when they were alone, or among other Irish people. Almost all the settlers had some language that was their own – German or Swedish or Icelandic or French – and their English was for use with outsiders. So what language did the Blackfeet speak? That he could speak at all, like other human beings, was a surprise for Sophie. The women who scavenged on the rubbish heaps of Greenough were as silent as trees.

'Take it,' said Sophie, not looking at him.

'Goodbye,' he said.

That was all. He left the cabin, unhooking a side of deer from the eaves outside. Then he walked away. She got up and watched him from the little window as he moved into the forest, disappearing from her view more quickly than he should have. Maybe, she thought, he was not real. Maybe he was some sort of ghost.

Kathleen – that is, Mrs Sullivan – complained that her children were driving her mad.

'Don't they play in the snow?' Sophie asked. She had been married for two years. The idea of children increasingly embarrassed her. Even looking at them embarrassed her. She did not envy Kathleen her brood, not at all. But she was always conscious that envy was the emotion Kathleen, and everyone else, attributed to her. Poor little Mrs Burns. Childless, God help her.

'They play in the snow. They slide on the lake. They ski down the slopes on those wooden yokes their father made for them. But it's dark most of the time and they have to be inside.'

'Why isn't there a school for them?'

'There's nobody to teach a school here,' Kathleen said.

'I could teach them to read and write,' Sophie said. 'If I had some books I could.'

Kathleen thought it was a good idea.

Ned did not agree. 'You can hardly read or write yourself,' he said.

What about the letter she wrote every month to her sister? What about the local newspaper she read aloud to him once a week? What about that?

'It's one thing being able to write a letter to your sister and another teaching children to write or to read.'

What would he know about it? Ned Burns, who'd been brought up in the bad end of County Derry, who'd seldom darkened the door of any school.

'Teachers go to school till they're eighteen years of age. Then they have to be apprenticed to a master teacher for six years. That's how long it takes to be a teacher.'

His scorn was so immense that she believed he must be right. But Kathleen was sceptical. 'Apprenticed for six years? I never heard tell of that,' she said. 'Anyway, what odds? You know more than the children anyhow,' she said. 'And more than most of us.' She did not say 'more than Ned' but that's what she meant. Ned could read a bit, and sign his name. But he could not read a newspaper. He couldn't be bothered, the small print hurt his eyes. And he had never written a letter.

'I suppose they get some sort of training,' Sophie said.

'We're not going to get a trained teacher out here in the back of nowhere,' said Kathleen. 'There aren't many like you here, either.'

'What do you mean?' Sophie was not being entirely disingenuous.

'A girl like you. A fine-looking girl who can read and write. Nobody knows what you're doing here.'

'I'm here because I'm married to Ned,' Sophie protested.

'Aye,' Kathleen said, looking curiously at her. 'Well . . .'

'I'm fine,' Sophie said. 'I like it here.'

'Well, that's grand,' Kathleen said. 'But you could spare a thought for the children.'

'If you can't have a child of your own I don't think you should interfere with other people's' was Ned's rejoinder to that. 'You think you're so clever but . . .' He did not finish the sentence.

The sun shone on the snow, and it was warm in front of the cabin. Light scattered across the trees. Sophie was inside, writing a letter to her sister. She told her about the attempt to teach, and, in a watered-down way, about Ned's reaction. Then she tore up that letter and started another one which made no reference to the incident. Sheila would probably agree with Ned. Or else she would use the information as ammunition against the marriage.

A knock on the door.

The Blackfoot again.

'What do you want?'

'Flour, please,' he said.

'I haven't got much,' she said, thinking, that's the trouble. You give in once and then they keep coming back. All beggars were the same.

'We have none,' he said.

'All right,' she said. 'But this is the last time.'

He handed her a small basket made of bark. She went to her flour sack, and scooped two scoops of the crunchy yellow flour into the basket. When she turned, he had come into the kitchen and closed the door behind him.

'It is so cold,' he said, by way of explanation.

'Do you go to other cabins? Like this?'

He shook his head, and smiled at her.

She smiled as well.

Then it started to happen. What should not have been possible, with a man like this, a man who was not real, who was a sort of animal. Blackfeet. Red men. Savages. She felt her heart change inside her. It changed so that she could feel it, she could feel her whole mind and body and soul begin to change, to ignite, and she felt this change as her heart tossing around inside her like a lump of butter in a churn and her muscles shivering. His brown eyes stared at her, as if he knew what was happening to her. But he couldn't have.

'Here is your flour,' she said, handing it to him and speaking in a cold, neutral voice. 'You'd better go now.'

'Thank you,' he said.

She wondered, later, where he had learned his English. Just hanging around the town? Or in some other way? There was nobody she could ask. She had no business talking to someone like him at all. The correct thing for a woman to do, when confronted by an Indian, was to scream her head off and run as fast as she could away from him. If Ned knew this had happened, he would probably strangle her.

She still read the paper. She read it on Saturday nights after she had come home from the store, when Ned was bathing his feet in a tub of hot water. His toes were almost frozen off sometimes, with the cold of the mine.

'Gold discovered in Yukon,' she read. 'Gold has been discovered in the Klondike region of the Yukon Territory in northern Canada. Already hundreds of eager prospectors have arrived in Dawson City, with a view to bettering themselves. The seams, which have been found close to the junction of the Klondike and Yukon rivers, are said to be exceptionally rich . . .'

'Gold,' Ned said. 'Gold is better than silver.'

'The Klondike must be an awful place,' Sophie said. 'Up there in the north. Haven't you heard of fools' gold?'

'You're such a fool you wouldn't know the difference between gold and silver,' he said. And he laughed. But she did not laugh this time, and let him go to the saloon on his own. When he came home he was very drunk. She pretended to be asleep. But he woke her up to tell her that several men from the village were planning to set off for the Yukon as soon as the ice melted. They hadn't needed to read about the gold in the paper. Already, somehow, word had reached Butte that there was more gold up there than had ever been found in the whole of North America before. 'It's for the taking,' he said. Sophie knew it could not be so simple, but nodded and pretended to agree.

Blackfoot looked about twenty years of age to Sophie, who was now twenty-two herself. His image was in her mind most of the time as she went about her tasks or lay in bed before falling asleep. (Ned seldom kissed her, or caressed her, any more. He was too tired, most of the time, after the work at the mine. When he came home at night all he did was eat his dinner, say the Rosary, and flop into bed.) It was a disturbing image, and she tried to dislodge it from her head, but couldn't. His tall, strong body clad in its beaver skins. His bronze face with its pools of dark eyes, its polished cheekbones. His hair fell to his shoulders, thick and opaque, unlike any hair she had seen. She felt her fingers itch to touch it just to find out what it felt like.

If he had not been able to speak English this would not have happened to her, she thought. Or if she had not been able to speak English, but only the Irish she had spoken at home, and still spoke with Ned. If he had only spoken his savage's language, and she her own, she would have kept away from him.

By now, four years after Ned had started his apprenticeship to the silver miner, he had learned all there was to know about the trade. He could locate a mine, he could drill and blast. He could identify different kinds of minerals. He could evaluate them.

'The value of silver has dropped,' he told Sophie. 'It's gone from eighty cents an ounce to forty cents.'

At first, Sophie did not understand how this had happened. 'President Jackson did it,' Ned said, neutrally. 'He devalued silver.' How could a man, even if he were the President, have enough power to change something like the value of silver? Apparently that is just what he had been able to do, by simply ordering it to be so. It sounded to Sophie like the wedding feast at Cana.

'Gold is the thing,' Ned said. 'We'll never get anywhere if we don't mine that.'

Then it struck Sophie that gold could change its value too. It struck her that it had no value. 'Why is gold valuable?' is what she asked.

'What?' Ned was incredulous.

'Can't its value change? If President Jackson changes his mind?'

Ned didn't appear to think so. Anyway he didn't give her an answer. His mind was made up. Already he had planned every inch of his journey, from Missoula to the Klondike. He would take a paddle steamer most of the way. Then he would walk from the Yukon fork to Dawson City. That was where the best gold was: clear, bright yellow, the most valuable kind.

'Why? It's nice to look at, but it's no use.'

'Of course it's use,' he said.

'What use is it?' Sophie persisted, as her mind wrapped itself around this idea. What use is silver? More use than gold. Silver knives and forks, silver cups and bowls. They last and last. They shine and can be shone up again, clean and bright as water.

'It's use,' he said. 'Don't be stupid. There's so much you don't understand.'

'I suppose so,' Sophie said. But she wondered. Gold. Why did they want it so much?

★ ★ ★

'Because it looks like the sun,' North Wind said.

'That's probably it,' said Sophie, although she wondered. Did it have some properties she was unaware of? Could it cure some pain? Could it endure for ever, like – perhaps – a man's lineage?

North Wind. That was his name, in English, but for a long time Sophie could not say it. It sounded so silly. 'What does Sophie mean?' he asked.

'It doesn't mean anything,' Sophie said. 'Names don't have a meaning.' He looked sceptical and as she said this she wondered if it was true. Edward. How could a sound like 'Edward' mean anything? It was not a proper word, just a name.

North Wind came to the cabin again and again, as the winter turned to spring. Ned had moved away, not to the Yukon, but higher into the mountains behind Greenough, the Bitterroot Mountains, where he was digging for gold.

'Do your people use it?' she asked North Wind.

'No,' he said. 'We use instead beads made from shells. Wampum.'

'The same thing!' said Sophie.

No, it was not the same thing. The shells lay everywhere, on the shoreline of the lake. On beaches at the foot of the high cliffs that fall into the Blackfoot river. The Indians did not blow up the mountains in order to get them. The earth gave them the shells, for nothing.

He came to the cabin for meat and bread. They both knew that was why he was coming. It was for no other reason. To him she looked old and pale. Paleskin, and she was very pale, even now, with her fair hair, her white peaky skin. Even her eyes were colourless, by comparison with his. Black hair, bronze skin, dark brown eyes. He was the colour of a dark forest animal, a fox, a bear, while she looked like an urban aberration.

He told her things. The names of the months. The month of the melting snow. The month of the greening grass. The month of the rutting stag. He told her about the animals in the mountains: the great brown bears, the thin mountain lions. One had come and taken a child away from the camp where he lived with his tribe before the snow melted. The lions were short of food – and he blamed this, like almost every misfortune, on the white settlers. He told her about the Great Spirit that inhabits the whole earth, that owns the forest, the mountains, the plains, the waters, the animals.

The Great Spirit sounded to Sophie like God. But she did not say this to the Blackfoot, who would have scorned her. He thought everything about the white settlers was stupid.

'Our land is more valuable than your dollars,' he said. 'It will last for ever. It belongs to the Great Spirit and white men cannot buy it, although they think they can. If they cut down the forest and blow up the mountain, the Great Spirit will punish them.'

But he did not know how the Great Spirit would go about this. In fact most of the punishment going seemed to be meted out not to the white men, but to the Blackfeet. They were half-starved on their cold encampment. Several of them had died during the winter – the miners had taken the lion's share of the game on offer from the Great Spirit, apparently.

'You have more guns' was the explanation he had for this. Guns, dynamite, steam engines: the Great Spirit was no match for these weapons. Yet.

Ned found gold. He came down from the mine and showed it to Sophie: nuggets of rich, dark, solid gold. He said fifteen decades of the Rosary in thanksgiving. Sophie's knees were worn out by the time he'd finished. Then he drank half a bottle of whiskey and tried to make love to her, but fell asleep before he could.

One of his colleagues took the nuggets to Butte to sell them. 'Our fortune is made!' said Ned.

Sophie had been excited when she held the rough, heavy lumps of gold in her hand. They glittered like the water in the lake when the sun shone on it in the middle of summer, sparkling it with a million diamonds. It was like holding that sparkle of sunshine in your hands. The darkness of the gold reminded her of the dark eyes and dark skin of the Blackfoot. Indian gold.

But she was not so sure about the fortune. 'What will we do then?' she asked uncertainly.

'Go somewhere,' said Ned. 'Out of this hellhole. Back east. Back to Ireland.'

When she walked in the forest she did not see the Great Spirit. But she heard the trees talking to her. She watched the light seeping through the high roof of the fir needles as she moved along the aisles. She watched the rich green and carmine carpet of berries sprouting around her toes.

Wrapped in her sealskin, she felt she was a seal. She felt she was a tree.

Naked, bathing in the deep dark pool of the creek, she felt she was a fish. A slippery salmon, fat and juicy, its skin the same colour as the shingle on the banks of the river.

North Wind came to the cabin while Ned was there, during the week of waiting for his fortune to be brought back from Butte. North Wind knocked on the door and Ned answered it. When he saw the Indian standing there, dressed at this time – it was the month of the long sun – in very little, he hit him on the jaw. Then he turned and picked up his rifle. By the time he had got back to the door North Wind had vanished.

'Fucking bastard,' said Ned. He was so angry that for a while he did not think to ask what North Wind was doing there. But later he remembered. Had Indians ever come to the cabin before? No, said Sophie, wondering if this lie were wise or foolish. No. Sometimes the women come, searching in the bins.

'Shoot them if they come here,' said Ned. His voice grew tender. 'You shouldn't be here on your own.'

'I'm used to it now,' said Sophie, as nonchalantly as she could.

'At least you won't have to be alone here again,' he said.

But the news from Butte was bad. The gold was not valuable. It was too dark.

'What?' Sophie could not believe this. 'It's still gold, isn't it?'

'It's gold. But it's gold that's no more valuable that silver.'

So it was true, Sophie thought. Gold was not always precious. Some of it was and some of it wasn't. Maybe it was not precious if you could find it too near home, if you came upon it too easily? Was that it? Or was it that someone decided, some powerful man sitting in Washington, that some kinds of gold were important and some were not?

'No no.' Ned would not hear of it. 'That's not why. It's the colour that's wrong. It's too dark. It's redskin gold, it's nigger gold.' Too dark. Only the white light blond gold of the snowy Arctic would be good enough for America. The gold of the Klondike.

'I'll stay here,' Sophie said, when Ned announced that he would go there, drawn to it as the bees to clover. Once you started on this road there was no turning back.

'You can't,' he said. 'It's too dangerous.'

'More dangerous than the Klondike?'

It seemed that her life had become a balancing act as she moved from east to west, choosing the lesser of two evils all the time. Ned was better than Sheila and housework in Philadelphia. Being alone in a cabin in Montana was better than working in a factory in Philadelphia. Now going to the Klondike with Ned was supposed to be better than staying in the cabin here. But her judgement was faltering. She could no longer weigh up one choice against another and see, quickly, which was the best. North Wind had skewed her power to do that, had taken away her ability to distinguish black from white, silver from gold, bad from good, good from better.

'There isn't enough money. You can't stay here.'

'If I taught the children they'd give me food and fuel,' Sophie protested weakly, but knowing as she said the words that they were true. She could stay here on her own and survive.

'Don't be silly,' he said firmly. 'You can't teach anyone.'

'What if the gold in the Klondike also turns out to be the wrong kind?'

'It's the right kind. And I'm going to get it,' he said. In spite of his experiences, Ned had not changed. He was still always convinced that he knew exactly the right thing to do.

When Ned had been on Granite Mountain, mining the dark and useless gold, this had happened. North Wind had come to the cabin when Sophie was washing clothes. She washed them, during the summer, in the creek, rubbing the hard soap on them and scrubbing them on her washboard. She liked to watch the suds dancing off downstream in the sunlight.

'You should not do that.' North Wind was suddenly there beside her. You never heard him coming.

'Why?' She smiled up at him.

'It poisons the water,' he said.

Of course. That was what she would never think of. 'It's just a tiny bit of soap.' She watched the white, lovely suds.

'Yes,' he said. 'But if all the white women do it, it is a lot of soap. Then, no fish.' He helped her fill a tub with water. Then he helped her wash.

'Do you do this at the camp?'

He laughed. 'No,' he said. 'Never.'

'Have you a wife?' she asked suddenly, out of the blue. Did they have wives? Not in the sense that she was Ned's wife. Not in the sense of a priest and Mass and signing your name in a book. A real marriage.

He did not answer.

She touched him then. He was kneeling at her big wooden tub, splashing some shirt around in the soapy water. She touched his slippery hand under the surface of the water. He took out both their hands and pulled her towards him, kissing her. He led her into the forest and laid her on the soft old needles. First he dealt with her nipples, kissing them until she twitched with desire. Then he turned her on her stomach, so that the pungent needles tickled her skin, teased her belly and her thighs. He slid into her from behind. This time what she felt was not the twittering of birds, but an overwhelming delight which encompassed every inch of her body, back and front and in and out, which seemed to wrap her and him and the forest and the sky together. America. Gold. Heaven.

Ned had to go to Missoula to get some supplies for the journey.

Soon after he was gone North Wind came in.

They made love on her bed.

'We are going away,' she said afterwards, the languor the lovemaking had given her body blunting the pain of what she was saying.

'Why?' He looked curious rather than dismayed.

'Ned wants to go to the Klondike, north of here.'

'I know where it is,' he said, patiently.

'Sorry. Well, you know why we're going then.'

'Gold fever.'

'Yes.'

'You will get rich.' He laughed. 'There's plenty of gold up there.'

'I will die, maybe.' She realised this was true.

'You will be all right in your sealskin coat. You will be at home.'

'I am at home here.' She realised this was true too. She had been here for five years. Ireland was a dim, unpleasant memory. When her mind moved to the Klondike, she saw endless snow. The snow was beautiful but even here she had learned what an enemy it could be, how imprisoning, how threatening of starvation and isolation. And here the snow lasted for about five or six months. Half the time the earth was green. There was hot, very hot sun. The water in the pools was warm, so that bathing was like bathing in a tub. Up there, the snow would last for much longer. Maybe it never melted? There would be no food apart from meat and fish.

'We move all the time.' North Wind had been on the move since the moment he was born – the year of Little Bighorn. He had moved farther and farther away from home, if home was the sowing fields, the winter hunting grounds. He had moved to the badlands.

'Yes. But we don't have to. We were doing well here.'

North Wind shrugged.

'He wants gold because he does not have a child,' she said.

'If he had a child he would need gold for another reason,' North Wind said.

'How many children have you?' she asked him, blushing suddenly and feeling weak.

'None,' he said. 'I have no wife.'

Her heart leaped. 'Why not?' she asked, smiling.

'I am young. Twenty-two.'

She had assumed they would mate as soon as they could, like cats or dogs. Everything she assumed about the Indians was turning out to be wrong.

'Would you like to be my wife?' he asked.

'I'm Ned's wife,' she said.

'Among the Blackfeet, if you get tired of one husband you can take another.'

'I'm a Catholic,' Sophie said. 'I couldn't do that.'

'If I kidnapped you, you would have no choice!' He laughed and gently pushed her down again, stroking her so that she laughed for joy.

They were ready to go. The mining tools were packed in one backpack, and food in another. All the clothes were in a lighter pack, which Sophie would have to carry. The cabin was ready to be closed up and abandoned. Somebody might come and take it over while they were gone. No arrangement was made, one way or the other.

'We might come back here,' said Sophie.

'Aye surely,' said Ned.

He went to Clancy's to have one for the road, the night before they were to set off for the steampaddle at Missoula.

When North Wind came, he was not alone, but accompanied by four other men. He did that to make it look like an authentic raid. He could see the headline in the newspaper. redskins capture white woman. It would absolve Sophie from blame, at the risk of starting a war, but it was so easy to give rise to a war that the risk hardly counted. A battle could start over a stolen sheep just as easily, or a frightened child. In addition, it would help to assimilate Sophie to the tribe. Abduction of a white woman they would understand.

The men were painted, black and red and blue stripes on their faces and bodies. One of them wore a war bonnet and the other three had feathers sticking out of their loose black hair. They carried machetes.

Sophie hardly recognised North Wind. She knew his voice, but apart from that he did not at all resemble the man she had got to know, taken to bed with her. He looked like a redskin. He looked like a savage.

She did what white women did, in these circumstances. As he carried her away on his horse – a mangy, underfed nag – she screamed loudly.

He clapped his hand over her mouth.

Already Kathleen Sullivan and all the little Sullivans were out. They were also screaming, at the tops of their voices, in their Kerry–Montana accents.

The Blackfeet did not know what to do with her.

'I'm happy now,' she said to North Wind. They were on the move again, moving to somewhere new where the Greenough gang would not find them.

But before they could dismantle the tepees and get out, Ned and Mick Sullivan, Mossie Fitzgerald and Miley Gallagher, Fritz Zumpfe and Jon Johannsen, and several others, converged on the camp. They carried shotguns, pikes, shovels, axes, anything they had available.

'Fucking savages.' Ned's voice was heard above the others. 'I'll rip them apart. Fuckers.'

Nobody was hurt.

A miracle.

The Blackfeet had run away, all of them. They were packed and ready to go anyway as Ned and his friends came upon them.

'Brave braves!' Ned said sarcastically. 'As soon as they sniff a real man, off they run.'

Sophie looked at him, neutrally.

'I'd like to strip their skin off and roast them skinless,' Ned said. 'Did they do you any harm?'

She did not answer.

'The poor wee woman's not right after it. No wonder,' said Miley Gallagher. 'Give her time. She'll tell you what happened when she's had time to let it all sink in.'

'Aye,' Ned said.

They went to the Klondike three days later.

Sophie had a baby, up there in the north, sometime the following spring. The baby was fine, a small light-skinned boy with black straight hair, not like Ned's or Sophie's. They called him Teddy. People often said to Ned, 'He's the image of you.'

Sophie loved her child. She fed him with her own milk, she wrapped him in furs, she sang to him and told him stories about Ireland, about the mountains, about the creek that ran sweetly outside her cabin in Montana.

Before Christmas, Ned hit gold – the pale gold of Alaska, which was the most valuable kind. His joy was boundless. 'By summer we'll be rich enough to go back home. We'll buy a good big farm in Derry and live like gentry.'

After Christmas the baby caught a cold. For two days the sound of his small cough racked the cabin and then, unable to get his breath, he died.

After that, the black sickness descended on Sophie, immured in her cold cabin in a land of ice. It descended on her mind and her heart like a blanket of black frost, blotting out every song and every flower that grew there, snuffing her flame.

Nothing ignited it again.

Ned prayed for her, night after night, in long litanies of supplication to his beloved Virgin. Mother Most Merciful, Mother Most Pure, Mother Most Renowned, pray for her.

After a while Sophie, who had not been one for praying before, began to join him in his prayers. Morning Star, Help of the Sick,

Comfort of the Afflicted. Pray for Us. She recited them not only in the evenings, kneeling at the rough wooden chairs in the cabin before bedtime, but all day long. Mother of God, Star of the Sea. She walked around the shanty town, wrapped in her sealskin coat, chanting these incantations, without cease. To the litany she added an epithet of her own. North Wind, North Wind, North Wind. Nobody noticed that it broke the rhythm of the song, or that it was in any other way extraneous. Nobody would have commented if they had.

It was generally thought, among the Irishmen, pious or secular, sensible or wild, who were hitting gold with Ned, that Sophie's ordeal in Missoula at the hands of the Indians had affected her brain, and that she was not quite right in the head.

THE DAY ELVIS PRESLEY DIED

Pat and Douglas are staying in the house — meaning the enormous grey stone pile that sits on the hill overlooking the lake. Jim and Margaret, Douglas's parents, have another residence, referred to as 'our own place', close to the edge of the wood. From the window of her narrow room Pat can see 'our own place': it is a log cabin, one of a cluster of such cabins, all nestling cosily into a backdrop of rich dark green spruce, fir, pine — whatever. To her all evergreen trees look the same. But she likes the look of them, always has: maybe what appeals is their association with Christmas, with snowy mountains and tinkling sleighbells, or with mountain walks, the idea of hiking groups of cheerful young people. Or maybe it is just their reliable colour and contours.

'Settled in?' Douglas asks. Pat has been in her room for five minutes. She has opened her big suitcase but has not removed any of the mountain of clothes from it. The bare boards of the room, the painted wooden wardrobe with its clatter of wire hangers, remind her of rooms in convents where she went on spiritual retreats as a schoolgirl. That such old, shabby, well-used rooms exist in the United States comes as a surprise to her. In Douglas's house, south of here, in Delaware, everything is plushly soft, deeply comfortable.

'Yes,' Pat says. She looks out the window. 'It's so beautiful.' She means the long blue lake, sheltered by spiky evergreens, the grey and black and silver mountains, the hundreds of wooded islands; those things, and the clipped lawns sweeping down to the edge of the lake. The wooden docks, the canoes gliding along the calm water. The clear summer sky. She does not mean the room, which disappoints her, although already some Americans might think this sort of worn-down austerity special and charming. Douglas does, apparently.

'It's not bad,' he says, glancing around at the bare cream walls. Maybe he's pretending not to understand Pat? She regards him with suspicion. She knows he hates her enthusiasm, her exuberant praise of landscape, her sentimental overstatements – the trite, unconsidered verbiage that flows out of her in her soft, excessively pleasant voice.

Pat is too eager, too eager to please and to be pleased. That is what he thinks. She is too readily effusive about almost everything. What a wonderful view, what a wonderful dessert, what a lovely carpet, what magnificent houses! She is exclaiming every five minutes. How can you believe a single thing such a person says?

Pat knows what she's doing wrong but can't help it. Everything she has seen since she came to America has seemed amazing to her. The words at her disposal, lovely, gorgeous, beautiful, seem the only ones suited to describe all this loveliness, of tree and landscape, of architecture and interior decoration. Of people. Of food.

What surprises her most is that America is both shockingly familiar and stunningly novel. For instance, the America Douglas belongs to, exactly resembles the America she has seen on television for most of her life. She walked into his living room and felt instantly at home. She'd been there so often as a child. On *The Donna Reed Show* and *The Lucy Show*. *The Honeymooners*. Real life is better than the sitcoms, because in it you see not just the living room, the staircase and the front door, but all the other rooms as well, the upstairs and the outside. You see the painted wooden gingerbread exteriors, you see the generous unfenced gardens, the clean, flower-edged winding suburban roads. You see the malls and the turnpikes and the highways. All that before you come to the mountains and see this: scenery more splendid than anything Ireland can offer. That also came as a surprise to Pat. She has not travelled very widely and has always been taught that Ireland is the most beautiful country in the world, without qualification. That is what her mother had told her. Her mother, her teachers, the Irish Tourist Board. Ireland, in compensation for its economic and social failures, was Miss World in the International Beautiful Places Competition – a dumb, and virtuous, blonde among smarter but uglier nations. That's why everyone in the world should take an Irish holiday. That's why millions of Irish emigrants weep and sing tearful songs about their homeland, remembering the unsurpassable natural beauty they have left behind them. But what's the fuss about? The truth is that America is not just a place where you can get a job. The truth is that it also looks nicer than Ireland. It is more beautiful, and sunnier, and there is so much more of it. You can drive for hundreds of miles through dramatic mountains, or deep forests. The sun doesn't disappear after half an hour, and the good scenery doesn't give way to flat boring stuff after half a mile. You do not have to anticipate a change, often for the worse, every five minutes.

America has been a stunning experience, for Pat. And Douglas doesn't like that. He wants her to appreciate America – his country. But he doesn't want her to go overboard with this appreciation. He wishes she knew when to stop. He wishes she could be less childish, more studied, and cool. Maybe he wishes she could be less Irish?

Douglas sighs and looks at her, his eyes ironic, but not really unkind. Suddenly he puts his arms around her. Their warmth, through the thin cotton of her blouse, abruptly seduces her emotions, so that she feels tears springing up behind her eyes – gratitude, though, rather than desire, is her overwhelming feeling. So much of the time he is impatient with her. The tension sears his forehead, tortures his face, and is to be heard in the dry, irritated tones of his voice. Then come the spurts of forgiveness, like a sudden pouring of warm sweet rain during a drought. She soaks up those rare moments like a withering flower, a browning scrap of sheep's bit, desperately clinging to the rock. She buries her head against his chest, trying to take every drop of kindness from him, as if that could sustain her for the next period of deprivation.

He kisses her. His mouth is warmer than hers. He has everything in abundance. He is a cornucopia, a fountain of gifts, for her, if only she could manage to take them. If she could find the way into him, for more than five minutes at a stretch, happiness, joy without end, would be hers. If only she could learn how to make her way through to him, there is no end to the bliss which he can give her. This is what she believes.

They hold the embrace for a couple of minutes: for several weeks, they have not had much of a chance to kiss in comfort. First, because they were separated: Pat was in Ireland, Douglas was here in America with his family. For the past week they have been together but in his parents' house. It's not that it is small. And they have often enough been left discreetly alone in the den. But even there, tucked underneath the house, on the wide old comfortable sofa, Pat has felt inhibited. At any moment, she feels, Douglas's mother or, worse, father might walk through the door and discover them. So just at the times when he wanted to be tender she has been anxious and resistant. She has kissed and hugged with one eye on the door. When she had her chance to love him and take his love, she ruined it all.

Now the bolt is shot on the door and Douglas's parents are far away, in their cabin. There is no reason, no logical reason, to be wary. Douglas, not releasing his lips entirely, nuzzling her hair, her neck, pushes her gently enough to the bed. It is a plain, narrow bed and the mattress is firm. It does not give under Pat's weight. But she manoeuvres her head on to the spongy pillow. She sighs, and gives herself, at last, to his kiss.

There is a kitchenette in the log cabin, where you can cook or make coffee. Jim and Margaret will eat their meals in the dining room, down in the big house, but they have this extra facility should they require it. When she has unpacked her clothes – a couple of white blouses, cotton flowered skirts, a light-blue silk shirtwaister for the banquet that will occur on the final night – Margaret makes a cup of herbal tea. She calls to Jim: 'Would you like some tea?' He answers immediately, in his round booming voice, 'No thank you, dear.' She doesn't take it as any sort of snub: they'll go to dinner in half an hour, and he seldom takes cups of tea or coffee, snacks between meals. 'I'm going to drink mine on the porch,' she says cheerfully. 'I'll join you in a minute,' he calls back equally cheerful. She can tell from the tug of his voice that he is shaving his upper lip, stretching his mouth to make a smooth surface of skin.

Margaret goes out and sits on one of the sunchairs on the porch. It is a substantial porch. There are four wooden chairs on it, as well as a low table suitable for cups or glasses. The porch has the same view, more or less, as Pat's room, namely the lake. All the cabins, and most of the occupied rooms, have this view. Only staff sleep in rooms that look backwards to the yards where the dustbins are stored, and to the wall of forested mountain.

Margaret surveys the scene and feels a great sense of relief. She it was who invited Douglas and Pat to share a week of the holiday with them. She wanted to give Douglas a break, and she wanted to show Pat this beloved place, the resort she had been coming to for forty years – as a child her parents had brought her here, driving up from Delaware in their big Studebaker, taking the train during the war (when Jim, already her boyfriend, was fighting in the navy). They had stayed in the house then; these cabins, although they look old, were built only ten years ago. But although she is glad she had had the bright, if expensive, idea, she was also glad she had decided to book them rooms in the big house (also an expensive idea). There is plenty of room in the cabin for the four of them. But she had believed that the young people would value some privacy. What she had not realised, not so consciously, was that she would value hers so much – that she would be so glad to be free of Pat. She is not sure what to make of Pat: she is a polite girl, and she looks all right, if not as pretty as Margaret would have liked, for Douglas. The neighbours who have met her have described her, to Margaret, as 'sweet': she has good hair, fair and waving, and long. And she has quite nice blue eyes, but there is something wrong with her teeth – they are uneven and turned slightly inward, like a shark's – they spoil her appearance, which is a pity, especially since they could have been corrected if her parents had looked after them in time. That might not matter if she were a livelier, wittier girl. But it is difficult to drag conversation out of her. She admires the scenery and the surroundings. That is gratifying, although sometimes Margaret has wondered if all the admiration is sincere. She also answers questions, but she seldom asks any apart from the most general. And she never proffers any information about herself. She is cheerful, but secretive. You never know what she is really thinking. Being in the company of such a person all day is a strain.

Now, however, thanks to her own kindness and foresight, Margaret can forget about Pat for a while. For a full ten minutes she allows her holiday mood to course through her as she sits in the evening sun. It is a most definite, tangible feeling, her holiday mood: a happiness which is a mixture of childhood memories, of the smell of the Norway spruce and the giddy glitter of sun on the water, of the excitement of the long drive up the tree-lined Northway Route to the lake. Even though the temperature is in the high seventies, there is a freshness, a crispness in the air here at all times. The air at home, where the temperature is in the high eighties, is leaden and humid. If the air conditioning is off for half an hour, you drip with perspiration. A walk along the sidewalk to the corner store leaves you washed-out, flaccid.

But up here, the outdoors is exhilarating.

'Ah, it's exhilarating,' beams Jim. He has changed into a check shirt and khaki shorts. His legs are tanned – it's late July, he's been swimming and sailing for months on the little lake at home. His stomach is protuberant in the shorts, but in a healthy way – it almost looks as if it is a firm extension of his toned, muscular body, rather than a flabby mess of a belly. He looks like a man who is well looked after, content with his lot. That is what he looks like, Margaret thinks, and a lot of that is thanks to her.

He ruffles her hair – blonde, a light fluffy bob – and drops a peck of a kiss on her forehead. 'Well?' he asks. 'Settled in yet?'

'Isn't it wonderful?' Margaret gazes at the lake. Her happiness is still welling up inside her, like hot water in a geyser. She knows happiness of this quality cannot last for long and she is making the most of it.

'Not bad,' says Jim. His voice is warm and kind. Margaret smiles, hearing the tone rather than the words. He sits down and opens a book, a book about golf. 'Not bad at all.'

What does he think about Pat, Margaret wonders, idly, and then answers the question herself. He probably doesn't think about her at all.

Douglas is the handsomest boy Pat has ever seen. It sounds like a preposterous boast, but it is really true. The first time she saw him, in a room in the college they both attended as graduate students in Dublin, she could hardly believe he was real. Real, and studying in this college, in the humanities faculty, where the boys were thin on the ground and usually smaller than the girls, much shorter than Pat, who is five foot eight. (The big sporty boys tended to select such subjects as engineering, medicine, or law.) Douglas was about six and a half feet tall. He towered over everybody. His face was classically handsome, his teeth white and perfect, his eyes a clean mid-palette blue. He had brownish-fairish hair, thick and wavy, falling in an undulating lock over his high forehead. Apart from a few spots, a sign of masculinity at his age, there was nothing the matter with him at all, as far as looks were concerned. If you were designing a blueprint for the perfect man, this would be it. So Pat thought.

She did not get to know him for quite a while. He spent little time in college, and seemed cool and distant with most people. It was generally assumed that he had a better and more glamorous life to lead elsewhere, that he was concerned only with what he was learning and, for obvious reasons, would not be interested in making friends with any of the ordinary students. Besides, Pat had a boyfriend already, a medical student whom she had been seeing for almost two years. Terry was the medical student's name. He was tall, but not as tall as Douglas. And he was handsome, but had a reddish, spotty complexion which detracted from his good looks. Douglas managed to be tall and well-built, with the solidity of a full-grown man, even though he was at most twenty-two. Terry, the same age, looked as if he was half-grown. It was not at all clear how he would finally turn out, although you could guess he would age well, if you were prepared to be patient.

When Douglas had been around for six months, somebody in the class held a party. She was an American girl called Rain. (Her father was Irish; he called her after the most typical natural attribute of the old country.) Rain might have been holding this party especially to get off with somebody – quite possibly with Douglas. Or she might have decided to have the party for fun, or from a sense of social obligation – she was the sort of girl who might act altruistically, without self-interest, because she was both generous and rich. So it was rumoured among the Irish students, who were all, in varying degrees, poor, like most Irish people in those days. Rain had a Fulbright scholarship, which was rumoured to be very large, and also a very large flat and a very old car. She had perfect teeth and a perfect complexion. Also serious ideals about her education and her subject, which was Medieval History.

Her flat was full of medieval reproductions – delicate blue and gold illustrations from books of hours, sculptures based on the Lindisfarne Gospels or the Book of Kells, a long tapestry which was a copy of a section of the Bayeux Tapestry, depicting small Viking boats on a smoky-blue stormy sea. She had bought these things, as well as records of medieval songs, plainchant and madrigals and carols, at museums and libraries around Europe: she'd been to Lindisfarne, to Iona, to Bayeux, to Clairvaux, to Chartres, to the museum of Cluny, to Canterbury. She'd been everywhere that mattered in the Middle Ages, even to Southwark on the London underground. To her, the Middle Ages were more than just a subject. They were interior decoration. They were blouses and dresses, long-playing records, and a hairstyle.

'She looks medieval,' Pat said to Douglas, at a certain stage in the party. 'Doesn't she?' It was a bitchy comment but it was true. Rain's plump high-breasted body, her soft oval face with its strawberries-and-cream complexion, her long ringlet of hazel hair, might have stepped out of the pages of Marie de France. Not Guinevere, nothing as hard and calculating. Not one of the wise beautiful fairy women, a Circe who bewitched men and trapped them in their apple-blossomed lairs. But one of the young, soft girls, the daughter in the Lai de Frêne maybe, whose mother locks her in a tower and spanks her daily as a punishment for her sexual misdemeanours, is what she looks like. Vulnerable, nubile, fated. Of course she plays it up, this look, with a velvet dress, wide batwing sleeves, dangling earrings: everything dripping, droopy, silkily soft. Summer rain.

Douglas laughed, and looked at Pat with admiration. Pat felt glad that she had managed to win this look for herself, diverting it from Rain. She elaborated. She trotted out the Lai de Frêne analogy and he took her hand, gazing as he did so over at Rain, who was frolicking with two of the lecturers, her large rump outlined against the flimsy velvet of her dress, and her round breasts showing their cleavage. Douglas had had about a bottle of red plonk to drink, at this stage – even Rain bought plonk. It was the mid-seventies; you could get only bad wine in Dublin then. Two-litre bottles called Nicolas or Hirondelle. Pat had had half a bottle already, which was enough to make her giddy. She smiled all the time when she was drunk, and burst into giggles on the tiniest provocation.

They went home together in a taxi. Home to Douglas's bedsitter, a room about one-twentieth the size of Rain's flat, about the size of a bathroom. They did not have sex. But they lay on top of the covers, kissing and wrestling, for whatever was left of the night. Pat drank Douglas's kisses as if they were spring water and she a camel who had plodded for weeks across the Sahara. She had not realised how serious her longing for real kisses was, until she tumbled into his arms and felt, for the first time ever, the urgency and energy of desire.

Meals at the lake are eaten in a big high dining hall, the walls and ceiling of which are panelled with dark wood. It is the sort of dining hall you associate with old universities. In such places, you usually sit at long narrow wooden tables, and are served by elderly Jeeves-like men in black jackets, or women who look as if they might have had an injury such as a blow to the head, or a baby who was taken away for adoption, in their youth and have never recovered from it.

But it is not like that here. The tables are suited to small groups, four or six, and are covered with cheerful gingham cloths, blue and white. A little bud vase holding a few daisies or a bit of yellow broom sits in the middle of each. At breakfast and lunch the dining room is self-service. At dinner, the waitresses are young, very pretty girls dressed in T-shirts and jeans. They are known as Muffins. The Muffins are the children of families who have been coming on holiday to this resort for years or for generations. Their reward now in their young adulthood is to be allowed to wait on table, wash dishes, clean bedrooms, and be paid for it, in the camp. Some of them look cheerful and happy with their work and others look disgruntled and incompetent, sulky sophomores dishing up baked potatoes, thick steaks, broccoli, creamed mushrooms.

Pat, Douglas, Margaret and Jim always eat dinner together, and usually lunch as well. At breakfast they sometimes miss each other: Douglas and Pat get up earlier than his parents, or get to the dining room quicker. It is, after all, in the house where they sleep.

Now they are eating dinner. It is the end of the second day of the holiday. They are summing it up. Jim wants to do this. Or maybe it is just a way of keeping the conversation going.

'The art class was good. I enjoyed it,' Pat says. She had spent the morning painting a bunch of broom stuck in a pottery jug, with a lot of other people, most of them old-age pensioners. Douglas had done this too, out of loyalty to her, although he has no interest even in the idea of painting. Pat, however, is devoted to the idea of many activities: painting, ballet, playing the piano, horse riding, mountaineering, sailing – activities which she did not get a chance to practise in her youth and which she thinks would be fun to try now. And apparently it's not too late. Look at the old women – and men – valiantly daubing at their easels, struggling with the jug of airy broom.

'Your picture was fine. It has something – a sense of movement.' Jim speaks not seriously, but with an air of conviction. Douglas glances at Pat with a glow of admiration and Pat feels inordinately grateful to Jim for winning this bonus for her.

'Yes it was lovely,' Margaret agrees. She is still happy. The day has gone off well, so far. All three of her charges seem content, which is all she asks for. 'Anyone like some orange squash?'

'Thank you, Mags, I'll have some.'

Douglas says, a bit surly, that he'll help himself. One of the things that irritates him is the way his mother is so helpful, just as it irritates him that Pat is eager to please. He thinks his mother treats him, and all of them, as if they were babies. Pat, on the other hand, likes having her squash poured for her, she likes to hear Margaret being solicitous about her health, her well-being, her happiness. At lunchtime Margaret insisted on buying Pat a tube of suntan lotion, and told her to rub it into her skin before going out again. Pat has not been mothered for a very long time.

'And how was the pony trekking?' Margaret asks.

'OK,' says Douglas.

'Go far?' asks Jim.

'No, not far,' Douglas says.

'We spent a lot of time learning how to sit on the horse and hold the reins,' Pat explains eagerly. 'So we didn't really go for a trek. She said we might go into the forest tomorrow.'

'Sometimes she goes right up and onto the ridge. You can see the riders from our kitchen window: strung out along the ridge, silhouetted against the sunset. It's quite a sight,' says Jim.

'Oh yes it is.' Margaret nods and smiles.

'I hate that damn horse,' says Douglas. 'A broken-down nag. I'm not riding her again if you pay me to do it.'

'Looks like you'll have to trek alone,' says Jim, cheerily, to Pat.

Pat smiles uneasily.

'Look.' Margaret is not deliberately trying to change the subject. But she has noticed one that is more interesting.

Pat sees it and her heart sinks.

A young woman so slim, so smooth, so lovely, that she seems to belong to a different species from all the other women and girls in the room. Star quality: perhaps what Princess Diana (now about fifteen and not a princess) had. Or Jacqueline Kennedy. Some film stars. Women who have style, class, sexiness, beauty. Pat feels like a worthless lump as soon as she sets eyes on this creature, who is clad in a simple white shift dress, sleeveless, the better to reveal her long brown arms, and short, to reveal her similar legs.

'Amy Brownlee,' Margaret whispers.

'She's the hostess this year,' Jim says. 'Yep. I met her dad last night. This is their twenty-fifth year at the lake.'

'Still haven't done as many years as me,' Margaret says. But although her tone is as ringing, as bright, as usual, her face is shadowed. Pat knows what she is feeling, if not thinking. She is feeling that Amy is a more fitting partner for Douglas than Pat is. It is what she feels, and Pat feels it too. But it is a feeling too frightening to be formed into a thought, much less a communication.

'Nobody can ever do that!' Jim says, pushing away his plate firmly. 'Did you know, Pat, that Margaret first came to the lake when she was four years old?'

Pat does, because all of them have told her so more than once. But of course she pretends she hasn't. Jim and Margaret between them repeat the story, or the linked stories, of Margaret's first visits to the lake. Douglas concentrates on his dinner, much too fiercely it seems to Pat. The furrow between his heavy eyebrows deepens.

Later when they are taking a long walk along by the lake she asks him about Amy. 'They know her parents,' Douglas says. He picks up a stone and skims it across the water. It's black now, shiny: there is a half-moon hovering over the trees, a sprinkle of stars. Pat knows she has to wait and hope that he decides to offer more information. He picks up another stone and skims it before doing this.

'We went to the same college, me and old Amy.' Pat smiles, as she is meant to do, relieved to hear her denigrated in this way. Old Amy. So there's something wrong with her too. Maybe she isn't clever enough? That would irritate Douglas, just as it irritates him that Pat isn't beautiful enough. He needs a girl who is both very bright and very beautiful. Until he finds such a girl, he is going to feel short-changed. He is going to sulk and wonder why he is unhappy. This is not something he has realised yet. Pat is learning to realise it, against her will, against everything she wants to know. It will be a long, tough lesson for her as it will be for Douglas, when the time comes to let the truth sink in. 'We went out a few times.'

'When?'

'Sophomore year. Second year.'

'And didn't you . . . like her?'

'She's OK.'

'Don't you think she's attractive?'

'She's OK,' says Douglas. There are many things he can't acknowledge, to Pat or to himself. He adds with a dry laugh, 'And her dad's a millionaire. They were all hoping we'd get it together.'

Pat says nothing, but she's grateful to him for his tact, for pretending that the important thing about Amy is that her dad is a millionaire – how that information diminishes her!

Douglas stops throwing stones. He links her arm companionably and they walk for a stretch, easy and happy almost as they used to be a year ago, when they first fell in love and when it didn't matter that Pat wasn't beautiful enough to compete with the smooth-skinned girls of America. They walk until the path ends and they are at the wood. Pat would like to go on but he won't let her. 'Poison ivy,' he says. 'We won't see it in the dark.' They have to watch out for poison ivy every time they come to the forest. It prevents them going most places. Pat finds it hard to believe in poison ivy. She can't believe that a substance so treacherous could grow everywhere, waiting, constantly, to trap the unwary. And they have never actually seen any: whenever she asks Douglas to show her some, he can't find examples. 'And then there's the snakes,' he adds, knowing she is terrified of them, like all Irish people.

'I'd like to walk back to the other end then,' Pat says. The meal she has eaten is still lodging heavily in her stomach, and there is nothing to do at the camp after dinner except go for a walk or go to the soda fountain and eat ice cream, or go to your room and kiss. It's only ten o'clock. Many of the campers, especially the young ones, will get up at six for an organised early-morning swim in the lake, so it makes sense to go to bed early. But Pat doesn't feel like it, not after that dinner.

★   ★   ★

Pat did not tell Terry that she had fallen in love with Douglas for a while. At first, anyway, she wasn't sure if this had really happened. Although she knew she enjoyed being with him more than she enjoyed being with Terry and she knew she enjoyed kissing him more than she enjoyed kissing Terry, it wasn't clear if this were enough. Terry she didn't like kissing at all, and she was impatient and often bored with him. On the other hand she liked him and trusted him. He was gentle, soft-hearted, reliable. And she knew that he loved her absolutely and completely, although she did not know why. He was like a devoted dog.

That, she thought, was the trouble. He loved her too much. No matter how cool and standoffish she was, he went right on being in love with her. A dog, and he made her feel like a fox being chased by a dog. A mean nasty cold and cunning fox, being chased by a kindly, tail-wagging dog who only wanted to play and lick her all over.

It had not always been so. Initially she had wanted him as much as he wanted her, loving his large blue eyes, his gentle manners. But very soon all that had changed, perhaps because he was too good, perhaps because he gave too much? Now all she felt was guilt. Guilt, pity, remorse. Why did she stay with him? Not from motives of charity. She stayed because she needed a young man, a boyfriend, in the background of her life. She needed someone to mind her, to love her, in the absence of a mother. (Her mother had not died. But she was in a psychiatric hospital, suffering from severe depression, so it was said. This had been going on since Pat was twelve years of age.) Terry had filled the role for a few years. He was there, to take her to movies and parties at the weekends, to be her escort when she needed one. She could talk to him about most things that concerned her – her studies, her exams, her father. She never talked to anyone about her mother. With him as a companion she had become self-assured and seemingly independent. She concentrated on her work and had become good at it. She had been able to streamline herself into an efficient, focused career woman. It was thanks to Terry that she was a graduate student, doing a Ph.D. Thanks to him she had been able to concentrate on her studies, and do well at them, because she didn't have to waste time worrying about matters of the heart. Terry was there for her.

She knew that he was the kind of comfortable, safe man any girl or woman should aim to have in her life. Looking around, it seemed that many of her friends had opted for relationships with men like Terry – certainly the girls who were not among the most lively, the most beautiful, the most sought-after. But how could you know this? How could you know anything about other couples' feelings for one another? Maybe dull, uninspired pairs were fired by hidden passions, invisible to the eyes of their friends? Or maybe many people felt no need for any sort of passion?

She could hardly say that what she felt for Douglas was passion: he kept it at bay, and anyway she was still too terrified of sexuality to allow herself true passion. But he presented her with a challenge. She knew she felt happy in his arms, satisfied with his kisses and caresses. To spend a night with him, locked in those arms, was not the trial it would have been with Terry. Far from it. She never wanted to leave him when the long sessions were over. (And he didn't want her to leave either. Not at the beginning. They would linger, drawing out their farewells, taking one last kiss, one last taste of the other's skin or hair, their bodies unwilling to separate until the moment when one of them, usually Pat, jumped up, as a lazy sleeper jumps from bed, breaking off the dream abruptly in mid-flight, and pulled herself away.)

Weighing the two relationships, the two men, in the balance, Pat did not know which was better. Sex or faithful companionship? Which was she supposed to choose? Which of these was true love? While she wondered, Pat continued to see Terry at weekends, and Douglas during the week.

After a while the problem seemed to solve itself. Gradually, perhaps through force of habit, Pat and Douglas became inseparable – they became one of the college couples that went everywhere together. (There were couples, it was said, who even went to the toilet at the same time, one – the boy usually – waiting outside the

Ladies until the girl was finished and ready to move back to the library or wherever they had been.) They read together, they had lunch together, they went to parties and to plays together. The barrier Douglas had erected around himself had broken down and Pat was admitted to his circle, the magic circle of Douglas and Pat. (What she did not know was that such a barrier can always be put up again, quite easily, by a man who has one to begin with.) Love. There was no longer any doubt about it. Pat and Douglas, Douglas and Pat. They were in love, they knew one another. Pat couldn't be apart from Douglas for long without suffering something that felt like real pain.

That is when she found out what love is and that is when she had to tell Terry – Terry who already knew, all too well, what it was, at least in its terrifying, unrequited or half-requited, form.

Pat would learn about that, too, in time.

Margaret and Jim are lying side by side in their double bed. They have just had sex, easy-going and pleasurable. Jim is in a joking mood, a more joking mood than usual. 'That wasn't bad,' he says, yawning. 'I think I can get to sleep now.'

'Thank you,' Margaret says, turning on her side to her bedside lamp and her novel. She is not being ironic: it is a habit she has, to thank him for this ritual.

'Do you ever think . . .' she begins. Then she stops.

'What?' He is alert. She can tell from the sharp rise in his voice that he thinks she is going to make some interesting revelation.

'Ah nothing,' she says then.

'Go on! It's not fair, starting on something like that. What is it?'

Margaret had been going to say, do you ever think how different all this is when you are young and in love? How there is less fun, in a sense, but much more joy? Do you ever yearn to be back there? Or to have that again? But she says, 'I wonder if Douglas and that girl will stay together?'

'Pat?' he says. He gets out of bed to get a sandwich: he is naked. That is another reason why Margaret decided to take a separate house from Douglas and Pat, that it is part of Jim's holiday to sleep naked and walk around the room and the house naked as much as he can. Margaret herself is always clothed, just now in a pale pink cotton shortie nightgown. She is thin enough to get away with it. 'Who knows?' he says.

'She's a nice girl,' says Margaret.

'Meaning?' He is in the kitchen getting bread and cheese out of the refrigerator: they have laid in some simple supplies.

'Meaning just that.'

'Meaning but. What's the but?'

'I don't know. I just wonder.'

'They seem to get along together all right.'

'Oh yes!' Margaret says, brightly.

'She's white. She's not a drug addict.'

'She doesn't even smoke cigarettes.' Margaret thinks it might be better if she did.

'But she drinks.' Jim laughs and wags his finger in the air.

'She drinks? How do you know?' Margaret feels puzzled.

'Did you ever meet an Irish person who didn't?'

There is a snake on the wall in front of the house. It is a thick, long snake, greyish with yellow marks, and it is coiled like a Danish pastry on a flat slab of stone, apparently asleep. Pat sees it and screams. Douglas is not as scathing as he might be.

'It's probably just a copperhead,' he says. 'But we'll report it.'

'What are the dangerous ones?' Pat asks.

'Rattlesnakes.' He tells her what these look like. Pat doesn't take it in. The sight of the snake on the wall fascinates her. She had visualised the local snakes as small and thin, sly wormy creatures sliding secretly in the wet grass, under the pine needles. But this is as big as any of the snakes she has seen in the zoo in Dublin, although their skin, as she remembers it, tends to be more yellow and brown, speckled like leopards. Or maybe she is thinking of 'The Speckled Band'. It looks like a grey, lumpy-skinned eel, except for its round desperate eyes, which it opens as she watches. It begins to flick its tongue lazily at flies.

Douglas is not afraid of the snake, but he is surprised by it. He stands in the hot lunchtime sun and gazes for a few minutes with Pat, his arm loosely hooked around her waist. She can feel his appreciation of her discovery. Quite by accident, she has measured up to his expectations. It can happen so easily. But it has to happen effortlessly, by accident. How can she figure out how to control a situation while not worrying about it? If she could only master that trick, she'd be all right. Douglas would love her again.

They go to talk to an official in the reception office of the camp, a well-spoken man wearing an outfit that looks like a combat suit. Her luck holds. They are the first to report the news. The man strolls out and looks at the snake with an expert eye. 'Not dangerous,' he says, winking at Douglas. 'It's just an old water snake. But we'll remove it straight away. It'll scare the children.'

So the snake is not vicious or poisonous after all, in spite of its terrible looks. It's just a fat harmless snake that came out of the lake to lie in the sun.

That there are snakes in the lake is unpleasant news to Pat, though. She had felt safe there until now, in the surprisingly cold water.

Terry asked Pat to continue to see him. They had been together for two years, and she had only known Douglas for a few months.

'How could I do that?' She was genuinely puzzled, even though she had in fact been seeing both men for the few months in question.

'Why not?' He looked cross, at this stage, rather than angry or upset. His face was very white under his reddish hair.

'I don't know. It just seems odd, that's all.' Pat was bored. That was one of her main feelings during this meeting, which took place in a public house on Suffolk Street. It was not as inappropriate as it sounds: they met at seven o'clock and had the upstairs lounge bar to themselves. The barman watched television discreetly in the corner, leaning against the shelves of jewel-coloured bottles.

'Relationships don't have to be so exclusive' was one of the things he said next. It seemed he had a theory about the situation, a compromise solution to which he had given some rational, sensible thought.

This took Pat by surprise. It simply hadn't occurred to her, ever. Relationships with men do not have to be so exclusive, when you are twenty years of age. You are not married to anyone. You can have more than one friend who is male, more than one at a time.

Is that what Terry was trying to say?

If so, it seemed to Pat that this was the most interesting thing he had said about anything in all the time she had known him. He was clever, he was supposed to be a good judge of situations and character, he was a good rugby player. In addition he was good-humoured. But Pat had never had even one conversation with him that riveted her, or even one conversation that had interested her in any way. And she still believed and hoped that such conversations were possible, that they were waiting there to happen, somewhere in her brilliant future. She still believed that, in the right company, she would be a lively participant in a brilliant, intellectual, sparkling conversation that would illuminate aspects of life, literature, philosophy, history. That for some reason no such conversation had ever come her way in twenty years she attributed to bad luck, lack of the right company. But one of the things she felt, sitting in this pub where wedges of silver dust danced in the evening sun, was that if Terry could provide her with even a hint of the sort of conversation she craved, they'd be all right. They could certainly go on being friends. But then, she thought, if he had done that she would never have 'gone off' with Douglas. He didn't make brilliant conversation, either. But he had so much else to compensate for that lack.

'I don't think it would work,' Pat said, drearily. Suddenly the smell of cigarette ash and beer weighed heavily on her. The seediness that all pubs carry within themselves, no matter how cosy or glamorous they pretend to be, became overwhelmingly obvious. Both she and Terry were drinking Cokes. But they had spent many many hours drinking other things in this pub and others.

'Can't I see you at all?' His face was weighed down with something else. Desperation, disbelief. Guilt struck Pat, but from afar: she heard its waves breaking on a distant shore. That she was the cause of this she did not really believe. That was a real illumination. It was not her fault that he was in love with her. She was the love object, that was all. He thought he loved her to distraction but how could he? In a way all his love was in his imagination and had nothing to do with her.

'What's the point?' Pat had an overwhelming desire to get away. She felt selfish, guilty, mean, horrible. But also cheated. She had done what she believed was wise and right for a girl: she had allowed herself to be loved. She had had a nice safe relationship with someone who was safe and reliable, someone who needed her more than she needed him. In so far as any advice on relationships had come her way, the gist of it had been that Terry was the kind of man to choose. She had taken that advice. She had done what was wise and right and look what was happening now. Disaster, for that nice reliable person. A broken heart for him and a guilty conscience for her.

A guilty conscience, and emotional danger.

Immediately after the encounter with Terry, she went to Douglas for comfort. At that time he was living in a tiny room on Camden Street. It was dark, its one small window looking out into a damp, mossed-over area. She came to him, walking, from the pub. It was summer then too, the summer before this one on the lake. She walked briskly along the empty, sunlit streets. Her head, her body were shadowed by uncomfortable, messy feelings. But above them floated a certainty that she had been brave. She had been loyal to Douglas, and straight with Terry, instead of duplicitous and self-interested. From Douglas she wanted praise for her good behaviour.

But what he said was 'It's your own business.' All her confusion, all her triumph and hope, were deflated. He was telling her then that he was not involved in the plot of her life, whatever she chose to imagine.

She heard him, and understood what he was saying. But she went on imagining another story for herself, in which Douglas played the leading role.

And they never spoke about Terry again.

When Margaret had started coming to the lake, as a child, the resort had been much smaller than it now is, and more overtly religious. There is still grace before meals (usually the hostess says it, in a low voice that does not carry well). There is church on Sunday and no alcohol. But in the old days there was a prayer meeting every morning, and Bible discussion groups in the evening after supper. Both were voluntary, of course, but many people, especially women, attended them. Margaret had attended them, with her mother and aunt.

That is where Jim had seen her, in the little wooden chapel, which is at the end of the village of log cabins. He saw her there one Sunday: he did not go to church on weekdays and he did not go to Bible discussion groups at all.

He saw her on three Sundays, spread over two years, in church. She would have been wearing a floppy muslin or silk dress, with a sailor collar, and a white boater hat, white gloves at the end of bare brown arms. The fashion of the thirties. Her hair was shoulder length, waved like Veronica Lake's, although not that brassy colour, a colour you would usually only achieve with chemical assistance. Margaret's hair was reddish then, what was called sandy. (Now it is the colour of Veronica Lake's, although its texture is different.) Her best feature was her mouth. It was wide and her teeth were perfect and perfectly white.

Jim saw her at other places as well. In the dining hall, of course, and walking around the lake. He must have seen her in the boats, since she went for a row with some girlfriends every evening. He had no doubt noticed her on the beach, in her puckered red satin bathing suit, with its skirt of spotted muslin half-covering her thighs. But he never approached her and she did not notice him at all, until her father told her he had had a note from a young man asking if he could ask her for a date.

A note from a young man!

Even her parents thought it was a little formal and old-fashioned. This was the year 1938.

'Well,' her mother gasped, smothering the suggestion of a sharp, ridiculing laugh. 'I . . .' She had been about to say 'I never!' Something like that. But she looked at Margaret, eating cornflakes, and stopped. Margaret was clearly impressed. So her mother said, 'Well, what do you think, dear? Will you go on a date with him?'

'James Henryson,' said her father, consulting the note.

'Yes,' said Margaret.

'OK!' Her father shrugged. 'What am I supposed to do next?'

'You'll have to write back to him and say that she will,' said her mother, having trouble suppressing her laughter this time. 'Tell him she will be honoured.'

Margaret stepped in and overruled this. 'I'll write to him,' she said. 'Give me that note.'

She had seen Jim. She had seen him on the golf course where she walked, along the edges of the fairways, with her friend Alison, spying on the young men who played there. She had seen him on the beach, and in the water, where he was a strong swimmer although not better than she was. She had seen him diving from Diver's Rock, a cliff about fifty feet high at the far side of the lake, where the boys went to show off during the afternoons while the girls sewed under the trees by the lakeside or discussed the meaning of the Song of Solomon or Noah's Ark with Miss Simpson and Miss Benson, the two old ladies who organised these events. Some of the girls, though, including Margaret, sometimes skipped these classes. They used the time gained to row across the lake to a tiny cove at the back of Diver's Rock. They docked there, and climbed to a stand of trees where they could conceal themselves while watching the young men run and jump from the edge of the cliff. Naked. Jim was one of the very best-looking of those who thus displayed themselves – he looked then very much as Douglas looked now: one of the stars. In men this is not as important, as excluding, as it is among women. If you have the luck to attract such a man, he is not necessarily a danger, but a prize you can take if you want it.

Margaret sat there reading his note to her father and feeling, if not thinking, these thoughts. His handwriting was enigmatic: it was elliptical, with long under-and over-strokes. The individual words were hard to decipher, but the overall effect was both very neat and very stylish. It was the most grown-up, the most sophisticated, handwriting she had ever noticed. Her own hand was rounded and clear, a childish style which seemed to betoken simplicity, willingness to communicate, honesty. What Jim's hand told her was that he was self-reliant and determined. She felt she would probably marry him.

The room, Pat's rather than Douglas's, although they are both side by side, continues to be their private meeting place. They do not have real sex, because Pat is not on the pill. This is another problem for them.

'I'll go to the clinic when I go home,' she promises.

He's not pressurising her. But it seems odd to him that they do not make love, make love properly, though they have been together for a long time. Pat is not sure whether it is odd or not. Her feelings about this most intimate of matters are influenced by outside forces. She has left the Catholic Church behind her, already sensing that it is consistently operating against her interests, against all women's interests. But she is not free. Social mores, convention, even the law, exert a considerable influence over her sexual life.

This is still a time when you would not be sure, in Ireland, what other people were doing, as far as sex was concerned. You think you know what people do in England and the Continent and America. They go for it. So Philip Larkin said in his poem. It began in 1963, about fifteen years ago. But in Ireland fifteen years isn't long – even if it's a whole childhood – and you couldn't be quite sure how long a fashion would take to catch on. The official line is clear: sex is wrong. The law forbids it, more or less. Contraception has just stopped being illegal for married people, so they are now permitted by the government to engage in sex whenever they like. But it is still illegal for unmarried people. You can't, for example, buy a condom in a shop or in a chemist's, still less in a machine in a student cloakroom. 'Going to the clinic' means going to an illicit clinic, operating subversively in a cellar in some quiet back street, run by feminists or perhaps English people. It does not mean going to the ordinary doctor. The ordinary doctor is not supposed to prescribe the pill to women who are not married.

On the other hand, everything one reads or sees in the movies or hears in popular music suggest that you ought to be sexually active. All these sources indicate that not having sex is abnormal – a crime against nature. So there are two diametrically opposite attitudes in the air. You can sin against the state, or you can sin against nature. In such circumstances, it is difficult to figure out what real people actually do. Which voice do they listen to? Pat is the sort of girl who wants to do what everyone else is doing – the right thing. But she isn't the sort of girl who would ask them what that is. What could she do anyway? Conduct a survey? Even if you could, the chances are most people would lie about it.

Douglas can be protective of Pat. She is his protégée, here in this strange land, in America. He knows what she is coming from – smallness, complexity, absurdity. Primitiveness. He knows but already he occasionally forgets that other world. Pat herself forgets it: the unheated house with its cheap rickety furniture, the ten-year-old car, the endless obsession with money. The father who is increasingly unable to function effectively even in the world he inhabits, whose old, uneducated country ways don't equip him to understand the mechanics of the modernising urban society he finds himself in. Her mentally ill mother. When Pat arrived in Delaware, a week ago, she and Douglas immediately understood that in Delaware, in America, she would never even have met someone like Douglas. The social gap would have kept them segregated at least until she had firmly lifted herself, by her own efforts, far out of her own sphere. The degrees from the unglamorous Dublin university and her illusions, her dreams, would not have accomplished that lift, as they did, or as she imagined they did, in Ireland. White trash, she probably was, in these people's estimation. Douglas knew it, the day she arrived, for a few days afterwards. It made him tender. He had selected her; he had brought her here. 'At least she's white!' It was a joke, but it was almost the only point in Pat's favour in middle America.

But after a few days they slipped back to their old roles. They forgot that Pat was poor and Irish. She became what she was in Ireland, in college: anybody's equal, Douglas's equal. His classmate in Medieval Studies. His girlfriend. His lover. His enemy.

Amy is at the beach for the early morning swim. A group of boys and girls gathers on the tiny stretch of shingle, laughing and exchanging greetings, like a flock of beautiful seabirds. Amy is the most attractive, and she is dressed in an all-in-one, modest, classy white swimsuit. Her tanned limbs show up very nicely against its pristine snowiness. Her hair is tightly wrapped against her head, encased in a rubber swimming cap shaped like a black turban.

Pat glances at Douglas, big and muscular and pale, in his swim trunks which are really shorts. He is not looking at Amy at all. He is looking at the lake, a pale grey in the morning light: it is 6.30 a.m.

'Taking the plunge?' he asks.

'Sure!' Pat has already begun to talk like an American: this process had started before she ever set foot in the country, thanks to Douglas's influence. For the rest of her life she will say 'sure' in the American way, and 'movie' and 'necktie'. It will not be noticed. So many Irish people have picked up Americanisms anyway, from television. Pat seldom watches much television, but who is to know that?

She places one hand in a position to hide the hairs which are showing, horribly, at the edges of her very skimpy brown bikini (the only bikini on this beach), and runs with Douglas to the edge of the water, and then into the water. She is not surprised by how cold it is, having swum in it already, but it is still a shock to the body. Douglas races out a couple of yards, then plunges and starts to swim. Pat would like to walk around, spend ages getting used to the cold, but since she has to do what people do here, and also hide those springy, sexual-looking hairs, she follows Douglas and immerses herself in the cold saltless water.

It is not as cold as it seems at first, and within a few minutes she is

comfortable. Douglas is a strong swimmer, he has swum out towards
the middle of the lake. The water is now full of swimmers. Everyone
is in, ducking and plunging, playing or swimming in a long line like
a plane going through the sky towards some invisible destination out
in the water. Amy's black turban is bobbing along like a cormorant,
making a beeline for – it seems to Pat – Douglas. By now he is a few
hundred yards away. There is no question of Pat pursuing him. She
will not swim out so far. She has always been taught to swim in
towards the shore or parallel to it, and that is what she is doing now.
Amy's black turban, other swimming hats, red and yellow and blue,
are making their way after Douglas, out to the middle of the lake.
She can see out there, far away, a kayak. She guesses that is what he
has picked as his destination.

The caps, and the sleek short back-and-sides of the boys make
their way to the kayak. Hardly any swimmers are left near the shore,
with Pat. She watches Douglas, a speck now, and the other specks in
pursuit.

She feels very light, like a leaf falling from a tree.

Her head is clearer than the crystal lake water. Gloriously clear,
glass, holy water. Light and free.

She swims to the narrow beach, steps up the rough, cutting
shingle to the rock where her big white towel (camp property, and
so appropriately pure and thick) lies draped. She wraps herself in it,
slips her feet into her sandals, and makes her way back to her room.

Just now she feels free. She doesn't care what happens.

In her room she showers, dresses, dries her hair and brushes it
more slowly and carefully than usual, backcombing it until it is a
glossy crest of gold around her head. She cleanses her face with a
tube of cream she bought at the airport, scrubbing the corners of her
eyes, the crease of her chin, meticulously. For days she has neglected
herself, meaning her skin, her body. Giving herself over to the
novelty of the holiday has been more than enough to use up all her
resources of energy. Giving herself up to her concern about Douglas,
about holding on to him or making him pay attention to her, has
been enough. The carelessness shows, at least slightly, in freckles,

spots where she didn't even bother to cleanse off makeup at night before going to bed, in the wild frizz of her hair, which is dry and needs conditioning if it is not to go mad. But she is not performing these rituals of cleaning and creaming, of brushing and polishing, in order to make herself more attractive to Douglas. Not really. What she is doing now is what women or girls do from time to time. She is pampering herself. She is restoring her own relationship with her real self, pulling away from that slightly crazed, neurotic creature who has no time for anything, for anything in the world, except one man. Applying a cream called Royal Jelly Face and Neck Moisturizer to her skin may not be the most profound or permanent path to her inner self, but it is faster than any other way she can think of right now.

By the time Douglas arrives back in the house she is sitting against the white pillow of her bed, neat and clean, reading a book.

'What happened?' Douglas has a white towel draped across his shoulders. Water drips to the wooden floor.

'I got tired. I came back.'

'You could've told me!' He speaks angrily but looks concerned.

'You were too far away. I can't swim as far out as you.'

'I was looking everywhere for you. I thought you'd drowned.'

He comes over to the bed and sits on the edge, in his wet swimming shorts. Pat puts her book on the floor and looks at him. She pats his hand, which is still cold from the lake.

'I'm sorry,' she says. 'I thought you'd have guessed.'

He shakes his head in mock disbelief. 'You thought I'd have guessed,' he says in a sarcastic voice. A sarcastic but relieved and friendly voice. Whatever it was Douglas thought he is not going to say, openly, to Pat. Just as he is not going to tell her what he thinks about Amy, or his mother, or anything much. Americans are reputed to be open and frank. Innocent, even. But they are no more open and frank than anyone else.

He gives her a warm, wet hug. Then they hurry off to breakfast in the big, beamed hall. Waffles, maple syrup, ham and eggs and sausages and hash browns, French toast and ordinary toast, orange juice and pink grapefruit juice and cranberry juice, cereals, cream, coffee, tea, muffins, bagels. What is on offer every morning. The atmosphere is buoyant at breakfast. The big hall hums with low chat, the sounds of people embarking on a hopeful summer day at the lake.

What Pat remembers is always the same. The name of the lake, which is stiff and upright, old-fashioned, the name of an English king. It is not the only name this lake has. Before it got its very English name, it had an equally unsuitable, very French name, which it had been given by Jesuit priests from Canada. A very Catholic name. And since the lake was clearly in place before those priests arrived here, it must have had another name too, an Indian name, rough-hewn and exotic as the names of the mountains that encircle it. The Adirondacks. It must have had such a name, given by the Iroquois, meaning something to them or perhaps not. Perhaps a name so ancient that nobody, no scholar, can discover its meaning. For so it is, often, with the names of lakes, and rivers. They have been there much longer than the languages that are spoken on their shores. And the people who lived on their shores had a name for the lake centuries and millennia ago. Those names, lake names, are the oldest words there are in human language, often sticking to the lake, surviving successive linguistic changes. But not so this great beautiful lake stretching from New York State to Lake Champlain. For some reason it has been named at least three times – maybe because it is big and strategic, and successive waves of settlers have needed to claim it as their own.

The name. And the high, stiff dark green trees, fir trees or pine, she still could not tell the difference, that grow all around its long, dagger-shaped shore. The higher rocky mountains that strut up into the sky behind the trees. Then the big outcrop of the camp, the old brownish crumbly-looking house with its tendrils of outbuildings.

Only after all that does she recall the water, the lake itself – blue, glittering, calm. The blue sky overhead. The sun shines all the time she is at this lake, one glorious day succeeds another, and yet the air is fresh, the temperature hot but eminently bearable. She knows that occasionally there must be less perfect conditions here. Maybe it rains sometimes, is cold. But she can't believe that it is so, not really. She has seen the lake only in this amazing light and remembers it as a perfect place, unblemished by meteorological flaws.

It is dinner time. Douglas, Pat and his parents are at their usual table, looking at their small plates of melon balls with mint, a starter which they will eat as soon as the bell rings and grace is said, by Amy. Amy is still in position near the door of the hall, dressed in blue this evening, welcoming the tardy campers with a smile and a nod, nothing in her expression or demeanour indicating that they are holding up the proceedings. That lack of expression expresses more disapproval than any pout or word could, anyway, to those who have the tendency to feel guilty.

Pat keeps glancing over at Amy, when she gets a chance in the gaps in the conversation that is going on, which is mainly a description of an outing Jim and Margaret have made to a museum in the mountains. The Adirondack Museum. Pat will have to go there, Margaret says. She will find the Native American artifacts, the illustrated history of the mountain area, fascinating. It includes a replica of a big Indian lodge, and several kinds of totem pole. Charcoal burners' huts, trappers' cabins and their tools. There is a film giving an account of the history of the lake region from the earliest times to the present day.

Jim talks about Davy Crockett. Or is it Daniel Boone? Pat gets the impression that Davy Crockett lived in the Adirondack Mountains, because he was a trapper who fought the Indians, like a lot of people here. (Later Douglas, complaining about his father, lets her know that Davy Crockett came from Tennessee and died in Mexico, at the Battle of the Alamo, fighting Mexicans with his bare hands.) Jim is not interested in the historical facts anyway, but in the stories. He tells a tall tale, the kind of tale associated most closely with Davy Crockett. It is a story about an encounter between a grizzly bear and Davy Crockett. He is telling this because he thinks Pat would be interested in it, and also because he is himself amused by these stories, which his own grandfather, the person he loved and admired most in the world, used to tell to him when he was a child. He does not tell Pat this, thinking it is less important than the stories themselves, as far as she is concerned. There he is wrong, of course. It is what surrounds these tales, which are somehow silly, that would ignite some interest in her. As it is she smiles politely, laughs unconvincingly, as she tries to think of some suitable response. 'That's a really good story,' she says sometimes, weakly. Or else she asks for clarification of some point, some clarification that she does not need. Were there a lot of bears hereabouts? Are they still there? Questions to which she knows the answers perfectly well.

Jim has not got to the end of his story when a commotion breaks out at the door, or what passes as a commotion in this intensely polite environment. A strange man has entered the hall. He is dressed in shorts. Nothing unusual there. Every man in the room is dressed in shorts, even now, for dinner. But his are different, crumpled and dirty, and instead of wearing the plain white or blue or lemon polo shirts that all the other men wear on top he is wearing nothing at all. On his head, nevertheless, is a baseball cap, back to front, which he does not bother to remove.

In addition, he is black. He is the first black person Pat has seen in the camp, she realises, although without much of a jolt – she has hardly seen any black people at all since she came to America, after the first half-hour at the airport.

As soon as they see this person Jim and Margaret cast down their eyes and start to eat their melon balls. The bell has not been rung, grace has not been said, but they do this anyway. Pat starts to eat too, obediently, but Douglas doesn't.

The man is saying something to Amy, who looks flustered. But within seconds other men, men who clearly have some management function in the camp but who are usually invisible, have moved up to the door and are engaged in conversation with him. Amy has disappeared – not disappeared, she is at her table at the head of the room, chatting animatedly to her companions. It is obvious from the way she is talking that she has something vitally interesting to say.

Before the main course is served they find out.

'They've found it,' Jim says to Douglas.

'What?' Pat has no idea what they are talking about.

'Oh nothing,' Margaret says. 'Some body.'

Meaning a corpse. It was found not in the lake but in the forest. A girl had vanished ten days ago, one of the Muffins. The black man – he was soon followed by some state troopers – had found her corpse when he was picking blueberries in a stretch of forest up the lake earlier in the afternoon. She wasn't buried, just covered by some branches and pine needles.

Pat asked Douglas if he had known about this, and why he hadn't mentioned it.

'We didn't want to worry you' is the first answer he gives. Then he shrugs and says, 'Anyway what's the point in talking about it? It's one of those things.'

One of those things the Henrysons didn't talk about.

While Douglas was home in the States, during the first month of the summer, and Pat was still in Ireland, she had gone to a barbecue on a beach near Dublin. The barbecue had been set up in the marram grass and camomile that grew at the back of the beach, and a camp fire had been lit on the beach itself, on the rough-grained, silvery sand. Many people Pat had been friendly with before she had met Douglas were at this party. They were either friendly in a distant way, chatting briefly to her but looking suspicious, or overly hearty. 'Long time no see' was something three different people said, at different times. 'Howdy stranger' was what the girl who had thrown the party said. In general there were no hard feelings. They were young, optimistic, forgiving. Not competitive. Grudges had not had time to take hold and harden, as they would later.

Terry was at the party. He came late. Pat had already drunk quite a lot of beer, and eaten several sausages and burned, delicious hamburgers, when he appeared on the path that ran behind the grass. It was almost dark at that stage. She was listening to a girl strumming a guitar and singing a song called 'Happiness Runs', a song with just these two words which she repeated hundreds of times in her high, tuneful voice. The words were rolling across the sand down to the waves breaking softly, but in a strangely abrupt way, on the shingle. Beyond the sea was spreading a milky, mild, darkening blue. A floating lighthouse flashed on the horizon every few minutes. The fire flames flickered.

Terry saw Pat before she saw him – in fact he had been tipped off by the hostess, if that's what she was. She had rung him and asked if he minded, she had asked Pat. He, being Terry, said he did not mind. But he wondered if it might have been more tactful of her to have asked him first, before she had already issued the invitation to Pat, instead of warning him not to come if he didn't want to risk seeing her.

He did not seek her out. He did not sit beside her. Instead he went and joined another group, a group that had congregated around the steel barbecue. They were somewhat noisier, drunker, than the people at the fire. They sat on the prickly grass and threw sausages at one another.

When Pat went to get another burger, she saw Terry. All he did was nod and smile. He did not even say hello. She returned to her spot by the fire, feeling chastened.

Something was happening in her relationship with Douglas at this time, even though he was not in Ireland. What was happening was that he was not writing to her, or telephoning. He had been gone for five weeks and in that time she had had one letter, although she had written several.

She was supposed to be going out to have a holiday with him in August, two weeks from now. Her ticket was paid for. This gave her a sense of security. How could he turn her away after encouraging her to buy a ticket? But although she believed a ticket so expensive would have to be used, could not be cancelled, she was apprehensive. He would have to get in touch with her before she left for America. He would have to confirm that he still wanted her out there, make arrangements about collecting her from the airport. Even if he did write to deal with these issues, what was going to await her when she got to America?

She sat at the fire and thought of this problem.

Later, she went and talked to Terry. He was talkative, as talkative as he had ever been, and not angry or in any way upset. It was as if nothing had happened. They had never had an intimate conversational style, there were no codes, no private jokes, between them: somehow their lack of common ground, their mutual lack of imagination or initiative, ensured that. Their lack of chemistry ensured it. He was like one of the many boys and men she knew slightly, her friends' boyfriends, her classmates, people she had known for years but with whom she could never have a real conversation. So far, in her experience, the only boys she could have a serious conversation with were boys she had at some stage been attracted to. With all others, some sort of barrier to conversational intimacy existed. With Terry that barrier still existed.

Why, then, did she put her arm around him, invite him to kiss her?

Habit, probably. And probably to test him, to find out if he was still there for her, if all failed with Douglas.

That was something she had not told Douglas about. The party at the beach. The fire, the mild sea. Her attempt to seduce Terry, to test him, just in case. Terry had returned the kiss, but then had walked away and had not come back at all.

Douglas told her a bit more about the murdered girl after they had said goodbye to his parents, and were driving back to Delaware in his big car – a Buick or an Oldsmobile, some car like that, bigger than any Pat had ever been in.

'She was a Muffin. Kelly Guildford. She was raped and then strangled.'

'By whom?' Pat is still interested in this story. Her interest seems, even to herself, prurient and vulgar. But it's there. And it seems to be inspired not so much by a curiosity about the details of the crime itself – which are, after all, fairly commonplace, and anyway not the kind of thing she takes any interest in – as by the circumstances. It seems so impossible that a Muffin could be assaulted in any way in this puritanical, sweet, precious, protected place.

'They think maybe the guy who found her.'

'The black guy?'

'Yeah.'

'Why would he report the thing?'

'I don't know. How could I know? It's what they're saying.'

'Who is saying?'

'The guys at the camp. My father. Amy. All that lot.'

Amy. But she doesn't care any more about Amy, who is stuck at the camp until the end of August and who lives in Washington, DC. She is still more interested in the dead Muffin.

'How did she get into that forest? Did she go there herself?'

'I just don't know,' Douglas snaps, gritting his teeth. His face is tight, strained to breaking point by his impatience with Pat and with everything about this holiday. 'What does it matter? She's dead.'

Pat wants to know. She wants to know how something as cruel and passionate as a murder, rape and strangling, could have occurred in such a sanitised, genteel place. There is something she does not know about that resort, she feels now. There are aspects to it that have been kept hidden from her, by Douglas and Margaret and Jim. They have all pulled the wool over her eyes.

Margaret goes for a walk in the woods. She goes alone, early in the morning before Jim wakes up, before the young people, Amy and that lot, are out for their swim. The sun has just risen over the mountains, and the lake is spangled, black and gold and red. The hush of the forest is deeper, cooler than usual, a dewy chill under the trees. She moves along through them, through the pines which are as high and bare as telegraph poles, long long pines, the foliage high above her head. Occasionally she hears a shuffle, a flurry, as something flies or runs.

She walks far into the forest, as far as the place where Kelly

Guildford was found. She finds the spot where she was buried, or covered – it is marked by a little rope barrier, red flags. The police and the forensic people haven't finished their investigations.

It is not different from other parts of the forest. You can see that the soil has been disturbed a bit, the pine needles brushed or moved to make a heap. Otherwise there is nothing, apart from the signs left by the police, that anything unusual has happened in this place. Once the flags are removed, there will be no sign at all.

'Where were you?' Jim is on the veranda, drinking coffee, when she comes back.

'I went for a walk,' she says brightly.

'By the lake?' He looks at her curiously.

'Yes. I saw the sunrise,' she says.

He gives her coffee, and they sit in their rattan chairs, looking at the lake.

'I don't think they will stay together,' Margaret says abruptly, without preamble, as she bites a muffin.

'No,' says Jim, unconcernedly. 'I guess not.'

'He's not in love with her,' Margaret says, calmly. 'I don't know why he invited her over, really. Poor thing.'

'Well, these things happen,' Jim says. 'It'll all work out.'

'I'm glad we were able to do this for her. Give her a holiday here, at the lake.' Margaret smiles, genuinely pleased.

'See Lake George and die,' says Jim.

Pat sees her and Douglas as tied by an elastic band. A longish elastic band, wrapped around them like a cat's cradle. It stretches this way, it stretches that way. He pulls away, stretching it to a taut rubber wire, ready to snap unless she moves forward. It is her job to keep that band flexible. It is her job, because Douglas does not even know it is there, he does not see it at all. That is what it means to be a young man. He is a young man of definite preferences, a deliberate, careful, pure man, the only kind Pat could feel anything for. But that means he has other things to do, he has no time to watch the progress of his relationship, to analyse and prod and test and know, and to remain silent. The watchful one will have to be Pat. That is the price she would have to pay to keep the connection going. She would have to be eternally vigilant.

She did not immediately know she cared about Douglas, even after the party at Rain's flat, and the kiss. A thing like that could happen. You could kiss someone and no more need come of it. That is what Douglas himself anticipated, and the thought relieved him but made him gloomy. He was very lonely then, alone and friendless, spending long evenings, weekends, alone in his gloomy flat while people in college believed he was going to hunt balls. Rain had said to Pat that she knew his type. 'He knows his cocktails,' she said, with a shrewd grimace. She told Pat that he went hunting in Kildare at weekends and was on terms of friendship with the aristocracy of Ireland, people the college crowd hardly knew existed. But she was wrong, they all were. Douglas was so isolated and beaten down that he did not believe that even Pat would stick with him.

A few weeks after Rain's party there was another party, hosted by the English department for its postgraduates. Douglas was not invited, since he didn't do English. He was sitting in the library, working, while the party was going on. But many of those who belonged to Rain's crowd were present. They drank wine in the common room and talked to the lecturers and professors, something they considered to be a treat. Somebody started talking about love, as people were wont to do. It was the subject that interested all of them more than any other. It was indeed the subject of many of the lectures, the courses, they attended. The study of medieval literature was the study of love. Some of those present in the room believed that romantic love had been invented in the Middle Ages (they were the ones who did French).

But even those who would question a theory that so limited the spontaneity of humanity were interested in the topic of love.

Soul mates. In the corner they were talking about soul mates.

'Of course,' one of the professors said. 'Fine. But my soul mate could be somewhere in South America. What use is that to me?'

The man who said that looked old and thin and disappointed. His wife was at his side, and did not react to his remark.

My soul mate could be in South America.

Pat saw, in her head, Douglas, sitting at his table in the postgraduates' library. She saw him, his head bowed over his books, engaged in the slow, painstaking work they all did: translating Insular Latin or Old English, checking every word, mind bent to the rigours of the task – the arduous, noble, old-fashioned task of learning an old language that most people in the world didn't care tuppence for. He gave himself to that hard work, as she did, without knowing why. They had risked a lot for old languages and literatures, just because they loved them. That they had in common. And now she knew he was there, alone and lonely, when she was enjoying herself, drinking wine with the professors, talking about soul mates.

A huge wave of longing, a wave of pity, overcame her.

Her soul mate.

Abruptly, she left the party, and ran along the long, dark corridors to the graduates' room.

He was there. It was ten o'clock and the whole vast college was empty. But he had waited, hoping someone – she? – would come.

Douglas's thesis is written. He has finished it more quickly than had been expected, during the summer. Already he has sent it to Dublin. He will come back to take a viva in September. But after that there will be no reason for him to remain in Ireland.

He tells Pat this now, on the way home from the lake.

'What are you going to do then?' She wants him to tell her everything. What he is going to do then, and then, and then. She wants to know. That he is going to ask her to come with him to America. (It would have to be a marriage proposal. She is not going to leave home for less. They both know it.)

But he tells her nothing.

And she can't ask. You can't ask a man like Douglas about the future. You could hear something very upsetting.

They are driving down the Northway Route, on the way back to Delaware. The lake is behind them – for ever or maybe until next year, until a few years down the line. She realises something about the camp. Temperance.

'Is it a temperance camp?'

'I suppose so, something like that.'

Something like that. It's not Methodist, it's temperance. That's what united all of those nice people. Jim and Margaret and Amy. An aversion to, a lack of interest in, alcohol. Pat had noticed no drinks but had not thought about it. She already knew the only cocktails his family drank were egg nog, cranberry juice with soda. At the resort, the word 'temperance' had never been used. Why should it be? Maybe in America you are more aware of the strategies people use to insist that their own culture is the norm than you are in Ireland, where most of the population colludes to shut out everything that seems alien?

They have the radio on in the car.

Rich music floats out into the crystal air, the dark green forest. Dory Previn is singing a song about a man she knows – probably André Previn. 'I know I know I know I know,' she sings, tragically. I know his face and his hands and his eyes. I know him out, I know him in. I know his lies. I know I know I know I know I know.

Pat in the passenger seat, Douglas driving, the music floating around them, the dark pointed evergreens. She loves this. This is where she wants to be. In the passenger seat, zipping along a wide blue highway, listening to a song that seems to her unbelievably true, a song she feels she could have written herself. The song of a woman who has given herself to love.

Suddenly the song is stopped. The fruity voice of an announcer breaks in.

Elvis has died.

He died this morning, this very morning. News has just come in.

Douglas and Pat are too young to have known Elvis as a star for themselves, if they ever would have listened anyway. The Beatles, they have experienced, just about. Douglas likes Peter, Paul and

Mary. The Byrds. Joni Mitchell. Pat likes Simon and Garfunkel.

Still. They know what he looks like.

An icon for their age, or the age before this one.

A diversion.

Pat observes Douglas's worried face, and feels a momentary relief. That he is shocked by the death of Elvis bodes well for her, she thinks. She does not know why, but she feels that it gives her some leeway. He will be easier on her for a while now, because of this tragedy. Tragedy that will be talked about. Talked about a lot, if they listen to the radio, watch television when they get home. It will divert his attention, and make him feel that having a woman in love with him is not the worst thing that could befall a man. Maybe he will understand what Pat needs? Maybe he will forgive her for not being good enough, perfect enough? Tell her what his plans are, that they include her? Maybe all the mistakes that surround them, soon may overwhelm and destroy them, will somehow vanish in the light of the greater tragedy, in the sticky sweetness of the Elvis songs?

The radio plays Elvis songs all the rest of the way to Delaware.

Long after this summer, when Douglas has disappeared from her life for ever, Pat meets Rain at a conference in Ottawa, where Rain has become a professor of Medieval History. She is very plump now, but still has a youthful, striking face. She is sharper than she was as a girl, and more impatient. Pat is still very thin. Her hair is fuzzy rather than wavy now, and is dyed a mixture of blonde and brown. Her teeth are still crooked but they are her own. She became a schoolteacher in the end, and teaches English, but has kept up her medieval studies, writing occasional articles and belonging to some learned societies. She did not get married and neither did Rain.

She talks to Rain about Douglas, and asks her if she has met him since they were all students together. Rain hesitates before she replies. Pat waits, wondering what sensational report is in store – Douglas has been in a coma for ten years? Douglas is on death row? Douglas is dead?

'He's a professor,' says Rain eventually, and names and Ivy League university. 'He did well. I'm surprised you haven't come across him.'

Pat, annoyed, mutters that she has lost touch with the academic grapevine. She reverts to the safety of the past, and tells Rain about the summer at the lake.

'Well, you probably had a lucky escape,' Rain says, in her husky, mellow, comforting voice. 'It would never have worked out.'

Of course it would, thinks Pat, even more irritated. How can an intelligent woman like Rain utter such a flaccid banality? Pat firmly believes that if she had handled things differently, if she had manipulated the situation subtly instead of clumsily, she would still be with Douglas. The people who get what they want are those whose controlling touch is so light as to be undetectable to the innocent, not those who are themselves genuinely innocent.

'And you're happy anyway, aren't you?' Rain asks, with an uneasy crooked smile.

Now it is Pat's turn to hesitate. She pauses, and in the pause, she remembers everything that matters: the snake, thick and roughly scaled, coiled like a cake on the hot wall. (By now she knows it was a rattlesnake, one of America's most dangerous reptiles, not a water snake at all.) She remembers painting the bunch of broom, and feeling pleased because, entirely without effort, she had managed to hive her picture life and flow and energy. She remembers the flowers on their long swaying rough stems, the paint wet on the thin paper, the old teacher in her flowery smock encouraging the motley crew ranged before her. Old men and women, Douglas and Pat, side by side, concentrating on their pictures. The pine trees, the silvery lake, a backdrop to the jug of yellow blossom. The morning sun hot on the nape of her neck.

'I am quite happy,' she says, realising that it is true. Nothing in her life has worked out according to her original plan. She did not marry Douglas, or Terry, or anyone. She abandoned her academic career almost as soon as it began. She is not rich, or powerful, or important. But in the mysterious borderland that separates dream and reality, the gap called 'anyway', she is happy – more or less.

NOMADS SEEK THE PAVILIONS
OF BLISS ON THE SLOPES OF
MIDDLE AGE

Mary steps out of her car, raises her umbrella, observes with pleasure her reflection in a rain-starred puddle: a shirred impression of smudged red, blurred green, spiked by the relentless rain of diamonds. Narcissus. What she sees is not herself but Leech's portrait of his wife – proud, slender, graceful, beautiful, her head cocked and cloched, her eyes full of mysterious knowledge. A woman of secrets, sheltered by her green sunshade, her yellowy cardigan, her olive skin, the contours of her body as green and fluid as those of the sea, the grass, the trees, the sky – a circle, a gentle rainbow, closed, complete.

Mary's umbrella is scarlet. Strident against the grey granite, jaunty as a red pennant on a summer cottage in some aged black-and-white photograph, brave in the wind, proclaiming holidays, joy, pleasure. Not her own umbrella, of course. In the past year she has owned and lost a succession of half a dozen, blue and green and yellow and black. All left behind, one after the other, in trains and restaurants and the fitting rooms of shops. The red she took by mistake from the boot of another woman's car, yesterday. She will return it to its owner, her friend Monica, next time they meet, if that happens and if she doesn't lose it in the meantime. Thus do the umbrellas of the world circulate, from hand to hand, finders keepers. Oddly, however, although Mary has lost hundreds she has only found one.

The drains are not coping with today's downpour, and the footpath is half an inch deep in water. Mary observes with pleasure her neat shoes, which are coping admirably, although they are designed to resemble ballerina's slippers. She shrugs comfortably in her khaki coat, feeling herself brave and lovely.

This is what love does for her.

Fills her with self-love, self-admiration. Transports her on heavenly wings from reality to the ideal. For her lover she is wondrous, heroic, an angel on tiptoe through the treacherous streets, an amazon hacking her way through jungles of stomach-deadening threats, of shattering deceits, of glittering risk and gleaming promises. A lady with an umbrella, alone in the rainwashed wildernesses of the heart.

Few people are about. Most huddle like sheep in the doorways of shops, or have stayed in their offices, waiting for the downpour to subside. Optimal conditions for an illicit rendezvous. Maybe today she and he can sit in the open, share a sandwich on a park bench, delight in the battering of the rain against the oilskin waters of duck ponds? The most brilliant days find them lurking in dim basements, darkest gloom of pub or café, the souterrains, secret panels, priests' holes of clandestine lovers.

Monday. Mary has spent the weekend in the country with two women friends: Monica, of the umbrella, and Elena. A surprising arrangement: although they'd been best friends at school, a close and dangerous trio, their contact terminated soon after they left. But over the past year or two Monica and Mary have renewed their old acquaintance – one gathers old friends as middle age looms, since the received wisdom suggests that new ones will be harder to find from now on. Over weekly lunches – Thursday is their day but there is no rule about it – they have brought one another up to date on their lives since eighteen. Latterly, Elena has joined them, escaping from her home to enjoy an hour of humorous, stress-free confidences over spinach quiche or salmon salad. By now they are calling themselves 'best friends' again.

Monica is a radio producer, married to a professor. Two children, the boy, Jason, sixteen, and the girl, Emma, ten. Jason, she thinks, may be doing drugs: his pupils dilate, especially at weekends. Emma, however, has clear and brilliant eyes. She is an A student with an exceptional talent for ballet – the Kirov has made approaches, but

Monica won't make commitments yet on behalf of a ten-year-old. 'We don't know how tall she'll be, for heaven's sake. Look at my husband!' He is six foot four, blond, always smiling. The male equivalent, like to like, she'd met him in her third year at college after dating three others – sixth school year, first college year, second year. Optimal time for mating, twenty-one, they married when they were twenty-three and he had already secured a permanent lecture-ship in Dublin's prettiest and classiest university, and Monica was on the first rung of the ladder in the national radio station, a research assistant in the media, one of the most sought-after jobs among college arts graduates at that time. Monica is the sort of woman who is brave enough to ask for more bread with the soup. The weekend away was her idea. She had been head girl in school and had taken the lead role in the ballet-cum-musical they put on for a whole week in sixth year. Some sort of made-up thing based on *Romeo and Juliet*. Monica had been Juliet, and the Romeo came from the boys' school down the road. He didn't have to dance so it had been a strange ballet. What he contributed was music and masculinity. No boy in their circle would demean himself by ballet dancing in those days.

Elena was captain of the hockey team and she played Juliet's nurse, a bit muscular and thin but otherwise convincing. She is still thin, and silent, but has developed into a smooth, svelte woman, with looks exceptionally natural and youthful for an Irishwoman in her forties. She could be a Swede or an aristocratic Russian. Athletes wear well, more so if they never compete and she hadn't, not since school. Few girls did in her day; ambitions in sport, as in everything, were modest. She became a civil servant and married a doctor, but now stays at home to look after their six children. They live in a huge bungalow in Greystones on an acre of garden which Elena tends herself, with exceptional skill. A woman's magazine did a feature on it once three years ago, including a centre-page panoramic shot – Elena in a straw hat and gardening gloves pretending to tie up a delphinium. Monica has shown Mary this. The conservatory and dining-room window are visible in the background, and from this Mary has formed her impression of Elena's house. They have never visited one another's houses, the relationship is lunch and girls only, the kind of thing that is supposed to be tremendously supportive and undemanding. As a rule it is.

Mary has one girl, Sonia, who is twelve. They live in a poky house which used to be corporation but which she owns herself. It is small but decorated with Mary's teacher-of-literature taste, wood and cotton rugs, books, several paintings by competent but uncelebrated contemporary artists. She has never married. Sonia's father, Keith, sends money and takes Sonia on holidays – camping in France, usually – every July. Mary teaches English and loves that, something which few people seem to believe. She has had several relationships with men before the one she is now having. There is plenty the women never tell one another. Their weekly meetings are never long enough to allow the disclosure of intimate secrets. That is the beauty of lunch.

Monica selected, booked, and then drove them to the hotel in Connemara. The plan was to eat a lot. This intention was declared at the hotel where they stopped for their first coffee, with scones, jam and cream. Mary felt a pang of anxiety: she wants to preserve her figure, slimmed down by two stone since she became involved with Michael, love and bliss now her food, not the cream buns and thick broccoli and cheddar soups, the potatoes *au gratin*, the lobster thermidor, which older women are supposed to crave. 'We must have our pleasures!' Monica laughed encouragingly, screwing up her eyes, speaking in the tone of good-humoured mock determination of which she has always been mistress. 'I'm getting worried about this,' Elena said smilingly at the third stop for coffee. Mary lapsed into silence, gloomily acknowledging to herself that weight gain would be unavoidable, and wondering how she could limit the damage. But what could three women do over a weekend, likely to be rainy? She consoled herself by biting into a cream scone. What could they do, except stuff themselves with calories?

Plenty. They organised a full, entertaining schedule. They went for drives, they went for walks, they went to an open-air museum, they slouched in a lounge and read the papers and drank gin and tonics. They slouched in one of their rooms and read novels – Monica the book that had won the Booker Prize last year, Elena a John Grisham, and Mary the novel which had won the Booker three years ago and which she had bought for fifty pence in an Oxfam shop. Mary read for most of the night. She knew the unspoken rule was that they should do everything together, even sleep, but she had been lately suffering from insomnia. She lay and read, and then lay awake and thought a bit about Sonia – staying with a friend from school – and a lot about Michael, whom she often slept with on Fridays: she has given this Friday up, for the sake of the girlie weekend. The thought of him still set her mind floating, away from the world of her bed, her head, away from the plod-plod of the routines which were now speedily eating up her days, faster than the mind could grasp. The image of him – his solidity, his invulnerable tough body, his ironic face, loops of thick, smooth hair – consoled her for anything, everything that is fleeting, flawed and ephemeral; consoled her for the sins and imperfections of her life, gave her a vision of eternity, opened her mind, she thought, as the minds of the ascetics have been opened. Kept her awake. Pained her body, but mildly, with desire. She would see him in a few days; waiting was not unbearable. Still, she cried silently, wishing for him, what she considered the other side of her, half of her apple, sleeping in Dublin, a hundred miles away, alone also. Perhaps Michael was awake too, thinking of her, their minds at one if their bodies were not? In the first months of their love they both lay sleepless much of the time, they planned to think one of the other at midnight, at two a.m. Not that planning was necessary.

Monica talked about old times over breakfast – old times one of the dangers, the test of the weekend. Mary had known it would have to happen, fifty or sixty consecutive hours being so much longer than one once a week with queues and choices of garlic or tomato or ham disrupting what conversational flow there is.

What she chose to talk about was the most dangerous subject for Mary: men.

They were under a billowing chiffon canopy in the middle of the dining room – at night this part of the room functions as a dance floor of some kind. Monica told them about a boy who asked her out when she was fifteen – already the undisputed queen of the class in every field, the most popular girl in the school. (Did Mary envy her? Yes. Everyone did, although they did not know it. Envy is one of the most common emotions, and the one least acknowledged, for obvious reasons.) Her mother would not allow her to go on the date, since she belonged to one of those generations which viewed sexuality as life's greatest danger. Monica had told him a lie, saying she was going out with another boy, and later he had found out about that (and, a year later, asked her out again). This person, called Sean, had phoned Monica the other day at the radio station and asked her to meet him for a coffee.

End of story.

Did she meet him?

'Yeah. He just wanted me to arrange some hype for a project he's doing.'

'Well, how was he?'

'Fine. Looked great. Always did. It was nice chatting to him.'

What Monica was saying is that he was still interested. All these years on. The persistence of desire.

'Will you see him again?'

She shrugged, bored with her own story. 'He said he'd ring.'

'And has he?'

'Come on. What do you think I'm doing. Having an *affair?*'

Mary thought of the first boy who asked her out. It happened at the second or third dance she went to, ever, and she was totally unprepared, shocked that dancing and drinking a glass of fizzy orange could so quickly land her in this dark territory where a complete stranger was asking to see her again. She was so scared she didn't even ask her mother if she could go (afraid that her mother, a more pushy type than Monica's, more earthy and ambitious in every field, would say yes – and she would have, delighted that her shy, gauche daughter had scored a little success, so soon, against all odds). Mary had rung up that boy intending to lie too, to tell the lie that had been Monica's truth. 'My mother won't let me date boys yet,' she'd planned to say, in her prim voice, creating in her lie the mother she desired, forging the respectable rigid protector she wanted, becoming her own mother. But she hadn't said it. She'd met him and gone to the pictures.

Mary did not tell the tale of her first date, a tale she has never told. She is not one to recount her sexual conquests, even those of the past, especially in this company, which never expected her to have any. Old taboos die hard. At school, girls like Monica were supposed to have the boyfriends, girls like Mary to become nuns. The belief among the girls was that men sought only perfection, of personality and physique; that the world was full of elitist predatory men hunting for the flawless; the world of men Mary found, of boys shy and frightened, striving, scared, much more anxious than she or any woman could be, had to await discovery beyond the school doors. That the world was full of men who would overlook almost any flaw in their search for kindness, friendship, warmth, was a discovery made later. That beauty would hinder as much as help most women she noticed only much much later, long after she realised, aged forty, that almost every girl is beautiful anyway. Only in schools and groups do the distinctions exist, and it takes queen bees to train the world to see them.

Mary discovered quickly the measure of her sexual power, as girls do, and was surprised at its extent. Her body, squat and square to Monica's fine, willowy tallness, was transmogrified into something energetically female by the time she was seventeen. Her freckles, frowned on as a major disfigurement, were after all a charm, like the carrot frizz of hair the school had laughed at (behind her back – it was a nice school, very refined). She was golden, sunny, electric, amber, speckled like a sandy seashore, a round soft hen. That men were drawn surprised her at first, but not for long – quickly she learned to expect love, and usually she got it. But in the company of these women she assumed her old schoolgirl role, became shy and plain and subdued. The passage of time has done little to change the relationship between these people. It's not just desire that persists, but also group dynamics. Deep down, perhaps nobody ever changes at all.

Monica, once started on this theme, continued to root around in the attic of the past, unwilling to abandon memory. She pulled out gems to display over the rashers and eggs. 'Did I tell you I ran into Penelope and Michael a while ago?'

Elena was puzzled, Mary punched in the gut.

'Michael Byrne, you know?'

Mary nodded, finding she could not speak. Why drag this up now? To her irritation, Elena encouraged Monica.

'Wasn't he in the bank?' she asked.

'Yeah, still is. Very successful, I believe,' said Monica. 'They live in one of those big old houses in Ballsbridge. In other words, he's a property millionaire.'

'I remember them now,' said Elena, who was also a property millionaire. 'How are they?'

'He was looking great. Penelope told me she was having a few problems.'

Mary forced herself to speak. 'What sort of problems?' she asks.

Monica looked closely at her, and Mary winced, convinced, for a second, that Monica knew everything.

'Health problems,' she said, and paused. 'But she didn't elaborate. Actually she looked very well, too. But then she always did.'

'She was very attractive,' said Elena. 'Didn't she do medicine?'

'Yeah,' Monica replied. 'She's an obstetrician.' She glanced at Mary again. 'I went out with him for a while, you know,' she said. 'With Michael. That was before he met Penelope, obviously.'

'Sure you went out with them all, Monica!' laughed Elena, giving her a friendly pat.

Mary sat, drained to sulking silence. She thought she would faint if she stood up at this moment; her throat was dry as paper while her eyes fought tears. Why does she react in this way? Shame, sorrow, fear, bitterness, envy. Anger. Doesn't Monica notice her discomfiture? Apparently not, because if she did she would stop talking about him. Monica is a compassionate woman. That is one of the problems. And she doesn't even remember that Mary had been in love with Michael.

Michael meets Mary at her home when he can, which is not often. His lovemaking then is as relaxed as if they did it every night: unhurried, skilled, practised — as is Mary's. They bring experience to their connecting, wide experience as well as distilled passion. His body — tall and powerful, with papery skin, rougher on him like sandpaper — empowers hers utterly, it is her perfect match. And he opens her up — she sees herself as a pod, russet and black, split, smashed to a pulp of pleasure. With him she feels bliss from the root to the top of her head, back and front, not the small pointed local orgasms many of her lovers have succeeded in producing. Pleasurable but limited. With Michael, her true love, emotion and mature physique combine to create more earthy and more transforming unions; she has not managed this with others, although she is gifted in her body, in her ability to enjoy sex, he claims — measuring her against what standard? Himself? His wife? Other women she knows nothing about? And he too seems gifted, to her. Potent, clever, desirous, patient. Time flies in that room with terracotta walls and Liberty prints, with its sullenly locked door, the short time they have together, and on the other hand those hours are eternity, all the meaning and reality of her existence packed into them. That he is not with her all the time seems after these hours irrelevant: he is with her all the time anyway, in her head, in her body, in her blood. He is hers and she is his. Marriage vows till death do us part are not stronger than what binds them. Love, body and soul and heart, essential, lasting through decades and decades of apartness.

At other times the separateness rankles deeply. Life is not only lived in a bedroom for two hours a week but in streets and living rooms and school halls and offices. In the structures of society, so-called permanent, the places that house all respectability, normality.

Today the shabby restaurant where she has arranged to meet him is almost empty, thanks to the pounding rain. She sighs with relief, glancing down the rows of tables. Now that she has reached the place undetected she glows with a small sense of achievement – these public meetings are fenced around with the worry: we'll be caught. Once in this very place, while they held hands over their sandwiches, Mary glanced up and saw Penelope, seated at a table with three or four women, laughing all over her beautiful suntanned face. She has never seen Michael so stunned – all the power vanished from him, the stuffing, his usually reddish face white as snow when she pointed out his wife. But even then they escaped – Mary slid away, along the side of the café, and Michael, his presence of mind restored, moved over and joined his wife and her party, thus avoiding the need to explain the plate of uneaten food opposite him at the table. Afterwards he and Mary had met in a pub, laughed weak and giddy with relief, like bold children who have got away with some outrageous prank. And Mary wondered why she had not used that moment, let them be discovered, as another mistress would have. That was the moment of testing, handed her on a plate like quiche across the counter, and she had handed it back, remained right where she was in the land of anomaly, adultery. Why? Because, a therapist would insist – from time to time she sees one – it was what she wanted. Deep down, really wanted. No commitment. No decisions. No moments of truth. Mary's natural habitat is the forest of ambiguity, where you don't see the wood for the trees.

Michael is at a corner table. She trips along, dripping, feeling glorious, all her nervousness vanquished utterly by the sight of him, as he sits, head bowed over a book, his hair dampened, some drops of rain still on the shoulders of his dark jacket. A mirage, an oasis, a drink of cold water for the parched. So it is every time she meets him – the morning is a series of obstacles to be overcome. Somebody is bound to notice something to pass some remark that will wreck it, some problem will arise, keeping her from him. But when she sits a few feet from him, hears his low kind voice, sees his warm face beaming at hers, all anxiety vanishes. She experiences perfect security. He is hers for three or four hours a week. Not much but still home for her tinker's heart.

Monica, who did her best to keep them cheerful, made jokes about having flings with men. 'I met a hunk up there!' she said, when she came down to dinner later than the others. 'Didn't you hear the bed creak?'

Elena cracked a funny rejoinder and Mary smiled, unable to think of anything witty to say. The distance between these jokes, which are frequent, and what she believes is Monica's and Elena's true attitude to sexual deviance is so unquantifiable. How far from the jokes to the dogma? What is in between? Mary does not know. She knows that these women, almost all the married women, joke and dream about deviance in order to keep it at bay, as little children tell jokes about dirty sex and lavatories. In reality Monica and Elena obey a rigid, but sensible and compassionate system of rules. Fidelity matters. Do unto others. How would you feel if . . .? Women should stand by one another at least as soon as they are married. This is one aspired-for sisterhood much more ancient than feminism, which Mary, like all these women, is supposed to espouse. The freemasonry of matrons. But when Mary catches a glimpse of that morality, glittering and gleaming at the bottom of a dark sexual pool, she knows she has been outside that club all her life, that according to its dimly grasped standards she is doomed and drowning. Drowning, she can see the bright clean pure empty banks but she can't pull herself back, back from her life which is, according to the accepted standards, the stuff of sleazy jokes.

Real true-life stories express the true morality less enigmatically.

Monica told these too, in a deadpan, compelling voice – she can tell stories, jokes and anecdotes, true life and false, as all the really grown-up, adult people can. Mary and Elena are girls still in the social world Monica is mistress of, they are like so many women-girls who will never grow to this level of competence, retain their shy girlish voices, their increasingly irritating slow-wittedness, until they kick the bucket. Monica was a storyteller when she was seven years old. It's something in the blood, like confidence, like wealth, like success.

A woman in their neighbourhood was a well-known tart. She had affairs with several men, anything in trousers was par for the course. Her husband was older than her, a nice man, everyone admired him, but she was a harridan. Everyone knew about the affairs, everyone. Including him. But for some reason he put up with them, he pretended everything was OK.

'Why?' asked Elena.

Monica sighed. 'I suppose he loved her. Not loved her. Didn't want to rock the boat. You know how people are.'

Mary nodded.

'Anyway, in the end she killed him.'

'She murdered him? How?' asked Elena.

'He'd a heart condition and she fed him on T-bone steak and chips.'

Elena smiled, her kind heart relieved. 'I suppose he could have cooked for himself.'

Monica looked cross. 'Sure, but he wasn't that sort of guy. And now he's dead.'

'And what happened to her?' asked Mary, picturing the woman. She could see her now, in front of her, blond, lipsticked, wielding a frying pan in a manicured claw.

Monica shrugged. 'She moved out of the area. They'd a big business and she got the lot. Sold it and moved on.'

'No kids?' asked Elena.

Monica shook her head.

The chiffon canopy billowed above them as they ate their enormous meals, drank gin and tonics, told these stories. The room was supposed to look like the harem of some Ottoman sultan. Mary thought if she were an odalisque she would long ago have been tied up in a cloth sack and hurled into the Bosporus. Or stoned to death.

In Dublin nobody throws stones. Not even stony words. At worst stony glances, occasionally the cut direct. Mary feels she tastes that knife edge more often than Michael, although he is the married one. To hell with them, she says to herself, gritting her teeth. What business is it of theirs? And it's none and they never betray her or him. Above all they do not betray Penelope, by hinting at the truth. Apparently not. People are kinder, gentler, more tolerant, than anyone could imagine. They protect everyone, the deceiver and the deceived. Another club, the club of those who know but hold their tongues.

Their conversations, like their lovemaking, have fallen into a pattern over the year they have been together. She tells him everything that has happened since they last talked, and then he tells her. So their lives, their ordinary little lives, have become the stuff of stories, riveting adventures that at least one pair of ears longs to hear. That in itself would be enough, for people of their age, to make the risk worth while. Much of their talk concerns their children. He has seen Sonia several times, and talked to her now and then. But Mary has never even seen his children, although she feels she knows them better than any other child in her life – apart from Sonia. Another cause for envy, sulking, another demon to assail her when she lets it.

His parents had not wanted Michael to marry her. That is how she reasons, knowing that such opposition stops no one.

Perhaps it stopped her? Their disapproval, real or imagined, took from her the drive she needed to take the relationship to its conclusion. She had let him go. She had let him find Monica. If it had not been her, it would have been someone else, some similarly strong girl–woman.

His parents knew they were much too young, eighteen and nineteen, peaked, when their affair was at its height. They encouraged him – and also Mary – to mix more, to go out in big gangs, to play the field. Sensible enough. Mary suspected meanly that their sense was seasoned with snobbery, and of course it was, it always is – only now can she see the inevitability of that, as she feels the same herself in relation to Sonia, her pride and joy, a girl of special class and nature. Mary's father was a plumber and her mother said 'dem' instead of 'those' and even 'I do be' – astonishing now to Mary how that woman clung to her dialect, retaining phrases and syntax which nobody has used since O'Casey, now to her wonder, then to her mortification. How did her mother do it? The thought of the wedding – his parents, teachers, refined, intelligent, cultivated (rather nice, rather what Mary would aspire to and become), side by side with hers. 'Would you pass us dem bottles of stout, please?' Mary, heartbroken when Michael gave in and started dating Monica, was even then relieved that she would not have to go through with that wedding.

She'd been happy with his parents only once. That was when she and Michael visited them one raining afternoon in Brittas Bay, where they were camping – because they were adventurous, ahead of their time. Mary's mother would have died rather than sleep under canvas, but Michael's camped in Ireland, all over Europe. They went for swims in the icy sea. They cycled until they were seventy, like people in Holland or Denmark. They wore shorts and funny peanut caps when all old Irish people wore grey suits and mantillas on their perms going to Mass.

The rain had beaten the canvas all afternoon and they had talked, cooked sausages, drunk tea and perhaps a glass of wine. What had they talked about? College, literature, history, people they all knew. She can't remember. But she remembers his mother, in loose beige sweater and khaki shorts, thin and wirily charming, and his father like W.B. Yeats in a navy jumper. Their sharp faces, which usually seemed to be laughing at somebody, were smooth and peaceful. They all laughed together that afternoon, even Michael, who all summer had been on edge and anxious (because already he was seeing others, he'd been to a film with Monica, he'd danced with her at an end-of-term party and had had letters from her – none of which Mary knew, as yet; all she knew was that she was losing her grip on him, that he longed to escape). Mary remembers that he sat with his arm loosely thrown over her shoulder – brave, for those days, with parents present – and seemed proud of her, settled in his mind. They had kissed, even, after the wine, and his father had planted a kiss on his mother's nose. The rain pinged cosily against the roof until eight or so, then gave up. The sky cleared, and they walked, all four, on the long strand, watching the sunset reflected gently in the quiet eastern sky, a smudge of peachiness rather than a blaze of glory, watery, the air clear and clean as a spring well after the day's downpour.

Afterwards Michael and Mary had gone back to town on the bus, wrapped in a sheet of bliss, love, relief. A winding sheet, as it happened, because the next week term started again, Monica returned and claimed him, as was her right. She was more beautiful, and came from better stock. Michael deserved her.

They are walking back towards his bank, under the umbrella. The rain has eased and there are more people about but they feel safe together, hand on hot hand, under the red shade. The overarching lime trees bolster their sense of security, the wide gleaming path is all theirs. Carefully they step around the puddles, their footsteps harmonising, their every breath in tandem.

Her eyes are on the path, shining, watching the trees and the houses reflected, moving, shifting, shimmering in the gleaming patches of water. She feels perfectly happy, as she always does when they are together, even though he was uneasy during lunch. She has walked with him on many paths, and always, as far as she can recall, his presence has imbued her with a deep sense of safety. None of the paths ever lead anywhere, at least never to the solid structures or enclosures that are the goal of real-life lovers. Not to a house, a church, a maternity hospital, a hospital ward. Not to a grave. Penelope gets all of that, the bricks and mortar of love, the cement, the house built on rock. She will get the grave too, the shared stone slab, words written in stone with a hammer and chisel. Her right, for being in the right place and state at the right time.

Mary gets the billowing tents, the sheets on the wind, the umbrellas.

The thought unsettles her momentarily. A gargoyle grins from the red shadow, prompts her. 'People notice, you know,' she says, with a candid opening of her little grey eyes.

'We're not having one of those conversations again, are we? At five minutes to two.' His face crinkles. Smile in adversity, one of any businessman's most important tricks. Or any man's at all?

'Monica knows.'

He starts, and the smile is wiped off his face. 'Does she? How do you know?'

'She told me she met you and Penelope.'

'Did she say anything else?'

'No. Not about us.'

'Then . . .' His banker's mind. His man's mind. If they don't say it directly don't worry about it. Never paint the devil on the wall. There's usually plenty of real stuff to worry about anyway.

She imagines he relaxes, and she follows suit, her body perfectly in tune with his. They take a few steps in silence, staring at the black shining pavement.

Mary remembers Monica's conversation. 'She said Penelope was having some sort of health problem.'

Michael stiffens again. 'Yeah,' he says. 'That's right. She is.'

Suddenly Mary knows what nobody has told her. But she asks anyway. 'So what's wrong with her?'

Michael thinks before replying, carefully. 'She's going to be OK.'

'What's wrong with her?' Mary raises her voice, so that Michael glances over his shoulder, worried that passers-by will overhear.

'Cancer,' he says despairingly. 'She's got cancer.'

'What kind of cancer?'

'Of the abdomen,' he says.

'And you didn't tell me?' She stares at him, shaking her head.

'I'm sorry,' he says, shrugging. His face is ashen. 'I tried to but . . . it seems so private. It seemed like it would be a betrayal, to tell you. Another betrayal.'

Mary continues to shake her head, hardly seeing him. She had imagined they were on a smooth mountainside, tripping through the heather. But they are in a deep clammy jungle. Invisible monsters roar in their ears.

'She's had a course of chemotherapy and has responded well,' Michael continues. 'She's probably going to get the all-clear.'

'We should do this again sometime,' Mary said, stupidly, when they stopped for coffee – no cakes or scones – on the way home. Monica and Elena looked surprised. Nothing had been acknowledged but of course they knew the weekend had been a disaster, although, unlike Mary, they did not know why.

Mary suggested mushroom identification. There'd been an article about it in a supplement she'd read that morning.

'Who wants to identify mushrooms?' Monica asked, airily for her.

'I wouldn't mind identifying wild flowers. Or walking in Wicklow.'

'It'd have to be spring or summer.' Mary thought she would actually enjoy that. A weekend involving activity, not thinking and reminiscing.

'You can't walk in Wicklow in the summer.'

'You can't?'

'Midges. Dreadful.'

'Mm,' said Mary. 'I've never noticed them.'

'Eat you alive.'

Monica left Mary at her bus stop. She wanted to drive her home since it was late when they reached town but Mary wouldn't let her.

'I'll phone you next week,' she gushed, effusing, trying to undo all the little hurts of the weekend, trying to forget the enormous hurt that she was still in the process of creating.

'Yeah. Keep in touch.' Monica's tone was at its driest.

'It was really relaxing.' Mary was so used to living a lie that she didn't know how to stop. 'Thanks a million, bye.' She raised Monica's umbrella over her head and hurried away.

'When can I see you again?' Michael asks.

The faint urgency in his tone lifts her spirits. In spite of everything, she wants him to need her. The emotions that connect her to him are mixed, to say the least. They include lust, nostalgia, revenge, affection. But however corrupt the concoction, it amounts to some sort of love: love which moves like a river from one place to another, speeding up and slowing down, spreading and contracting, drying up, flooding. It is polluted and subversive, but that doesn't mean it isn't as real as the official version, blessed by church, state and family, buttressed into safe fortresses with walls six feet thick. Mary, long-time dweller in the thin tents of the heart, the transient pavilions of bliss, believes, by now, that it means the opposite. We erect banks and castles and laws, but nothing we do can successfully civilise love, or the other great force that controls us all.

Mary believes this, but she looks questioningly at him.

Michael shrugs. 'I know, I know,' he says. 'But what about me?'

Mary loves him. But whenever he reveals his love for her she is taken aback to realise that he is not a pawn in a game of chess, a football being kicked from one side of the pitch to the other, tough as cured leather. His vulnerability always startles her, perhaps because he looks so powerful in his coat of armour: his immaculate suit, his snow-white shirt, his suave and smiling face. She makes the mistake of taking all that at face value. But in the shadowy forest of middle age, nothing can be interpreted literally. Under every shining surface lurks a life.

They are standing beside Mary's car, at the end of the one-way street on which Michael's bank is situated— a house as substantial as any in the world, two hundred years old, brick and wood, solid timbers, solid money, solid families, solid professional work holding all this cement and stone together. It's still raining and the umbrella is over them. It doesn't hide them from anyone but she positions it so they feel hidden; ostriches, they do what is most dangerous, they kiss, on a busy street corner at five to two on a Monday afternoon. Three buses, a taxi, porters at a hotel, about two hundred people, pass them by and not one sees them or passes any remark.

'I don't know,' says Mary, although, at this moment, she believes she knows better than she has ever known anything. Even her certainty includes the possibility of uncertainty, however. That much she always knows. She hands him Monica's umbrella, to protect him as he walks back to work, and steps into her car.

SEX IN THE CONTEXT OF IRELAND

'And a one! And a two! And a three!'
'Hooray hooray hooray!'
'Down the red lane!'

We raised our glasses and swallowed the drink in one enormous gulp. Then we each grabbed a cup of water and cooled our burning throats.

'Your only man.' Lilly sat heavily on to her chair and shook her head from side to side, like a dog that's been for a dip in the river. Molly Malone closed her eyes and sank on to the bed in the corner, out for the count already – not long for the world, as thin as a whip and with two red spots on her cheekbones now that had not been there five seconds ago.

I felt the hot methylated spirits sink through my body. My gut, my stomach, all the veins of my body until I was glowin like a sunny day at Dollymount. Like the sun itself.

'I feel like the sun itself,' I said stupidly. Meths did that for me, let me say things I'd normally keep to myself.

'Would you listen to your one.' Lilly, her purple dress slippin down her white arms, came over and patted me on the breast.

'Hands off,' I laughed. 'You sneaky little thing. You haven't paid for that have you?'

'What's a touch between friends.' I pushed her away and she pretended to topple over on to the kitchen floor. Her purple dress flopped around her thighs.

'Nice garters. Pity you forgot to get stockings,' I cried.

'Scrounger wouldn't give me any.'

I sat up, fed up all of a sudden, and took another cup of water.

'That'll make me job all the easier!'

Molly turned in the bed, moaning.

'Should get her thrun outa here,' Lilly said crossly. 'She'll infect the lot of us.'

'That's what I think,' I had to agree. Poor old Molly. 'Couldn't we get her up to the Union?'

'Do we hate her enough to do that to her?' Lilly went to the breadbin and ripped a bit off a black-crusted turnover.

'Don't be robbin the crust, you bowsie!' Molly said, waking up all of a sudden.

I giggled, I couldn't stop myself. I went into fits so I did. Molly staggered to her feet and went over to attack Lilly, who was twice the size of her. Lilly waved the black turnover aloft, over her big yellow bun of hair, dry as straw. 'Catch as catch can catch as catch can!' she sang. 'Finders keepers losers weepers,' I sang from my corner, between bouts of gigglin. 'Molly ye'll be the deatha us, so ye will.'

The door opened.

'Janey Mack sure it's only four a clock. I'm on me half-day,' Lilly began.

I stopped gigglin. The man wasn't Jockser, our bully, but a stranger, a thin man with a hat on his head which he didn't bother taking offa him, and a papery white skin. A little nose like a rabbit's and a grey suit. Not a customer. Not that I knew of. Jockser would never a let a customer walk into the kitchen like that anyway, in the middle of the day.

'Mr Murphy,' said the man. He had a woman's voice, thin as a blade of grass. 'Frank Murphy of the Legion of Mary. And this' – a woman in brown, ugly as the devil, a big nose like a foghorn on her – 'is Miss Moriarty. Can you spare us a minute or two?'

Ye coulda knocked us down with a feather. Molly snuck back into bed and covered her head with the blanket. Lilly took a big drink of water and stood with her back to the wall of the kitchen, near the door so she could run off. I didn't know whether to laugh or to cry and I just wished Jockser would come in and look after us. We pay him enough God knows.

Maybe ye're askin what I'm doing here, in a kitchen in Monto? A nice girl like me in a place like this! Maybe ye're not askin at all maybe ye couldn't give a sugar but I'm goin to tell ye anyways like it or lump it, so I am. Stop saying so I am I can hear ye sayin now, talk proper, talk so we don't hafta strain our delicate ears to listen and to understand what it is ye're sayin. Well I won't and if yez can't understand it's your loss.

I came a me own free will. Nobody forced me. Nobody came and dragged me be the scruff a the neck and said now Bella you go on the game or we'll bate the livin daylights outa ye. I heard about the place from a frienda mine up near where I used to live, be the name of Edie Catskins (I ask ye!). Mountjoy Square. Me da had a room in the back of a house there, or a bit of a room I should say, himself and his new missus and their dozen childer, the gifts of God me da calls them, joker that he is — all me precious gifts from the Man Above that'll look after their oul da in his old age if he lives to see it. Or if they live to see it. Foura them are dead already, of one thing and the other. Starvation if ye want to know the real name for what killed them, though the priest said it was TB in one case and other things in others. Me stepbrothers and sisters. Ye can see some a them if ye like. They beg on Sackville Street that they're after callin O'Connell Street now. We still go be the old name. It's the same if ye're running from the peelers, runnin after the nobs beggin for a penny or a cuta bread and runnin away from the peelers beggin for yer life.

Me ma died when she was havin me, her third, and then Da had skipped it off ta England and we were takin in be the nuns in the Good Shepherd Convent down the street from where I'm standin now.

I do often spit when I pass it God forgive me.

Me brother and me sister died in there.

I do hate talkin about the place or thinkin about it.

All I'll say about it is this. The sound. The blow of wood or leather on children's skin. That was the music of the Good Shepherd. The feelin. Hunger. Fear of yer life. Hate of the nuns. Freezin cold.

The weak died. Me brother. They beat him to death I swear to God. Nobody would believe me of course and I know you won't either. A nun bet him till he died and then she sent him out in a white coffin and said, 'He is gone to a better place.' The priest gave her a big smile and patted me on the head. This is at the funeral up in Glasnevin. The paupers' plot, do ye know it? Most of me family's in it at this stage, it's me back garden. I never told anyone what I knew about me brother. He was six, he'd golden curls. That's what they hated. They were always hacking off his curls but they'd grow again and they kinda blamed him for that though he couldn't help it. Jeese thank God I've black hair straight as a yardstick, they didn't mind that. When they cut it it stayed flat and cut for a while and didn't start springing back out like daisies in the park the minute the fella cuttin the grass turns his back. A martyr for his curls, poor Eddie. The screams of him when they bet him. He didn't know to keep his mouth shut. That was a rule of theirs when they were at ye, ye were supposed to keep quiet, I suppose now that I'm out it was so people passin on the street wouldn't hear. They do hear. I do hear screams meself sometimes and I passin on me way up to the shops and I do think of the poor childer in there. Me heart goes out to them but what can I do? Nobody ever did a thing for me either. Or Eddie that they murdered God forgive them! Women and men on their way to Mass or the novena up in Gardiner Street. They woulda heard the screams of him. Janey ye would've heard them on the moon, he'd lungs like an ox when he got worked up. Nobody paid a blind bit of heed. I do think . . . I know if ye want to know . . . that the people of Dublin like that sound, the sound of poor childer bein beaten to death. I don't know why they like it but I know they do. Otherwise they'd do something about it.

Before the Free State got into bein it was better. So Lilly says. She should know she was there. It was never good but the nuns were more afraid of the police and there was some inspector came around and asked questions. 'Now that we're free God help the children of

Ireland,' she said, rolling her eyes up the heaven and then giving a laugh. 'They'll hafta look out for themselves now.' She didn't give a sugar, Lilly, for anything but the next drink and the next dress. Mad for clothes and nothing else.

Me sister died of natural causes. That is to say, hunger.

Aided and abetted by other things but I'll say no more.

And I escaped. After three years of them, when I was nine years of age. Me da came back and married me new ma and he came and he took me out and up to the room in Mountjoy Square. Sure I thought I was made! Even when I saw he'd two new kids already and another on the way and two in the Angels' Plot, he half-filled that Angels' Plot, the same man, couldn't keep his hands offa his woman, or any woman, and maybe he didn't know that one thing led to another either, if ye know what I mean. I know ye wouldn't credit it but he was innocent, me da, big blue boy's eyes and a curly head, the same as poor Eddie's. Always ready with the laugh and the joke. The bit of an oul jeer as well. Women loved to be jeered by fellas like him though. It got him all the way to . . . well what me clients hafta pay me for, mind you the ones that come here couldn't hold a candle to me da in more ways than one. If they could it'd be an easier job but if they could they wouldn't hafta pay. Ye can't have it all so ye can't in this world.

He took me outa the Good shagging Shepherds to mind his brats so he did. But it was a blessed release so it was anyways.

Is there one good thing I can say about the nuns before I move on to the Square afore I forget? There is. Sister Assumpta. Once she gave me a cut of bread and sugar after findin me cryin in the middle of the night and tryin to scale the ten-foot wall with bits of glass stuck on to the top of it after Mother Christopher of the Holy Angels had been havin a go at my holy backside with her holy mother and father of a bamboo cane. There was me grabbin at bits of buddleia with me little hands tryin to get a foothold in the rocks and I would've made it I would so. But she snuck up behind me like a thief in the night – they're quiet, nuns, they're made like that so they can sneak up on children and catch them, and they have soft rubber shoes to help them in their sneakiness. She said in her silky soft voice, 'Arabella Brazil!'

I fell to the concrete yard like an apple that was after gettin knocked offa a tree.

'Are you going somewhere?'

'I'm just havin a climb sister.'

'I see. You are fond of gymnastic exercise?'

'Oh yeah I am sister.'

'In that case, come with me.'

I thought I was for it.

They often talked like that. Made a laugh of it. What they were goin to do with ye. I do believe sometimes they thought it was just a game. Sometimes a few of them would come to watch while one of them was doin it, as if it were something to enjoy like a play in the Theatre Royal.

She walked across the yard (for all the world like the yard in Mountjoy). Insteada goin into the hall, where they usually did the beatings (so lots of people could have a ringside seat) she turned and went into the coalhouse.

I'm not jokin ye.

The coalhouse!

'Sister!' I knew ye weren't supposed to say anything when ye were up for a hidin. Everyone knew that. It would make it all worse. They sorta wanted ye to stay quiet. The hidin was sorta partly to make ye stay quiet altogether, I think. They hated children making any sound at all, even talkin. I do think what they really wanted was a world where all the children were deaf and dumb and for good measure mentally handicapped as well. Only a course then they wouldna had anything to do. But now their job was to make the children they got dumb and mental. Deaf maybe too because boxing ears was a favourite sorta sideline sport.

'We'll get dirty!' Getting dirty was one of the things you could never do, on pain of the usual.

'Come in and stay quiet.' She pulled me in after her and shut the door behind us.

Then we were in pitch darkness.

The coal. The dark. Her black habit.

After a while I could see her white wimple and the sort of huge stiff collar thing they had on, like a bib, over the chest, hiding what they had of breasts.

A lot in Sister Assumpta's case.

She had me feeling them in no time at all.

Feelin them.

'Go on. Don't be afraid!' she said. 'Aren't they soft and delicious?'

Janey Mack! Well ye probably know yerself what big boobs feel like. Bird's Jelly Deluxe.

Meanwhile she was into my drawers.

It wasn't half as bad as the hidins.

What did I care? Sometimes I even got a bit of a thrill outa it.

I don't fancy Bird's Jelly Deluxe to this day. But she was clean – apart for the coal acourse. When she broke me in she used to get me in cleaner places. The laundry. I'm not jokin ye.

And afterwards the bread with the black crust, buttered thick all the way to the edges, and dipped in sugar.

Sister Assumpta.

She wasn't the worst.

Me good word for the Good Shepherds.

I've a good word for me stepmother too. Elsie. She wasn't the worst.

A small, good-looking little one. Black hair like me own, down to her waist, thick as a river. She wound it up at the back of her head in a pleat, showed me how to do mine. Enormous grey eyes and a lovely smile. Me da was lucky to get her. Wouldna, of course, if he hadn't got her expectin first. But he did of course, being my da. She was fonda him anyway though her own mother wouldn't speak to her at all on accounta her marryin him. She coulda done better, with her looks. Hard to say. Some young fella with a trade or that. Instead of him, fifteen years older than her and with a wife in the grave already. All he could do was labour on the docks. Strong as a horse and he didn't drink all the time. Some of them never brought home a crust. He gave her half of what he earned and the rest went on porter. Still she had her work cut out, putting bread on the table. Bread and tea, that was it. Coddle once a week if we were lucky. Her good suit and his pawned every Monday (I didn't have a good suit otherwise that would've gone in too). She had to char. Up in Phibsborough for some oul one, gave her half a crown for scrubbing her house down twice a week. Old dresses, stinking, I couldn't bear them.

I charred too.

Once she sent me, me ma, to do an interview in Jacobs. She seen an ad in the *Daily Mail*. GIRLS WANTED. GOOD WAGES. REFERENCES ESSENTIAL.

'You'll be made up,' she sighed. Meaning we'd all be made up. Wages once a week. I pictured meself in a little white cap and overall like I seen the girls wearing. Bags of broken biscuits ye got, white bags packed to the top with them. Goldgrain. Mallas. Kimberleys. They have them still, they never change their biscuits. Mikado. You could smell the jam for the mikados and the custard creams, the yellow ones with red jam in the middle, all down Bishop Street round the Whitefriar Street when ye went there for the Blessing of the Throats. (They needed blessing, what hadta go into them.) Sticky, hot, sweet smell. Sometimes I usedta go there just to get that smell. Made ye terrible hungry for biscuits was the only thing.

The minute I walked into the room I knew be the way the two men looked at one another they wouldn't be takin me.

One of them had a striped jacket and the other had a black jacket. The one with the stripes had a big handlebar moustache. It was him looked at the other one as much as to say 'Would ye look what the cat dragged in?' He twirled the end of his moustache, like one of them fellas at the circus. The Ringmaster.

'Name?' asked Ringmaster.

'Arabella Brazil.'

'Miss Brazil. When were ye born?'

'What?'

The Ringmaster twirled his moustache again. They do grow them moustaches so they'll have something to fiddle with. Some men are born fiddlers, can't keep their hands quiet.

'When were ye born?'

'Twenty-first of February 1907.'

'Where were you educated?'

'Convent of the Good Shepherd, Beresford Street.' It was outa me mouth before I could stop meself.

Ringmaster raised his eyebrows, which kinda matched his moustache. He probably fiddled with them too sometimes.

'The orphanage?'

'Me ma died. Now me da is married again. I'm out.'

'They let you out did they? The good sisters?'

'Yeah. He came and got me so he did.'

'You're Catholic of course?'

'I didn't know they only took Prods,' me ma said.

'Sure the dogs on the street know that.'

I don't know was it true. Mary Murray that lives down Hardwicke Street got in. She does the fig rolls, she's a fig roll girl. Holy Joes the lota them, always on their knees. She says the Angelus out on the street even in broad daylight with everyone lookin. For whom the bell tolls, me da calls her.

'What about Mary Murray?' says I.

'She musta lied to them.'

'She wouldn't,' I said. 'She's real religious.'

'Two-faced bollocks, all them Murrays, their uncle was an informer. Hadta scarper to Australia after the Rising. A castle hack.'

'I never knew that.'

'That's how she got the job now that I think of it. If I was a bettin man I'd put a shillin each way on it. They musta known. Jemser the Informer Murray. He's done well they say out there. Lord Mayor of Van Diemens Land or some such thing. Tellin on the convicts.'

'I never knew that. I woulda lied too.'

'Ah ye were never much of a liar, Bella me darlin.'

It was him suggested it.

'Ever think of talkin to Mrs Catskins down the way? She might fix you up, a charmer like yerself?'

'Ah go on!' started me ma.

'It's better than scrubbin floors,' he said. 'As long as she doesn't take to the jar she'd be landed. Look at Pussy Catskins! How do you think she started?'

Me ma blessed herself but she said no more about it. I wasn't her daughter, I suppose.

Mr Murphy sat on one of the chairs as if it was a hot grate and him a cricket trying it out for the first time.

Miss Moriarty stood in the door, blocking it but letting in a terrible draught. Molly started coughing under her blankets.

'Would you mind if we said a decade of the Rosary?' Mr Murphy asked. His thin voice was very soft, as if he was afraid to raise it. Also pleasant. One of them pleasant voices. Soft as rubber shoes on a nun.

'What, here?' Lilly looked shocked.

'Ah sure let them if it's what they want!' Bessie Boland spoke for the first time. She sort of nodded at Lilly as if to say, let's be careful.

'Fire away,' said Lilly.

'Would you care to join us?' he asked then.

'Yes,' said Bessie. 'Sure we'd love ta!'

I couldn't believe me ears.

The next thing Bessie and Lilly were on their knees, their heads stuck down on to the seats of the chairs. Mr Murphy was sayin the First Glorious Mystery in the voice that sounded like the cat that's got the cream. Miss Moriarty, God love her, I never did see a woman as unfortunate in the physiognomy (but a course I hadn't seen the half of them yet) answered in her slow sorrowful country accent. Bessie and Lilly sort of mumbled.

I had to leave the room.

Of course I go to Mass of a Sunday and so on. But I had such a fit of the giggles that I had to leave.

I went off and found Jockser.

'They're the Legion of Mary,' he said.

'What's that?'

'Some Holy Joes. Want to convert yez from yere sinful ways.' We were in Mrs Guerin's sheebeen, down at the Five Lamps.

'So what are ye doin letting them in?' I asked.

'Ah . . . better let them,' he says. 'Trust Jockser. I'm afraid they might be in cahoots with the police.'

'I thought ye always said the police had promised a hundred years ago to let us alone?'

'There hasn't been police for that long, Bella.'

'Pardon me ignorance.'

'But ye're right. They've always left us in peace. But what's after happenin?'

'We're free.'

'Ireland is free. The Dublin Metropolitan Police is now the Gawrda Sheehauna.'

'Them Irish names is always bad news.'

'Especially for the like of us Irish means crawthumping.'

'God help us all.'

'Ah, it'll all turn out for the best. They'll never . . . go for us in a big way.'

'No?'

'How could they? Sure half the government is down here of a Saturday night.'

'In Pussy Catskins' caves?'

'Where would the bees be but where the honey is?'

'Has that fella Cosgrave been down?'

'Confidentiality is assured. If ye pay Jockser sufficient,' he said. 'Go back to work. It's all hours. I'll have customers for ye now. Wash that puss of yours and put on your Sunday best.'

I went back to the kitchen.

They'd taken Molly.

'Ye let them?'

'Sure you were sayin yourself that she should be put in the Union!' Lilly had done her hair up and put on kohl and lipstick.

'And is that what they've done?'

'They called a cab. She went in style.'

'We'll never see her again.'

'Good riddance. I'm after throwing away her blanket. She was crawling. She'd everything.'

'Maybe we should get rida the mattress?'

'Maybe she'll give them a dose?' Lilly laughed and handed me a cup of tea. 'God did you ever see the cut of the pair of them! Mr Murphy and Miss Moriarty! Wouldn't know his arse from the pit of his arm. Pardon me French.'

'So what's he doin down here then?'

'Good question, Bella.'

I'd seen his eyes. And hers. All lit up, twinkling. They couldn't keep it out. Thrilled with themselves. Gawking at us like childer staring at a shop window full of Peggy's Legs. An eyeful, is what they were after.

Pussy Catskins fixed me up.

'You'll do,' she said, giving me the once-over. Me in me birthday suit. She had me parading up and down the room she has, her showroom, where she keeps all the clothes.

'Not everyone does but you're a good-looking lassie, so you are!'

She was lovely. I always thought that even when I seen her when I was a girl. She was as neat as a button. Navy blue suit with a lovely little tight jacket. Big white lace collar. Her hair was brown, silky, always clean, tied back in a soft sort of a bun I never seen on anyone else. White skin and the loveliest soft red mouth. She used all sorts of stuff, creams and powders, lipstick. But ye'd never guess. She looked like a lady, from top to toe. I woulda given anything to look like her. And she was forty-three, with a husband in the bank and three grown daughters, one the spit of herself.

'I'll lend you the price of a gown,' she said. 'And other things you'll need.'

Her showroom was festooned with the most gorgeous dresses I ever seen in me life. Pastel colours. Sky blue. Pink. A yellow like primroses. A few dark ones too, like the ones she wore herself, but she sorta ignored them.

'Too old for you,' she said, when I fingered one. A brown velvet. It looked so classy. Cream collar, little black ribbon at the neck. Gonny mack! I woulda sold more than me virtue to get me hands on it.

'The lemon would suit you. Try it on.' She pulled it off the hanger. Lemon silk, with white lace at the neck and in ruffles around the hem. I put it over me head. She patted it into place, then got me paradin again.

'Yellow is your colour!' It looked as if I was havin no say in it. 'Then you'll need shoes, and underwear.'

Pussy was the lady had them all. I left decked out in new clothes from inside out. Not a stitch that was not brand-new. I owed her ten pound.

'Ten pound!' Let me tell you. Da got two shillings a day on the docks.

'You'll earn it soon enough,' she said.

I laughed. If she was willing to take the risk who was I to argue?

She didn't tell me about the interest till I thought I'd paid the ten pound off, a year later. And be then I needed another dress.

'That's Pussy,' laughed Lilly. 'Ye'll be in debt to her till you go up to Glasnevin.'

'But jeese! Why didn't somebody tell me?'

'Did ye think she was the sisters of the Good Shepherd?' Lilly didn't believe that I was only after finding out about the interest. She didn't believe I could be so green. But I was.

At least I had the dress and the other stuff.

And the work.

Ah gonny. The less said about it the better.

Sometimes it wasn't too bad.

And sometimes it was, God forgive me! The filth of some of them. The things they wanted me to do to them. I'll spare yez the details.

Mr Murphy could fill yez in. He found out everything.

Couldn't hear enough. Filth. Some get their fun outa doin things and others outa hearin about other people doin them and if ye ask me he was one of the second lot. Ye'd see his little watery eyes glistening when he listened – Lilly told him things that never even happened, just to see how he'd take it.

'God bless you, God bless you' was what he used to say, Mr Murphy. But you'd see his feet twitching under him. He couldn't control them. And his hand sneaking down to check that nobody could see what was happening in other places.

Miss Moriarty came only one more time, two weeks after her first visit.

'Poor Molly passed away!' was the first thing she said as soon as she walked in the door of the kitchen. I was eating bread and sugar, still a bite I fancied. Lovely bread from Johnston, Mooney and O'Brien, the crust black as mahogany.

'The Lord have mercy on her,' I said, mumbling because my mouth was full.

'She'd a lovely death.'

'Were you there yourself?'

'I was. She gave birth to her baby and then she died,' said Miss Moriarty, 'thanking God for taking her and thanking the Legion for having rescued her in time.'

My ears pricked up. 'But I thought yez were . . . Where was she, when she had the baby?'

'The Good Shepherd, where else? In the loving hands of the holy sisters.' She sat down, spreading her big bottom over the small chair. 'Would you ever give me a cup of tea if it's on it love? I'm perished with the cold.' Big smile. The nose sticking out over the table like an eagle's beak. All them Legion women had noses like that.

'Ah Janey, poor Molly.' I wanted to kill her, there and then. 'Yez said the Union!'

'Did we?'

'Yeah yez did.'

'Well that was Mr Murphy's suggestion. I don't think he realised she was the way she was until we saw her sitting up in the cab.'

I'd seen girls having babies in the Good Shepherd. It's not something I'd want to see again. Much less put a pal of mine through it.

'She was very happy. You should have seen her face. So peaceful.'

Glad to be going. And no wonder. The grace of a happy death. The sooner the better, if you were in that place.

'And what happened to the baby?'

'Hm?'

'Her baby?'

'It was baptised straight away.'

'Was it a boy or a girl?'

'God you're nothing if not inquisitive. It was a girl if you must know.'

'And where is she now?'

Miss Moriarty shrugged. 'The sisters will look after her. Give her a good Catholic upbringing in their orphanage. They are heroes, those nuns.'

I couldn't even speak.

I should tell yez something about our life in Monto.

The red light district. The only red light district to enjoy police protection in all of the British Isles, if you don't mind.

Some protection! You'd get bet up as quick as you'd get a cup of tea.

I don't know how many of us there was. Girls. So-called. Some of the girls were nearly forty. After that they hadn't much left in them. It's not that our clients were all so particular. Wouldn't want to be, the cut of them. But there's a limit, I suppose, and somehow nobody much beyond that was here. Where they went I don't know. A good lot wouldn't have lived much longer. We get diseases, you pick up things, it's a professional hazard and the hospitals, since the Irish took over them, weren't places ye'd want to go to. Turn you in as soon as give you a bottle of medicine. Probably there were about a hundred of us. We lived mostly in the brothels, we'd our own quarters there. Separate from the workplace in many instances – I had a room I shared with Lilly and another girl, but we worked in separate rooms. We had rooms under the ground, in the caves. That was a compliment, if you don't mind. I don't want to be singing my praises, but the youngest and best-looking girls

did the caves, where the big shots came. Judges, fellas from the Castle,
from the government. Men who had a bath two or three times a week
and had a white collar fresh and stiff every day. Money to burn, not that
they paid more than they had to. Still it was the best side of the work, all
things considered, even though they were usually old and had funny
requirements. Not to mention accoutrements. I've seen quare things, I
can tell ye.

All the girls were minded by 'bullies' – ours was Jockser,
afore-mentioned. The bullies' job was to get the clients, make sure
they didn't cause trouble, and take care of them if they did. The
bullies were supposed to get fifty per cent, us fifty per cent. On top
of that the bullies paid the rent for the houses, if they didn't own
them. (Jockser didn't. Pussy Catskins owned our house, and two or
three others. She'd started off as a girl herself and done very well.
Some oul codger – rumoured, by some, to be the Viceroy – had
fixed her up with a big house up on the Square, where he could see
her in comfort. She'd never looked back after that. Beautiful, Pussy
was, and also cute as a fox. Never drank. Saved every penny. She
could be rulin the country, Jockser said. She'd twist you round her
finger, she knows more than the Pope himself or the King of
England.)

The bullies did other things as well. Like beating up the girls, if
they were out of order. Or if they owed money, which they usually
did, to Mrs Catskins, and weren't payin.

The system was that she gave you your first outfit, to get you
started, on credit. You would never pay off that debt in a year. So
then you'd be in a position where you got your next outfit from her
as well. And so on. If ye fell behind with the repayments, or tried to
scarper, as some did, the bullies gave you what for. Half-killed you.
Or killed you outright. More than one girl never left Monto alive.
Who'd ask questions about a whore? The bullies would lift her up
and dump her in the bay, or catch the train and put her somewhere
up the Dublin mountains, mountains covered with bluebells and
heather in springtime and no wonder, with all the girls' bodies that
are buried up there in shallow graves, pushing up the flowers. I do

often think of it when me sentimental old codgers sing songs or get one of us to. 'The violets were scenting the woods Norah displaying their charms to the bees . . .' Ah Janey Mack! If they displayed all they had to display, them woods. The pine forest. Pining is right.

I paid me ten pound back fast. I got a good lump regular from a man high up in the courts.

'There's interest on top of that,' Pussy said with a cute little smile. I knew she wasn't pleased that I could pay her back so fast.

The interest was ten pounds again. I got it from him, as an advance – she hadn't counted on that.

Jockser came into me room the day after I paid it back. Now it was his turn to have a little smile on his face. 'I called in to Mrs Catskins today,' he said.

'Here's your fiver, Jockser,' I said before he could say another word.

I won't say he was gobsmacked.

He raised his fist and hit me a blow in the mouth knocked out one of me teeth. I picked it up and stuck it back in but it fell out again anyway, while I was asleep, and I swallowed it. That's why I have a gap in me teeth.

'I take the money from the customers, not you,' he said, laughing at me. I lying on the floor with me mouth pouring blood. 'Remember!'

That was all he done.

It was worth the loss of the tooth to be free of Mrs Catskins. After that I went to Clery's and did me shopping in a shop with the best of them. Half the price of Mrs Catskins' stuff they were too. The ones in the shop, the men and the stiff fat ladies in their smelly black dresses stretched over big behinds, sniffed at me as if I was a rat and them cats tied up and unable to get at me. But they took me money. I tried on whatever I fancied and they had to let me, and then they had to sell to me. C'est la vie as the judge says. You know what it means? So I won't insult ye be tellin ye.

Three years I'd been there when the Legio Mariae came in. Frank Murphy et alia to you and me. Another three years and I'd a had enough put together to buy a little cottage in the country – or in Skerries or Rush, somewhere like that. Me ma and da coulda left their bit of a room and come out with me. Or . . . whatever.

Not to be.

'Can't I entice you to one of our novenas, Bella?' Frank was having tea. With him was another sister, a Miss Ní Choincheanain this time. A lot of them had names in Irish. Weird. Nee this Nee that. Long noses thin mouths big hair spotty skin. That's what Nee means if you want my opinion.

'No,' I said.

'Bedad you're the hard woman.' He winked at Miss Nee Colcannon, who was new. Always as I said a new one, a different one. The competition to get to us was that fierce.

'So many of the girls have come by now,' said Colcannon. 'They love it. They are changed beyond recognition.'

'Yes indeed,' said Mr Murphy. 'If you saw the serenity, the peace which descends on them when they hear the word of God again, wild horses wouldn't keep you away from our novenas, Bella. They are special.'

'I'm sure they are,' I said. 'But I'll do without. I had enough of the Good Shepherd when I was up yonder.' I jerked my head in the direction of the orphanage.

'Oh yes. The nuns did their best. Look at you, a credit to them in so many ways!' Frank gave me the once-over – for all his holy jopery.

'Compliments fly when the gentry meet,' I said, pouring him a fresh cup of tea.

'And Bessie and Lilly have both left you now,' he said.

'And poor Molly Malone,' I said. 'What ever became of that baby of hers?'

'You'll be delighted to know that the baby has been given up for adoption to an American couple. It's a new project the good sisters have. Good Catholic American couples – and I assure you there are often no better Catholics, Irish extraction of course – are often looking for healthy babies to adopt. The nuns have decided that this is the ideal answer to . . . well you know the situation.'

'Yeah.'

'Boys are most sought-after, of course. So usually the girl babies are left with the nuns, which is appropriate enough, you will agree.'

Seein as they killed my brother, how could I argue with him?

'But Molly's baby – Goretti, they called her – was an exception. A most fortunate exception. She has been sent out to New York.'

'Good for her. I suppose they pay for this?'

'I'd know nothing about that.'

'I suppose not.'

'I have, I must say, had a hand in arranging some part of the project. I take credit for that. I had a meeting with a friend of mine in the Department of Foreign Affairs. Thanks, I may say, to my personal intervention, the scheme can function easily. The babies don't even require passports. They are simply let slip quietly out of the country as if they had never existed, and nobody is any the wiser.'

'Why? Could I not slip out of the country if I wanted to?'

Frank laughed, not unkindly. 'I wouldn't put it past you, Bella. But normally there are protocols to be observed.'

'I might have to slip out,' says I, teasing him, 'if all the girls slip out of this place and go to live in your hostels, doing novenas all the time.'

'Indeed and you might,' he said.

'Are you serious?' I asked then. Actually Bessie and Lilly still worked. They just kept outa the way when the Legion was in town. They went to the novenas to keep in with the Legion, who gave them a good supper after the prayers, but they held on to their jobs. What else would they do? Go to Magdalen homes, was the best Frank could offer. Be slaves for the nuns. Go way outa that!

'I have never been more serious in my life,' said Frank. He looked around at our kitchen. A bit of a kip. Jockser shoulda gotten old Catskins to paint it once in a while. The yellow paint was peeling down the walls like it was a banana. It was damp too and there were ratholes everywhere. 'I and my fellow legionaries . . .'

'Not many fellows . . .'

'. . . Sister legionaries will not rest until this whole district is closed down.'

'Sure what good will that do?' I asked. 'The girls will just set up elsewhere. It's because they know that that the police have always left Monto alone.'

And because the police occasionally use Monto, I did not have to add.

'I used to think that might be an argument. But what I have seen, the miracles of conversion I have seen with my own eyes, in recent months, have led me to change my mind. They have, Bella. I now know that this whole terrible industry can be simply eliminated from Ireland.'

'It's the oldest profession in the world, they say,' I said. 'If you eliminate us . . . sure you might as well talk about eliminating everything. Every bit of carry-on.'

Miss Colcannon looked tight-lipped.

'I will,' said Frank, calmly and quietly. 'The Legion will eliminate all sexual activity in Ireland. Nothing less will satisfy me.'

Miss Colcannon uncrossed her legs and blessed herself. 'Amen!' she said, in a mother of sorrows voice 'Gurbh fada buan tú!'

'We will be the purest, holiest, most chaste nation in the world. We have that potential. I see it all around me, in the faces of my sister legionaries . . .'

You'd see it there all right.

'And most of all here, in this district, the historic red light district of Dublin, the major blot on our Holy Catholic and Apostolic soul.'

'So you plan to put me outa a job?'

'I'll give you due warning, Bella. I would not let you down.'

But he did, the effer. We should never a let him in, soft-spoken oul pervert that he was, barefaced liar and hypocrite.

Only a few weeks later, one Saturday night, he had the whole place cordoned off be the police and raided. After a hundred years. Five hundred years.

There was hurrying and scurrying, I can tell ye! More be the clients than us. They ran through the warrens underground and came up somewhere – I believe outside the Pro-Cathedral. Probably got last confession and a novena before going home to their holy wives and the Rosary.

I jumped from the first-floor window and sprained me ankle. I'd me money in me shift. I tried to drag meself down the street and out on to Amiens Street but a big policeman got me and pushed me into a Black Maria.

The Joy.

They took me money offa me and said they would give it to the poor.

The poor. Where did that leave me!

I got six weeks. Prison. Better than the Good Shepherd. But when I got out what do you think?

Frank Murphy had burned down Monto. Burned it to the ground.

There wasn't a bit of it left. My house, all the houses, the streets, the shebeens. Nothing. All the bullies and the girls and the clients. Gone. Gone like they'd never been there and all there was left was a black, razed patch of ground. It looked so small. It looked like somebody's back yard.

I went home to me da. Mrs Catskins was still in the Square, so I called in to her.

'The girls are working the canal now,' she said. 'Outdoor work. More risky. The police are after them all the time.'

'I thought they looked after us.'

'It's the Free Staters,' she sighed. 'Them and the Legion of Mary!'

'What is wrong with them?' I asked. 'Why can't they leave well enough alone?'

She shrugged.

'They're religious,' she said. 'Religion is a dangerous thing. They don't like people like us, religious people.'

'He told me he wants to eliminate all sexual activity from Ireland.'

Pussy Catskins smiled her cute little ladylike smile. 'It's worth a try!' she said. 'I don't think he'll succeed. Now, can I do anything for you? You look like a girl could do with a fresh frock or two?'

'No thanks Pussy, thanks all the same.' It was my turn to smile sweetly. 'I'm going to England.'

'To England?'

'I think I'll try me hand at life in London, or Liverpool, or somewhere like that,' I said. 'There's lots a sailors there, isn't that right?'

'I believe so,' she said primly.

'And it's not a Free State, is it?'

'No.' She shook her head.

'And there's no Legion of Mary there either, is there?'

'Ah Janey, Bella,' she sighed. 'Who knows?'

THE MAKERS

David sits over a blue bowl of tomato soup, spooning it to his mouth with the caution he reserves for all foods that are not sweets wrapped in plastic, bought by himself in the shop. Even though he likes tomato soup, has indeed requested it himself, he isn't taking chances. You never know where a slimy scrap of onion or a gritty seed, a sliver of garlic, might lurk, waiting to invade your body, uninvited.

His mother watches him from the other side of the table. Three o'clock. He's just home from school. Since eight, when she waved him off, a minute snail in a navy tracksuit carrying his enormous schoolbag on his back, she has been alone. She has, in those hours, performed a few tasks: carried clothes from the washing machine to the line, watered geraniums in the conservatory. She has painted a picture, or rather has painted at a picture which has been long under way and which may never get finished, for all she knows or, in her present mood of lassitude, cares.

She stares at him. The vermilion soup travels from the bowl to his mouth, slowly and surely, seven or eight times. It has passed the test. He is also eating white bread, taking the middle bit out and leaving crusts in two golden rings on his plate. There is a glass of milk in front of him and he sips that from time to time as well. It's an unusual day for more reasons than one.

'You like this soup?' she asks, in grateful wonder.

'It's all right,' he nods. He doesn't smile but his face is neither angry or anxious, as it usually is, at mealtimes.

'Good,' she says. 'It's healthy – relatively.' Healthier than fruit gums is what she meant. Healthier than gobstoppers.

'But I couldn't have the same thing every day, could I?' He opens his eyes wide. They are not particularly big eyes but his habit of widening them makes them seem big. Their colour is a clean morning blue.

She is not sure of his drift. 'Would you actually eat it, if we had it every day?'

'Yeah.' He lifts the spoon one more time, then lays it firmly down on the cloth. There is some red soup in the bowl but not a lot.

'I'd like chicken soup too,' he adds. 'I'd like to try that. And the farmhouse vegetable.'

'Great.' She smiles. Chicken soup. Farmhouse vegetable. Is he serious? She scrutinises him more closely. His head looks like a flower, a heart-shaped blossom, pink and white, with the petals of straw hair fluttering in his eyebrows. He'd hate to hear that description of himself.

He stands up. It's not nice to be stared at. 'When caveman discovered the wheel did he make a wheelbarrow? Is that the first thing he made?'

'Gosh, I'm not sure.' She can never remember anything about prehistory, which interests David more than any other kind.

'I'll ask Dad. I think that was the first thing. He watched a stone rolling down a hill, and then he put a hole in it and made a wheelbarrow.'

'Probably,' she agrees. It sounds likely enough.

He pushes the petals of hair from his eyes. 'Can I get my hair cut? Now! '

'Sure. I'll ring them. No time like the present.'

No time like the present. That is not her phrase; she's stolen it from David's father. And the present is not Marie's time, not any more. Recently she has moved to the land of put-it-off. She's taken up abode in the land of dreams. When she phones the hairdresser there is no reply, much to her relief. She feels much too tired to walk all the way to the village, and back again, just to transform David from a flower to a scrubbing brush.

'Monday,' she tells David. 'Maybe he's closed on Mondays? Like, eh, the National Museum.'

'Mm,' he agrees, pulling at his fringe. 'Or maybe he's cutting someone's hair and can't come to the phone. Try again later,' he orders. 'Try again in five minutes.'

'I will,' she promises meekly.

David goes to his room to do his homework and she goes to her room, also with the intention of working. When she gets there, however, her eye alights on her bed – wide, silky ochre, seductive in the soft glow of the afternoon. The cat is asleep in the middle of it, curled into a neat, firm ball of white fur, catching the sun.

Marie lies down beside her, and lets the sun warm her face.

Her daddy got the flu on New Year's Day, as he had every New Year's Day for ages: the effect of too much excitement over the Christmas holiday. Marie's mother got it too and a few days later phoned and told Marie this in her weakened voice, the voice that made Marie grit her teeth and arch her back, that made her snap and snarl when she should sympathise and love. It was as if she still needed her mother to be invulnerable, immortal, and could not yet face the reality. A cry for help, a litany of graphic details followed. Diarrhoea and kidney trouble, weak spells and vomits. These were her mother's symptoms. 'And how is Daddy?'

'He's very chesty. But he's got the inhaler and he's doing his best. I think he'll be all right, please God. But we haven't had a bit to eat in three days and I woke last night and the sweat was pouring off me.'

'Have you had the doctor?'

'I rang him this morning. He's to come later.'

This was the third day of the new year. Marie was at work. As well as the painting she has a part-time job in a gallery in town, and it is there, in the middle of the afternoon, that she receives this call from her mother. Typical. Every year her mother makes this phone call. Marie has to drop everything and run to her rescue. Her mother is a person of exceptional optimism, energy and good humour when she is well. But even a pinprick of illness punctures her utterly, robs her of every vestige of courage. Death's door opens when a common cold tickles her throat. Marie thinks she knows the reason for this hypochondria: her grandparents died when her mother was four or five. But understanding the cause is not enough to make the effect easy to tolerate. What Marie's mother needs is Marie's sympathy. And that is just what Marie cannot give. She has none. Or if she has, it dries up into a hard ball of resentment and disbelief when these crises occur. All she can think of is time, and where she is going to find it. There is no time in this life she has made for herself to care about ailing parents. There is not time for anything except the next deadline.

Marie went to visit her parents the day her mother phoned. She bought tomato soup and fresh bread and lots of mineral drinks in the nearby supermarket, then walked to their house, her own childhood home. It was dark and spitting snow, very cold. But inside, the silent, neat house was a cosy nest – they'd got central heating a few years earlier, and the old rooms which had always been freezingly uncomfortable every winter until then were transformed utterly.

They were together in their high lumpy bed, her parents. Her mother lay back against the pillows with her eyes closed. Her father was sitting on the edge, his legs dangling to the floor, working on his breathing.

'I tell him to get up. He's better off up. He'll never shake that phlegm off his chest if he lies down. But he gets tired.'

Her father smiled weakly at her. He had the merriest smile, and small wide cornelian eyes which often twinkled in amusement or joy. They did not twinkle now. He sat on the bed, his grey and red pyjamas neatly buttoned, labouring to do this most natural thing. His breath came in thick, sticky whoops.

'He's got the antibiotics. He'll be grand, please God.'

'And have you got antibiotics?'

'No. I've to take fluids. I'm dehydrated. That's what caused the weakness. All the oul vomiting, and the sweating.'

Her mother overflowed with liquids, darkly swirling. Words

poured from her in a rich stream, tea from a spout. Desiccated inside, her silent father struggled for air, smiling, taciturn. The difference. So it had been, always. The melancholic and the choleric? Life does not yield such easy contrasts. Her father was not really choleric. His lungs were dry, after years of smoking, of working in air thick with sawdust, the dust of concrete and asbestos, but his temper had always been sanguine.

Marie made them soup and buttered the bread and poured the juice. They tried to eat. Afterwards she tucked in her father. His body which had been stocky and thick was thin, hollow, although the shoulders remained broad. His legs were so skinny that they made tears come to her eyes.

Her mother cheered up considerably after the meal, although she ate none of it. So it was always: all she needed was a modicum of attention, proof that she was loved, or at least supported, by her family. Her father did not need this proof. He was cheerful, with or without attention. He took life as it came, and didn't believe in worrying unnecessarily.

Marie pulls the quilt to her chin, stretches her legs, tries not to disturb the cat. She closes her eyes. Tiredness weights her stomach, drags her blood earthwards. Now that the days are long and light and fine, she feels there is no night, and one day blends into the next as charmingly as all the frilled trees in the gardens form great, cushioned banks and waterfalls of light, translucent green. Getting up in the morning is easy, and every day seems like a holiday, weightless, freefalling. All tasks – work, painting, housework – have grown simpler. But today in the heel of the afternoon this exhaustion descends, and all she wants is to shut her eyes and return to the dream landscape she left behind her the night before.

Daddy's flu became pneumonia. This, too, had often happened. The doctor asked, 'Would you like to go to hospital?' and Daddy, who liked hospitals, said yes.

Marie went to see him on his first night there. He was sitting up in bed wearing a white gown, with an oxygen mask over his face.

'How are you?' Marie hugged him.

'Grand,' he said, smiling broadly. 'This yoke is bloody marvellous. And I just had my dinner. I feel great, to tell you the truth.'

He looked happy. He was in a ward with about six people. One man read a book. Some were looking at newspapers. Two of them were up, perched on the sides of their beds, talking to one another. Nobody looked sad or very ill. Besides, there was no television. A blessing.

'The nurses are great. One of them is from Sligo. She's a lovely person, a really lovely person.'

He felt safe in this hospital, where he had often been before. The doctors, the nurses, the medicine, the oxygen – he knew they could help him. The ward was coloured softly, like the inside of an ear, and it did not have a smell. Marie loved it too. The high beds you could see under, the tight white coverlets like envelopes, the flesh-coloured curtains looped like loving arms at the ends of the beds. She'd only been in hospital herself once, to give birth to David, the best event of her life. So her associations were brilliantly rosy. Like her father, she loved the orderliness of the place, and she loved the cheerful, workaday atmosphere. A hospital, they both knew, is a place where people come to be refreshed and rejuvenated.

'Your mammy didn't come today but she'll be able to get in tomorrow.'

'How is she feeling?'

'Ah she's still only middling. But she's going to try to get in tomorrow anyway. Is it still snowing?'

'It's stopped now. It's OK.'

'Are you on your way home from work?'

'Yes.'

'How is David?'

'Great. Still on his holidays.'

He talked and talked, through the oxygen mask, sometimes removing it to emphasise a word or a sentence, to make himself plainer. His talk was all of ordinary things, of how he was feeling and what he would do next, of his medication. Sometimes he referred to the nurses, already counting them as friends, after one day. It was talk without much substance but he spoke eagerly and with excitement. He nattered, in fact.

This was a man who had never had one real conversation with Marie, in all the years she was growing up. He had always been kind, gentle, considerate. But he had not talked.

Instead he had made things – for her, for her brother, for their children: her cradle, modelled on one in which a queen of England had once lain as a baby. David had lain in that cradle too. Later, he had played with a painted train, rocked on a horse carved from pale, gleaming elmwood. Her father's communication had been with his hands, in objects built or made by them. Now for the first time, when he could not breathe without artificial aid, he wanted to communicate like other people, with words. Marie listened, pleased, her heart warming inside her. Her mother never stopped talking. Talk poured out of her, a torrent of commentary, conjecture, opinion. And her talk, excessive, sometimes became wearisome. Marie knew she could listen to her father for ever.

'I'll probably come on Saturday,' she said. 'I've visitors tomorrow night.'

'Fair enough, Marie,' he said. 'Don't you be driving in here in this bad weather. I'll be grand,' he said. 'Beidh mé go breá. Slán leat anois.'

She grasped his hand, which had been a huge paw of a hand, every finger thick as a thumb, and now was bony with veins gnarled and tumescent as an oak, purple as aubergines.

'See you soon.' She kisses him.

She doesn't want to talk Irish to him. His first language. His first language is a dialect that hardly anyone speaks any more, a dialect of Ulster Irish, on its last legs. There are some people – Marie's husband, Karl, is one, and he is right about many things – who would say that it is because nobody shares his first language that Daddy never speaks much. Marie is not sure about this. It must be strange, all right, seldom if ever meeting someone who really knows your own language. But plenty of people overcome this difficulty. Karl, for instance, is German, but he has plenty to say in English. And Daddy knows English perfectly well, just as well as anybody else in Ireland. There is more to it than that.

All her life Marie has been busy and energetic, working stolidly if not brilliantly; a day when she has not learned or written or painted or made something she considers wasted. She sits on committees and boards, she does two or three jobs, she keeps her house in order. She has passed heaps of examinations, given hundreds of talks, participated in umpteen projects. Besides all that she loves to cook and bake, to sew curtains, to paint rooms and paper them, to walk and to swim. Her life is packed with activity. But when people remark, as they often do, 'How do you get the time to do it all?' Marie feels annoyed, or accused. Why? Who is accusing her, and of what? All she knows is that she is not happy unless her hands or her feet or her head are totally engaged. Baking bread or scrubbing floors or walking five miles across a mountain. Painting is the best thing of all. That is like harvesting corn with a sickle. It is like designing a house and then building it, stone on top of stone, with your own two hands.

That is what Daddy did when he was a boy, eighty-odd years ago. There is talk in Ireland of the terrible poverty of the past, and Marie knows it is true. Her mother refers to it, tells her stories, usually about other families, thankfully distant, miserably unfortunate cousins. Stories of toddlers gathering brosna for fires, of no food and no money and no boots and no heat and no hope. Terrible humiliations. Daddy never told such stories. He did not think of his family as poor, although they probably never owned any money at all. They were medieval. Not cavemen, but medieval. In his house, the cloth was made from wool that his mother and sisters spun. It was dyed the colour of rust with lichens from the rocks, yellow with weeds from the ditches, deep brown with black ink from the bog. Their food was grown in their own fields, their meal was thrashed in their barn. They fished in the bay and salted barrels and barrels of herrings for winter.

Even their house they had built themselves, and furnished it with simple, beautiful furniture, because his family were weavers and masons as well as fishermen and farmers. Hunters, gatherers, tillers. Makers.

They always had plenty to eat and, it seems to Marie, warm and beautiful clothes to wear. And the house, as Marie pictures it, was also warm, electric with life – with the slap of the churn and the whirr of the wheel, with the hopefulness of baking bread. The Middle Ages. Only a few things in that house could not have been there if he had been born in 1312 instead of 1912. His father and mother could not read, even, and had never been to school. But they could spin, they could make clothes, they could make tables and chairs and houses and fish with many kinds of hooks and nets. They never stopped working. And that is what lies behind Marie's life. Centuries of people buzzing about their work of survival, like bees in a hive. That is what her father did. Worked. He did not talk, because his language was no longer spoken in the world he inhabited, and besides he had chosen a wife who could do all the talking for him. And he did not write poems or stories. But he worked happily. That was his prayer, his mark on the world and his legacy to Marie.

He went to hospital on Thursday and that is the night Marie visited him and had the long chat. On Friday she had a visitor to dinner, Amy Murphy, an American woman who was in Ireland for a few weeks to do some research on Irish artists. She was a small, chatty, kind woman, an excellent guest. She presented Marie with a bunch of yellow freesias, her favourite flowers, the flowers that smell of damp green meadows, of spring rain and of ethereal perfumes. They talked happily about the latest exhibitions, and the latest scandals. They ate something light and good and Marie was complimented on her cooking, as she usually was, as she expected to be.

The conversation was so lively that they all forgot about the last train, so Marie and Karl drove Amy home to her hotel in town. The snow was falling lightly again, in the dark blue streets, but the roads were not dangerous. On a whim Marie decided to drop into the hospital. To her surprise, Karl did not object, although it was not exactly visiting hour, being past midnight.

They had to go in through the casualty department, and traverse many silent corridors, lighted and warm, but empty, to reach the ward. Daddy had been transferred to the coronary unit. The nurse there was friendly and spoke in a low, kind voice. There was nothing wrong with his heart, she said. Don't be alarmed. They merely wanted to monitor it while he underwent some treatment for his kidneys. His kidneys? Yes. The medication for his lungs had affected his kidneys in some way, so they were not working properly.

Daddy was sitting up in bed, delighted to see Marie and Karl.

'I'm grand!' he said. 'You didn't come all the way from Killiney to see me, did you?'

'We had to leave someone to town anyway,' said Marie. 'So we dropped in.'

'I'll be here until tomorrow, I think. Will yez be in tomorrow?'

'I will, probably. I might bring David.'

'Yeah. Bring David. I'd like to see him. How is he?'

'Fine. Your breathing is better?'

'Much better. They're great in here, they couldn't be nicer.'

His eyes twinkled, and his face was merry. The light in the ward was soft and yellow, and the room soothed with the familiar sounds of patients snoring, the regular comforting bleeps of machines that minded them, like watchful angels, as they slept.

The next day Marie put Amy's freesias in a small green jug and brought them to the hospital. She thought their spring colours would appeal to Daddy, who was fond of flowers. She thought he could lie in bed and look at them, when he was too tired to read or think.

But when she arrived in the ward, Daddy was lying on his back, his face crumpled, his eyes almost closed. His breathing was heavy again, gnarled, clotted, tangled. He looked cross.

'He's not responding to the treatment,' the nurse said. She motioned Marie and David outside to the corridor. 'The doctor will talk to you soon. Are you the closest relatives?'

Marie knew then.

'Yes,' she said. Her mother was still at home, sick with the flu.

'It could be a few hours, a day,' said the doctor, a tiny Oriental woman with skin as smooth as the lining of a nut. 'We don't know. We don't know why his kidneys have failed and we're trying to find that out.'

But it was clear from her tone that they would not find out.

'Oh.'

'He could have dialysis,' the doctor said. 'But he is not a good patient for dialysis. His heart is weak and then he has the lung disease.'

'What chance does he have, if he gets dialysis?'

'I think if he goes on the machine he would not be able to take it. He'd go.'

Marie thought of dialysis as something painful, like chemotherapy. She thought of her father spending his last hours hooked up to a machine, in pain. She reiterated the doctor's comment that dialysis was not a sensible option and the doctor nodded eagerly.

'We can try to make him comfortable,' said the doctor. 'I think that is the best thing now.'

Comfortable. Marie had thought of dying as a quiet and simple task. She had thought people lie calmly in bed, breathing softly, and that one breath is weaker than the others, and that is the last. She had read of final words, of *bloscadh an bháis*, where the dying person wakes up as bright as a bird and says goodbye to the family gathered around the bed. When the doctor said 'comfortable' that is what she imagined: they would make it peaceful for him. They would create a state of quiet and ease and painlessness to move him gently from life to death.

But that is not what 'comfortable' meant at all.

Daddy died after three days of struggle. 'He's not in pain,' the nurses said. How did they know? After the first day he was dumb; he could not talk and tell them. But he looked pained. His breathing was loud and noisy like a damp engine, his skin looked sore and tender. His eyes sometimes half-opened, and what you could see in them was torture.

Sometimes the nurses gave him sedatives, and he had some peace. At other times, they gave him treatments – changed the tubes that failed to draw water from his kidneys, put other tubes down to his lungs to extricate the excess liquid that clogged them. After these treatments, he breathed easily for half an hour or so. Marie did not witness the insertion of the tube, the suction of the lungs, but she felt it in her own body. She felt the intrusion and the pain. She thought of her father as a hapless victim, lying speechless, dying, on a high bed, while nurses circled saying, 'He feels no pain', inserting tubes into the centre of his body, inserting needles into his skin, needling him and turning him and twisting him. On the first day, when he could still talk, he said, 'Leave me alone', his profound patience at last exhausted. But they could not leave him alone.

Marie's heartbroken mother and the other members of the family said it was for the best, that they knew what they were doing. Marie said nothing. She noticed that the treatments varied. On the day shifts, the nurses attended to him every half-hour, and what they did seemed to depend on the personality of the nurse on duty. Some were brisk and sharp, and worked hard, helping or annoying Daddy. Others were soft and gentle, and gave him sedatives to help him sleep. The night nurses were the best. They left him alone, administering morphine, often at Marie's request. The nights, Daddy's last nights, were closer to her idea of what death should be than the days. The days belonged to someone else. To the hospitals, the nurses, the doctors. They had to be filled with activity. For Daddy, night cannot have been different from day except in this, that during the day he was constantly bothered by the hospital staff, and during the night he had peace. Marie sat by his bed and held his hand and asked for morphine, and sometimes he even slept, and his face was at least calm, not twisted with pain and despair, as during the day.

Three days. It was like labour. A long labour, leading not to a new life but to the opposite.

He died after the nurse had inserted the tube into his lungs for one last time. That was his last experience of life on this earth: three strangers in white sticking a plastic tube into the centre of his old, wise body, and sucking water from his lungs.

He had been born in a small country house, in a room with his mother and a midwife. He might have heard, soon after his birth, a seagull screaming. Or, more likely, the cranky squawking of hens, or the sombre lowing of the cow in the byre across the street. The medical equipment in the room where he was born might have stretched to a pair of scissors, a bowl of hot water. The light would have been dim: the shadowy amber of an oil lamp, if it was night; a slender ray of misty sunlight if it was not, because the window in the room would have been tiny. And he died in a room blazing with electricity, with wires attached to many parts of his body. He died with a plastic tube scratching his lungs, the centre of him, where the first, the simplest, the most natural function had happened.

In the paper the notice said 'peacefully'. And Marie, Marie's mother, everyone said, he was lucky. Daddy was one of the lucky ones.

Marie has always wanted to work and produce, and if she is not doing that she feels unhappy, anxious, even guilty. But now there is a change. What she wants to do is nothing. She would like to lie in bed, with her cat and like her cat, for days and days and days. She would like to spend her time sleeping and dreaming the long, lazy dreams she loves. Instead of wrenching from them abruptly in the mornings, losing them, she would like to stay in them until they fade away of their own accord. Then, if she must get up, she wants to sit and stare at the garden, to move through the house from room to room, silently and quietly. That is what she would like, for a while, until she has sloughed off her skin, until she has turned inside out and started again, until she has dreamed her fill.

David comes into the bedroom. She opens her eyes.

'Look what I made, Mammy!'

He hasn't been doing his homework, it seems. He shows her a robot, a robot that moves with the aid of a small engine and can carry a tray from one side of the room to the other.

'Do you like it?'

David is small for his age, still very childish for ten. His hands are soft and tiny like starfish. But his eyes are wide and they twinkle when he is happy. And with his little starfish hands he is always busy, building and moulding and making all kinds of things. The house is full of his productions.

'It's lovely.'

He pushes his petals of hair from his eyes. 'Did you ring the hairdresser again?' he asks suspiciously.

'I'll ring him right now.'

He smiles, points bossily at the telephone, and readjusts his robot. Marie starts to dial.

AT SALLY GAP

There are many kinds of love but one that everyone wants. True passion. The perfect union of body and mind and soul. Ecstasy – with a man on a bed.

There are other kinds of love, obviously, and they are not to be sniffed at. Friendship, companionability. Filial love, parental love. It's nice to experience all of them as well. But not as nice as the other kind. Not as rare, not as special.

There are other kinds of ecstasy, apart from sexual passion. Transcendance, via nature, beauty, contemplation. Solitude. The cloud of unknowing, the centre of the circle, the dancer and the dance. Intellectual ecstasy, so unfashionable it is seldom talked of, hardly acknowledged. The passion of the mind intensely at work, grappling with a problem, arriving at a solution. The passion of the exploring mind making a discovery, experiencing illumination.

That's all very nice too, and you can reach it on your own, which makes it both easier and harder. But it's not as good as the other kind. Why?

Not as physical. Not as tender. Not as emotional.

Orla lies awake at night, thinking things like that. Her bed is wide and comfortable during the day, but at night the sheet crumples under her and feels as if it were sprinkled with biting crumbs. She turns the heating off at night but still feels too hot. Or else too cold. She glances frequently at her bedside clock. One o'clock, four o'clock, five o'clock, six o'clock. All these times she sees every night. In between she is either thinking or sleeping. She knows she sleeps because there are dreams.

It is a long time since she worried about this sleep pattern. It has no effect on how she feels during the day. Tiredness is not a problem, as it was when she had small children. Having small children meant being tired all the time. Having grown-up children means never being tired at all, even when you don't sleep well at night. Having small children means you always sleep well at night, for as long as you can, anyway.

They decided to drive to Glendalough. It was a sunny, blustery day towards the end of March. Clouds, white and black, scampered across the stunning blue sky. Showers threatened.

'It'll be quiet down there today,' Patrick said firmly, turning off the dual carriageway at Kilmacanogue.

'Yeah, I suppose so. Apart from the foreigners on buses.' Orla spotted a coach already, silver and beige, squeezing along the road between the rocky outcrops and picket fences like a fat overdressed woman climbing a mountain path.

'You're not worried, are you?' He patted her companionably on the knee.

'Well . . . why should I be?'

'Exactly. Going for a walk among the ruins is not a crime.'

It wouldn't be, if he had mentioned it to his wife. Or if she had mentioned it to her husband. If it wasn't a crime, why didn't they do that?

Orla is over from England for a few weeks, to bury her mother. That's how they put it still, here. She always sees herself with a shovel, digging a hole in an old, ivied graveyard, while her mother waits patiently in her coffin on the wet grass. Orla in overalls and wellington boots, sweating as she works. The clay grey and stony and heavy. The sky is usually March, in this image. The time had been appropriate. Her mother obliging, going as the daffodils blossomed all over the gardens of Dublin, yellow hopefulness under changeable skies.

'We decided to go for cremation,' her sister had informed her, with a fleeting smile that brooked no argument. 'I assumed it would be all the same to you.' That quick smile again, as much a challenge or taunt as a gesture of friendliness. 'That's fine,' Orla had said. Of course it was simpler not to get involved in this. 'Thanks for making all the arrangements. You're great.' She kissed her sister on the cheek. The simper came and went rapidly, to be replaced by tears. They glistened dangerously in her eyes as the two of them moved through the doorway, crossed to the car park. Orla put her arm on her sister's arm for a few moments. Her sister did not shake it off. But she shook her head vehemently, shook away the trace of emotion in her eyes, smiled her grim smile as she pushed the button of her car alarm. The car, a dark blue Toyota, new, flashed its lights, and Orla felt a little safer for a second.

Her mother had died after an illness of a few months. Cancer. She had been diagnosed in January and Orla and Sarah had come over for a few days, to visit her, before the first session of chemotherapy. Her mother had been at Kathleen's then, comfortable in the guest room. Kathleen had a large house now, in Killiney, a house with wide windows and views of the Irish Sea. Her mother could see Dalkey Island if she sat up in bed, as she did most of the day. She could see the ferries to Wales, white galleons, cheerily buoyant on the intense blue sea, setting out, coming home, the eternal pattern repeated four times a day.

'Musha I'm only middling,' she had said to Orla. 'Only middling, alanna.' Her mother spoke like that still, like someone from the thirties, which of course she was. She could speak in other more modern dialects but usually chose not to when she was with her family. When Orla had been young she had hated this habit. She had been convinced that her mother was using her quaint old expressions on purpose to irritate and upset her children. 'A pinch of salt,' she would say. 'A haporth of flour.' 'Ne'er a drop of milk in the house.' Drinks were always measured in drops, salt in pinches, flour in haporths. Flour, or was it cornflour? 'Don't spoil the gravy for a haporth o' cornflour', that was it. She said these things, and also the Rosary, and the Angelus, at six o'clock, wherever they were, as soon as she heard the bell toll. The Angel o' the Lord declared unto Mary. It all hung together in Orla's mind, praying and bells ringing and haporths of cornflour. A malicious, shameful mixture.

Now Orla wished she had taken notes. She wished she could speak like that herself. The English of Forth and Bargy. Mixed up with the English of Rathmines, the English of RTÉ, and other kinds as well.

'You look . . . not too bad.' Orla kissed her mother, whose face was warm and soft as a peach. In her blue nightdress against the white pillow, she looked peaceful and at rest. There was a soft-yellow-shaded light by the bedside, a pitcher of water, a bowl of grapes. She had been listening to the radio when Orla had come into the room. Mike Murphy's booming, comforting voice had filled the room.

'I do have terrible pains sometimes. I do be in agony. But for that again I feel grand.'

'That's good.'

'But sure after the oul chemo I'll probably go to pieces altogether.'

'For a little while. And then you'll feel much better. You'll be up and about, even.'

'That's what they say. But I don't think they know themselves half the time, to be honest with you. I think they do be only lettin on or chancin their arm.'

Orla had stayed for four days then, at the end of January. She had stayed all that time in Kathleen's house, mostly in the sickroom, tending to her mother and listening to her. Her mother had wanted to talk. Not, after a while, about her illness and the doctors, although for as long as Orla could remember illness had been a favourite topic of conversation with her. But about her childhood, and about Orla's father. Orla had heard a lot of the stories before but now she heard a few new ones. 'I wish I'd've wrote it all down,' said her mother. 'And I wish your daddy had written it all down. But it's too late now.'

'When you feel a bit better we can do that,' said Orla. 'Or I can get a tape recorder and tape it. Then it'll be there even though you haven't written a single word.'

'I used to drive into Ferns every Saturday in the donkey and trap,' said her mother. 'And I always had a bag of Kerry Creams to eat on the way home. I used to eat around the edges of them, nibble away, and I'd keep nibbling and nibbling until I got right in to the middle of the biscuit. That's what I used to do. To make them last longer I suppose it was. God the childer nowadays would think you were mad! They'd think bad of even eating a Kerry Cream if they got one. The young one here only eats chocolate biscuits. "No Nana, I only eat chocolate biscuits," she said to me a couple of days ago when I gave her one of them digestives Kathleen does have in her tin: "Dark chocolate for preference". I ask ye!'

Orla stayed until her mother was installed in the hospital ward, and left then, the night before she was going to have her first go. 'Say a prayer for me, alanna' had been her mother's last words to her. 'Yes,' said Orla, who did not pray. 'I will. I'll be thinking of you. And I'll be back soon again. I'll see you soon.'

Her mother had not answered that.

When they reached Glendalough, the car park was full of cars and coaches. People swarmed over the churchyard and along the lakeside path, the green road.

'We can't get out here,' Orla said.

'OK.' Patrick looked at her critically. 'What would you like to do then?'

'Go somewhere else.'

He sighed but started the car again.

She looked regretfully at the valley. The steep mountains, the brilliant blue lake fringed with pale gold sedge. The stone church and round tower.

'It's unbelievable, isn't it?'

She meant, the stunning romantic beauty of the scene. If you were imagining a perfect nineteenth-century European beauty spot, you could not do better. Mountain and lake and sky and tree. Waterfall. The medieval monastic settlement graciously crumbling into all the natural wonder of it. Girls in red anoraks and cheerful green hiking boots hung over one of the little wooden bridges, watching the stream babble over the rocks.

'I suppose so.' He was annoyed after all.

'I used to come here a lot when I was a child. We used to drive out on Sunday afternoons.'

'It seemed like a longer drive then, I'd say.'

'I used to look into the river, like that girl is doing. I'd stare and stare at the water, sparkling along. Hoping for something.'

'What?' He sounded interested, at least.

'I don't know.' Orla looked back at the valley. 'I didn't know then either. But I know I believed there was something there. You know, some sort of illumination, or truth. That sounds daft, doesn't it?'

'Daft. Only English people say daft.'

'What do Irish people say?'

'Crazy. Or funny. Or weird.'

'Well. You know what I mean.'

'Not really.'

'No. Well neither do I. But I thought there was something there and if I stared for long enough I'd have it. I suppose it was just youthful romanticism. Optimism. I thought I was so clever, you know, and so different from everybody else.'

'You are.' He laughed.

'But not all that different. Then I thought . . . I don't know. I thought all kinds of amazing things would happen to me.'

'Because you stared at a stream?' His voice was dry and friendly. She loves it when he teases, even a little. She giggled and put her head on his shoulder, not even checking to see that nobody was looking.

Orla lives in Bangor, in an old stone farmhouse on the road to Caernarfon. Her husband is a lecturer at the university, in English – he specialises in Chaucer. She has worked there too, as a tutor, as a temporary lecturer, and, lately, helping in the library. Although she is well-qualified – she has a doctorate – she has never worked seriously at any job. Her husband had been her professor and it seemed that

marrying him had been the zenith of her career. Looking for a job in
Old and Middle English had been difficult, anyway. There were very
few positions. She would have had to travel much farther than Wales,
and keep on moving, before hooking a real permanent job, the kind
he had. When they had fallen in love and decided to marry, marriage
had seemed preferable to struggling on, writing out applications
every year or two and packing up to go to some other city, some
other country. She'd been twenty-seven when they married, and had
felt quite elderly. Most of her friends had been married for years.
Kathleen had married when she was twenty-two.

Kenneth – he was never called Ken – was ten years older than
Orla, but they never noticed that this mattered in their relationship.
Physically he was active and fit – he liked to walk in the mountains
near where they lived. Maybe he looked older than her – but that is
not the kind of thing you notice, once you have been together for a
while. His hair was grey, of course, grey turning to white. But maybe
Orla's was too. It could be almost any colour now, under the layers
and layers of dye that she had put in it. Black and brown and
chestnut and rosehip and God knows what else. They're supposed to
wash out but a residue seemed to remain always, leaving its mark –
usually a pale orange – on the hair near her temples.

He knew much more than she did about medieval literature,
about mythology, about the classics, about history: his general
knowledge relating to anything up to about 1900 was immense. She
had always deferred to him there. But he knew nothing about
contemporary life, literature, culture, politics. So a balance of kinds
was struck.

Orla did not feel second-class or inferior. Even though she had
never had a full-time job, even though she spent a great deal of her
time at home, planting flowers in her lovely, crowded, higgledy-
piggledy conservatory and quaint old garden, and looking after the
house which is full of unevenly floored, lopsided rooms, she felt his
equal. Even though he earned most of the money and the prestige.
She took all this in her stride and did not wonder about it.

Kenneth and she had had two children, a boy and a girl, soon after they were married. The boy was still at school, and at home. The girl was at Oxford.

Kenneth and Orla used to quarrel a lot when they were first together. But now they never quarrelled, they had reached some sort of equilibrium. They went for walks together on Sundays, tramping all around Snowdonia. They drank wine with their dinner on Saturday and Sunday, and sat afterwards, chatting idly, for an hour or so, before Kenneth vanished into his study to work and Orla sat with a novel, or, more often of late, in front of the television set. She had begun to watch soaps, something she would never have dreamt of doing when she was young, or even a few years ago.

Kenneth never watched television, except for Welsh-language programmes and a channel which showed French movies. She watched them too, and felt a lift of achievement when she under-stood the French. But if Kenneth didn't turn on such programmes she didn't bother doing so herself.

What she had become was lazy.

Too lazy to learn, too lazy to read anything difficult. Too lazy to bother much about her appearance. She seldom visited the hairdresser. Her wardrobe had not been replenished in about three years. She had let weight creep on to her thighs and hips – they were disgusting, laden with loose fat flesh, spongy like sheets of thick jellyish foam someone had laid over the real flesh, the real Orla. She had let it creep on not because she liked to eat or drink all that much, but because she couldn't be bothered weighing herself, keeping her body under control. It was as if she had let every aspect of her life slide. This had happened when Sarah, the daughter, had gone to Oxford and Matthew had started studying for his A levels. She'd moved offstage, somehow.

Kenneth didn't care how she looked. They never made love – her choice, but he didn't seem to notice, or mind much if he did. He was the typical absent-minded professor. His life was lived inside his own head. His enthusiasms were huge, demanding enormous time and energy but, it seemed to Orla increasingly, childish. He, and all his colleagues up at the college, seemed to be playing elaborate intellectual games all the time. Did Chaucer intend 'The Wife of Bath's Tale' for the Wife of Bath or for the Shipman? Kenneth had devoted years of his life to an investigation of this question. Was *Beowulf* based on a historical character who had lived in Sweden or in Denmark?

Did it matter?

To the world?

It made Kenneth happy. Tired but happy, like children coming from a picnic at the seaside. He emerged from his long sessions in front of the computer rubbing his reddened eyes and luminous with the joy of intellectual activity. The mind needs exercise as much as the body does, and benefits from it as much too. Kenneth was a kind of mental athlete, immensely fit. She knew about that. That feeling of well-being that comes from intense thinking, problem solving. Using words and sentences to get to the heart of a problem and find a solution to it. The sentence first the way of simply giving voice to the thought, and then the thought itself, so that you discover, again and again, that language, prose, is thought. Prose is the thread that brings you into the profound depths of the mind, the sparkling stream that leads to the source of knowledge, as well as the symbols that you bring out from the well and use to express what you found there.

She knows this, in theory, but it's been too long since she visited those places deep in her own mind. What did she bring forth? Nothing that seems to matter or to have lasted even in her own memory.

'Don't stay too long,' Kenneth had said, putting her on the boat.

'Not this time,' she promised. She wished he could come with her. But he had his job, always a good reason for not making trips like this. He hated visiting her family, but never said it.

'Not the next time either,' he said.

'I'll do what has to be done' was all she said. She saw him going to his car – a green jeep – and driving away, as she stood at the window of the ferry. Watching someone you love drive off in a car is unsettling. It gives you a sharp insight into how separate they are from you, and you from them. They are so alone, all of a sudden, at the steering wheel of their destiny, without you beside them for company and control.

She shook off the sense of abandonment by getting a drink at the ship's bar. She shook it off by dipping into one of the glossy women's magazines she'd brought with her in her Times Past tote bag, covered with Latin ex-libris. A clever disguise for a heap of *Cosmo* and *Image* magazines.

He turns on to the military road at Laragh and takes the road to Sally Gap.

'I don't think I've ever been on this road.' Orla looks out at the ash trees, the tangled brambles. The road is narrow and deserted. She feels relaxed already.

'Ah you must have been.'

'Maybe I just don't remember. I think I was at Sally Gap, but we didn't go this way.'

'You would have come up from Blessington, maybe, with your father. Or through Enniskerry.'

'I've no memory of it at all.'

Patrick rolls down his window a little, then lights a cigarette. He doesn't ask her if she minds. He knows she does not, not in the sense of minding the smoky car, although she can't understand how he can go on smoking, someone whose mother-in-law has just died of lung cancer. They've been through all this. Kathleen doesn't nag him about it, just sets her mouth in that grim line, half-smile half-grimace, when he lights up. It's one more thing she turns a blind eye to.

Patrick is a businessman. He owns three dry-cleaning shops in various suburbs near Killiney, and usually works in one of them himself, in the office, no longer out at the counter. He employs ten people and will expand again soon. The DART stations could take a lot more cleaners. There's only one so far, at Pearse Station. Patrick plans to open three more probably over the next six months.

He seems playful and innocent, often making jokes. But underneath there is a layer of sense and even cunning, which a successful businessman has to have. And underneath that is another layer, of wisdom. He knows something about humanity that Kenneth probably does not know. So Orla senses. Sensing that this is there, in him, buried under his other personalities, is probably what made her fall in love with him. Also he is very attractive, stocky and blond. His skin is clean and cream-coloured, his eyes a very pale blue. But he exudes virility, in spite of all this pale creamy colouring.

Orla may be falsely attributing some of his spiritual characteristics to him. But his physical ones are definitely there. He is an intriguing, complex physical type. Women are always attracted to him. Poor Kathleen. The set of her mouth is not accidental. Since she married Patrick she has had to turn away, remain calm and philosophical, remind herself that she is his wife and that nothing will ever change that. He strays, but will not stray far. He will always come back.

They see a pheasant. It crosses the road in front of the car, then dawdles by the ditch, pecking at the grass.

'Oh! Stop!' It's not that she doesn't see them often enough, even in the garden at home. But this one is particularly spectacular. His golden and beige feathers glow like a Byzantine treasure. His green head, capped with crimson, is delicious. And he's so nonchalant, tame as a farmyard fowl. They mustn't shoot here.

'Delicious,' she cries.

'Delicious enough to eat,' says Patrick, before he can stop himself. Predictable. If she were younger, if she were his mistress and she were younger, he would say, 'Like yourself.' Predictable. But he doesn't, because she's not. Those slabs of shaking thigh. That round face, ready to collapse into hills and shelves of wrinkled jowl any day. He is in love with her, but it's not her body that attracts him.

The tree-lined road soon gives way to mountainy farmland, or bungalow land. Little green fields patchworked over slopes, bordered by stone walls or high hedges of gorse. The gorse is in full bloom. Great bushes of bright yellow – even through the cigarette smoke she can get a whiff of its burnt butterscotch smell. It's always elusive anyway – strong and elusive simultaneously, so that you always feel you are just about to fill your lungs with its sweetness. But just as soon as you prepare to suck all that yellow honey air into the centre of your body, it runs past you.

'It was worth driving up here, just to see this,' she says.

'Isn't it out in Wales yet?'

'I haven't been into the hills for a while. Maybe it is.' She thinks that in a way this landscape is a mirror image of what she has left behind her. Half the jigsaw here, half sixty miles away on the other side of the pond. And then, other features are so different. The white bungalows, mainly, that are everywhere in Wicklow. The painted towns. Over there, stone cottages carefully preserved, towns that are all grey, everything in them built of big grey granite blocks. The coal mines. Why are there no coal mines or quarries in Wicklow when Wales is so full of them?

'There were gold mines here,' he answers this question. 'Lead mines. Copper mines. And look at this.' Acres of bogland. They are climbing now, up the mountainside. The little fields have disappeared and instead there are swathes, sweeps, vast expanses of heather-covered bog. Dark burnt purple leggy clumps of heather, pale straw clumps of withered grass. Purple and straw, purple and straw, as far as the eye can see.

'Turf. It never got a chance to become coal.'

'It never will now. Half the chancers of Dublin up here at weekends, footing their bit for the winter.'

'Do they still do that?'

'You bet.'

They come round a bend and see a waterfall. Silver water tumbles down a rock race into a meandering snake of a stream below. Dashes from a grey ridge to the pastoral valley – it looks pastoral from up here, deliciously cosy and civilised.

'I've never seen that. I've never seen that waterfall. Isn't that amazing?'

Kathleen had all the work and responsibility. In and out to the hospital every evening. Days and days of leave from her job in the civil service, used up on her mother's illness. Orla should have come over. She should have come over, or she should have taken her mother back over to Wales.

Kenneth wouldn't hear of it.

'We haven't room,' he said. Not strictly true. 'You don't have to go that far. Can't she be in hospital?'

'She doesn't want to be,' Orla said. 'And I don't think they'll keep her anyway. Not unless she's very bad. Beds are in such short supply.'

'I thought Ireland was in a boom phase,' he said. He never went to Ireland. It was too like Wales; he didn't like it. During the summer they went to the south of France. They have a cottage, smaller than the house at Bangor but not altogether dissimilar, in the Cevennes.

'It is. But they still can't cope with all their sick people. In fact I believe they are closing down hospitals rather than opening them.'

'This is not a hospital, Orla. And you are not a nurse,' he said. He left the sitting room then and went to his study. Ten minutes later he came back and said, 'Do whatever you think is best.'

Orla looked up from the newspaper she was grazing on. Irritated, because something about Sunday newspapers always irked her. She got three of them and browsed through all three, being irritated by their silly impossible recipes, their advertisements for horrible vulgar clothes costing about a thousand pounds per garment, their silly articles about teenage pregnancies. Their assumption that everyone was a millionaire. Orla always felt poor and unsophisticated and stupid after the Sunday papers.

She gave him a hug and said 'thanks'.

That had been last Sunday.

Since then, her mother has died – Kathleen and Patrick at her bedside. There's been the funeral. Crowds of relations from Wexford and Tipperary, drinking tea and whiskey. People she hasn't seen for decades and people she thinks she never saw. Patrick.

They've been doing this for ten years.

Flirting. Not that either of them can flirt. But they've been conscious of a mutual attraction. Over the dinner table, over the fireside table in Kathleen's sitting room. On hikes up the side of Mount Snowdon, on the occasions when Kathleen and Patrick visited them in Wales.

There have been times alone. Half a dozen of them, at most. Hours snatched here and there during holidays. Kisses, hand clasping. But mostly this relationship has consisted of yearning. Vague yearning at that, yearning without much of an end in view. Yearning that has been more a sense of mutual liking and friendship than anything more focused.

Now it's focused. All of a sudden it's focused.

She is here without her husband, or her children – Matthew came over for the funeral but has gone back. Kenneth and Sarah did not come. It's the first time this has happened. That she has been here alone.

Kathleen is somewhere. Out somewhere. Not at work yet. She gets five days' leave for the death of a parent, so she's taking a well-earned rest. She's gone to a leisure centre for a day. She suffers from arthritis in her knee, so this is not half as luxurious or frivolous as it sounds. Hot jacuzzis and massage give her a bit of relief, for a while. Her mouth is set in pain, physical as well as mental.

After the waterfall the landscape gets barren and wild. They are on the mountaintop, a wide plateau of heather and peat. The sky is blue as the Mediterranean, the clouds have all disappeared. The road cuts straight through the bog like a silver ribbon and it is free of traffic.

But is there anywhere to hide?

The heather.

Deep and thick, high as your forehead when you're out in it, even though it looks short from the car.

Nowhere to hide the car but what matter?

They get out and walk through the bog, with difficulty, clambering over the humps and roots. The sun that shines so brightly is not as warm as it looks, not warm as it was down in the valley. The wind is ferocious, whipping their hair roughly and biting their faces. They cling together battling in the wind, their words get carried away on it before they really hear them. After a few minutes they sit down and find themselves sunk, and, they hope, covered by the rough heather.

He has brought a tartan rug from the car.

Not ashamed to plan in advance.

Although in the car she had not known that this was going to happen, she acts as if she had anticipated nothing else. And her body copes admirably with the occasion. She is excited, passionately excited, from the moment he takes her hand to help her over the heather. His hand is big, hot, helpful. Its touch on her waist, as he propels her along, makes her want to cry for joy. His touch on her face, as they lie on the rug, sheltered by the high rough growth, makes her laugh. That this can happen. That it can still happen.

Afterwards they drive past Kippure – a stand of pines, the first trees for miles, and the two transmitters – and downhill to Sally Gap. A spider of roads going in four or five directions. He takes the one marked GLENDALOUGH. 'But we've just come from there!' she protests, weakly, still soft and easy from what has happened. She nestles to him in the car, his tweed jacket. She won't want to leave him, she wants to cleave. That's what happens to you. You can't bear to separate.

'The wind has twisted the signs. Or gurriers. They're all facing the wrong way,' he explains.

He'd know that, of course.

So they go down the mountain, down to Glencree, a patchwork of fields and bungalows, down to the familiar silver peak of the Sugarloaf, down to Killiney. The coast.

The sea.

In the house, her sister's house, her mood changes.

Kathleen has been cheered up by her day at the leisure centre. She has prepared a special dinner, with good wine – it's Orla's last day in Ireland. There is a fire dancing in the grate and the sitting room looks clean and sparkling, with great blue vases of daffodils near the window.

Kathleen is dressed differently from usual. Usually she wears tight-fitting suits, clothes in off-beat colours – murky pink, lilac – that look uncomfortable and unflattering. Now she is in a kaftan, silky and gorgeous. Its colours are crimson and dark green, and there is gold in there somewhere. Under it, black silk trousers, loose and light. She even has little gold slippers.

'My harem outfit,' she says, in her tart voice. 'Got it in Turkey when we were there last year. Patrick forced me to buy it, didn't you darling?'

Patrick smiles ruefully. 'Yes, love,' he says.

Orla slugs back some wine. She is wearing green corduroy pants and a thick woollen jumper. Her hair is tangled like a gorse bush and her face is red and patchy from the wind and from kissing Patrick. Although she can smell fresh air from her skin, she feels messy.

'Maybe I'll change,' she says. A delicious lassitude has taken her over. All her muscles are relaxed. The heat of the fire is balm to her face and she feels she cannot bear to move from the deep comfort of the sofa.

'Can't stand the competition?' Her sister grins, not kindly.

'That must be it. You do look stunning.' Orla is too lazy to catch any hint of malice. A hint of more malice than is normally present, that is.

'A bit late for that,' Kathleen says. 'Since the deed is done.'

Patrick glances anxiously at Orla. Then he asks, blandly: 'Did you have a good day at the pool?'

'Delightful, thanks, darling.' Kathleen gives her little smile. 'Did you have a good day in the mountains?'

'I was in the office,' Patrick begins.

'I know exactly where you were,' says Kathleen.

He smiles now, a big, disbelieving smile. He stretches and looks quizzically at Kathleen. Orla wonders what he is going to do next. She is a spectator now at this drama. She can get up and go. It occurs to her that this is what she should do.

'That's good,' says Patrick. 'Now can we eat dinner? I'm hungry and I'm sure you are too. After all that swimming.'

'I haven't been swimming, dearest,' Kathleen smiles. Orla notices a lump in the big pocket of her kaftan. It could be a bottle. A book. A knife. A gun.

Kathleen is mad enough to kill her. Suddenly Orla realises that her sister has always hated her. She has hated her. The grim smile, the tight-lipped jokes, all make sense. The reluctant visits, the dearth of invitations. They have never gone shopping together. They have never had a tête-à-tête, a girly drink. Always meeting at funerals, at their mother's house, at Christmas in the bosom of their families. Orla has always liked Kathleen but Kathleen hates Orla. It's clear. And now at last she has a real reason for hating her, and a motivation for hurt. *Crime passionnel*. That's all it would be. You read about such things more and more, happening in Ireland. Not called *crime passionnel*, of course. But somehow the criminals, the people who wield the knife or the gun, get off the hook. Out of control. Justifiable rage. Kathleen would know that she'd be freed by any jury. A woman betrayed so cruelly by her sister, a few days after her mother's funeral.

Orla drags herself out of the armchair. Her limbs are leaden. She might have taken some drug, instead of air and love at Sally Gap.

'So what have you been doing?' Patrick drinks his wine.

Orla slides out of the room. She hears Kathleen's voice issuing its tart, crisp statements, as she climbs the stairs, fetches her bag – not bothering to pack what is not in it already – and comes back down. She stops to listen at the door of the sitting room.

'You're always doing this to me. But you're not getting away with it this time.' Kathleen's voice is louder now, high-pitched, hysterical.

'I did nothing,' he says in the exasperated tones of the righteous being accused in the wrong.

'You went off somewhere with her and did it. My sister. It's disgusting.'

'Listen, you should see a doctor. I didn't. Of course I didn't. It's a mad idea.'

Orla feels the strength seep back into her limbs.

'I see you and her. Making eyes at one another. Don't think I don't notice.'

Orla puts her bag down on the hall floor and takes off her coat. She goes back into the room.

Kathleen is crying now, her silken robe spreadeagled across Patrick's shoulder. He is patting her head and comforting her.

'I'll get up the dinner,' says Orla. 'All right?'

She takes the first ferry home next morning, leaving Dun Laoghaire at eight o'clock. At nine thirty she is in Holyhead. That's all it takes, to cross that mythical stretch of water, the stretch that separates two civilisations, so insistent on their difference. That is all it takes to be in exile. One and a half hours by Seacat.

During the crossing she does not ponder much on anything. Patrick in the mountains. The shoots of yellow gorse. The intense azure of the sky. The shock of sexuality. Love. Love.

She's awake again. From now on she will not be lazy. She will be energised, alive, sensitive to all of life's possibilities. You'll be long enough in the grave, alanna, her mother used to say. Used she? Life is short. Make the most of it.

Matthew is there, in his green wax coat and his golden hair, when she gets out of the boat. She rushes to him and hugs him.

She will never go back to Ireland. She will never see Patrick again. And she will not miss him.

This is what she believes, for the moment.

THE TRUTH ABOUT MARRIED LOVE

Where are you most married? Your kitchen, your garden, your sitting room? The restaurant where you celebrate anniversaries? The church you got married in? Your bedroom?

Eric is lying against a heap of white pillows on the wide orthopaedic bed Sarah bought the year they got married and moved into this house. There are a few stains and holes in the mattress, puncturing its cheerful brown and orange cotton cover, but otherwise it has borne up very well, considering it's twenty years old. Hard to believe. Where does the time go to? It's twenty years old but it still looks new to Sarah, who still feels she is a girl, not married at all, not the mother of two big children taller than herself or their father. The bed used to be in the smaller bedroom in the middle of the house and the big front room used to be Eric's study. But six years ago they converted the garage and moved Eric's books downstairs. Sarah painted the big room white, and stencilled green and blue flowers on the wall around the door and window. She got the floor sanded, so it is a sweep of nut-warm golden wood, and replaced the old beige plush bedhead, which she had thought lovely when she first got it, with a simple bit of carved Mexican pine. The few bits of furniture match, and she has hung some cherished pictures, too personal to hang downstairs, on the walls: a blown-up photograph of a basket of blueberries she and Eric picked on holiday in America; a jokey poem his sister wrote when she and Eric got married; two still lifes, colourful but not skilful, that Sarah painted during her summer holidays. There is a radio and a CD player in one corner, a blue chair near the window.

The best thing is the view. When you sit up in this bed you can see through the window a wonderful expanse of sky and sea, marred only by five black telephone wires which cross the bottom of the window like lines in a music book. Starlings on the wires like notes of music. White seagulls floating past, a few terns diving far out. On the horizon, ships passing on their way from Ireland to Wales. A floating lighthouse, the Kish, flashing a friendly warning.

She likes to sit there, beside Eric, to ruminate and gaze. The sea and the sky are always changing. Sometimes smooth and cheerfully blue, sometimes calm and milky, sometimes grey and angry. Many more changes than you can describe or recall. As you stare you register them. 'Look out,' she says to Eric. He glances up from his book and looks out for a few seconds. 'Lovely,' he says, in a tone of exaggerated admiration. 'Bee-yootiful.' He makes big eyes and grimaces, then returns to the pages of his book. 'Aren't you glad,' she asks, 'to have this to look at, while you are lying here?' 'Ooh yes,' says Eric. 'I am very glad indeed.' 'It's a privilege,' Sarah insists. 'I am so grateful for it.'

But that is not what she has always said. Far from it. Often, to people who say, as they invariably do, 'You've a great view,' she has said, 'Oh, you get to take that for granted, I'm afraid.' Then she'd go on to complain about being so far from the city. Travelling for nearly an hour to get to work. The children setting off at a quarter past seven to make it to school by nine o'clock. The traffic. She might also mention that the area they live in is itself not fashionable, not one of the better residential areas. But she doesn't bother, usually. It seems snobbish. Also she doesn't need to. Most of them can fill that in for themselves. Dublin people know their residentials, down to a *t*. Some of her friends occasionally remind her that she lives in an area that is not one of the more desirable, in spite of its fine views, its backdrop of mountains, its foreground of beach and sea. All cancelled out, for the truly perspicacious, by the council housing estate which sprawls to one side of the village. Beauty is not valuable if poor people share it with you. That's how it is, in Dublin, and probably in most other places as well.

Sarah has not always been so appreciative of her view, of her house. Or of her husband.

She and Eric met at work; they were, are, solicitors. Eric was a senior figure, although not a partner, in the large firm. Sarah was a secretary, hoping to take her examinations at night and part-time and finally become a solicitor herself. She had not worked for Eric at first, and only saw him fleetingly, in the big glass lobby, filled with potted palms like a hotel. He was a tall thin man, about forty or forty-five, with an abstracted, distinguished look. Different.

'He's English,' Julie, one of the other girls, explained to her. 'That's why he's tall and lean, not round and fat like all Irish lawyers.'

It was true that most of the men in the firm were thickset and well-padded, if not really fat. Brown or fair hair, blue eyes, broad cheeks and big teeth predominated. They looked, all of them, a bit like President Clinton or Kennedy. That seemed to be the physique of the Irish bourgeois male, strongly represented in the legal profession. They were seldom very tall, and they all smiled and laughed a lot and made plenty of jokes. Smooth as cream on apple pie, or the top of a pint of stout, they were. It was fun to work for them.

Eric looked more anxious, and also more spiritual, than the rest of them. He had a serious cast of mind and an Oxford accent. His fund of jokes was relatively small – which didn't mean he didn't know any. But he was able to talk for five minutes at a time without making a wisecrack, which marked him out as unusual in Hayes, Brown and Murphy Limited. It also, in combination with his accent, height and figure, gained him a reputation for being highly intelligent. He speaks seven languages, was one of the things people said about him. Including – and this was the clinching factor, the unquestionable mark of linguistic genius – 'including Irish'.

Sarah was intrigued by him long before she went to work in his particular office. Intrigued, but certainly not in love. She was amorously occupied with another man at the time, a young man called David, with whom she had been conducting a relationship since secondary school. David was now studying at the university. Commerce. He wanted to be a chartered accountant, and swore that he would earn £20,000 a year before he was thirty or feel a complete failure. Sarah felt this ambition was unrealistic – she earned £5,000 herself – but she didn't say so. Probably she was wrong. David seemed to know everything there was to know about money, a topic on which he could hold forth with a quiet, firm authority at any time of the day or night, if provoked. He was handsome too, in the style of the solicitors: blond curly hair, which would recede but had not yet started its retreat; twinkling blue eyes; a mouth poised to laugh.

What struck Sarah first about Eric was that he was sad.

He saluted her gently each morning when he came in, and sometimes looked at her with such an expression of weariness in his long, brown eyes that she longed to ask him what was wrong, longed to comfort him.

'Can I get you a cup of coffee?' was all she could offer by way of consolation on these occasions. He usually accepted it with a smile. But when she brought it into his room she would find him deep in files, with no trace in his eyes of the sadness she had detected outside. He would glance up, absent-mindedly, and sometimes mutter thanks. Sometimes not, sometimes he would not even glance up.

She learned something about him one day when she was taking a letter about a case involving a legal separation.

'Oh dear dear,' he said. 'The trouble these people let themselves in for.'

Sarah glanced up, surprised.

'The law in Ireland makes life difficult for them. As if it were not difficult enough already.'

'You mean because we have no divorce?' Sarah glanced idly at the letter she was writing in Pitman shorthand. 'I suppose so.'

'Ours not to reason why.' He continued to dictate the letter.

'He's divorced himself.' Julie knew everything. 'He came over here six years ago. He used to live in London.'

Sarah was surprised. Somehow she had managed to think of Eric as unmarried – there was something celibate about the way he looked, the stillness of his eyes – and unavailable at the same time. She had never imagined him as a man with a sexual past.

'I think there is a child,' Julie said. 'He has a daughter who stays with him sometimes. She comes here. A big fat girl with jet-black hair. Sort of . . . jolly-looking.'

Sarah had not encountered this person as yet. Still, she felt uncomfortable, hearing her described in these slightly pejorative terms. Already she was feeling protective towards Eric.

A week later, two things happened, one in Sarah's head and one outside it. What happened in her head was this: she was walking along the quays, from O'Connell Bridge up to Ormond Quay, where the office was. It was a fine morning in April. The Liffey danced along, bright as bluebells, under the white arches of the bridges. Beyond that, the white balustrades of Ormond Quay sprouted tufty shoots of buddleia, freshest green, stretching out over the water. Into her head sprang an image out of nowhere: herself and Eric in a tight embrace, kissing passionately. She tried to push it away but the image lingered for several minutes, as she walked slowly along by the river. The kiss was long and passionate, and even though she attempted to dislodge it from her head, she enjoyed it.

When Eric walked into the office later in the morning, and nodded to her, she did not feel embarrassed. She tried to match him with the picture that had come into her mind earlier, but couldn't. Not yet.

The second thing that happened came about, by some extraordinary coincidence, that very night. David and she were supposed to be going out, to the pictures or something. The plan had been vague. She was to meet him in town, outside the GPO. She waited for half an hour, then three quarters of an hour. It had become chilly. The twilight filled O'Connell Street with a ghostly, grey dimness. She shivered in her raincoat and felt her face grow pale, cold and tense. It seemed that people were eyeing her curiously. After an hour she caught the bus and went home.

She telephoned David. He'd forgotten all about the date. Even though they always met on Wednesdays. 'I'm sorry. It just slipped my mind.' She had felt angry but he sounded so contrite that she believed him. 'We'll meet tomorrow instead. All right?'

'OK,' she said.

The following night he told her he wanted to break it off.

She went around feeling numb for a few days. She was twenty-one and had been going out with David since she was sixteen. Everyone had believed they would get married as soon as he finished his degree, in September. Sarah had not quite believed this herself, but she sometimes pretended to herself that it would happen. Although she had felt for months that David was anxious, and had been afraid, she had not prepared herself for what seemed to be the finality of this.

She told nobody. But Julie found out anyway.

'It might be temporary,' she said sympathetically. She was twenty-five, married, and had seen a lot of relationships crumble and form, form and crumble.

'It might be permanent,' said Sarah, feeling the first crumb of hope she had had since the break-up.

'Try not to take it too badly even if it is,' said Julie, making her feel sad again. 'It's not the end of the world. There's more where he came from.'

'The fourth-year céilí in St Malachy's?' Sarah responded. 'I suppose so but I doubt if they'd let me past the bouncers.'

A week later she caught sight of David, *bras dessus, bras dessous* with a girl she had not seen before, a girl who was both smaller and prettier than Sarah was herself.

That sight was so upsetting that she had to take the rest of the day off work.

Eric noticed her pale face or the rings under her eyes, or something. He was especially kind to her for the next couple of weeks. Then he asked her, awkwardly, if she would have dinner with him one evening. She accepted.

★ ★ ★

Eric's face is swollen to twice its usual size. He can talk, but in muffled tones, and he can't eat any solid food. Sarah makes soup for dinner, and a very fine porridge, a gruel, for breakfast. Luckily he is very fond of porridge.

'Delicious,' he splutters, as best he can.

'But why is your face swollen like that?' She touches it gently and he winces. It is dark, about eight o'clock in the morning, the week before Christmas.

'Is it swollen?' Eric asks. 'It feels . . . all right.'

'Does it?' She finds this hard to believe.

'Sore, inside, but all right otherwise.'

'Maybe we should ring the consultant?'

'Don't do that. I'll see him on Wednesday. I'm perfectly all right, darling. Don't go making a fuss.'

Sarah gives him some aspirin and leaves him alone in the room, which she has made as comfortable as she can. There is a big jug of salt water by his bed, which he is to sip from time to time to clean the wound in his mouth. There is a flask of tea and a plate of soft cakes on a tray, in case he feels hungry. She has moved the CD player close to the bed, so he can change the discs without getting up. And she has put a hot-water bottle under the duvet, for comfort, although the room is warm and in fact it is clear that Eric is running a temperature.

He is retired now from Healy, Brown and Murphy Limited, and she works as a solicitor with another firm in town. She drops the children off to school on her way in to work every morning. Today is no exception, although she worries about leaving Eric alone. The minor operation he had at the dentist's last week is turning out to be more of a problem than anyone had anticipated.

'What's wrong with Dad?' Sheena, the elder girl, asks.

'He's pretending to be sick.' This is Joey, the boy.

'He's not, is he, Ma?'

'No no.' Sarah is not concentrating on what they are saying. She is thinking of Eric's swollen face.

'He is. He's a chancer. He's not sick at all, sure he's not, Mam?'
Joey speaks emphatically. He is fourteen years old. Until he was
twelve, Eric was his hero, his best friend. Then Joey had his growth
spurt, and at the same time as he grew in stature, his love for Eric
turned sour, turned to mistrust and scorn. 'You miserable dwarf!' was
one of his kinder appellations for his father.

Sarah presumed that the idea of his father being ill was something
he wasn't ready to cope with. She tried to shut Sheena up – Sheena
often had to shut up, to act the adult, when Joey was around. Mostly
she was able to do it. Old before her time.

'Of course you should ring the consultant!' It wasn't Julie now – she
was still with the old firm – but another confidante. 'For heaven's
sake. They charge enough.'

Sarah rang from her desk. She spoke first to the secretary. Then
there was a scuffle of feet. The doctor being called from his work,
knife in hand, green-gowned.

'Is there a problem?' he asked.

She explained.

'I'm not surprised,' he said then.

So if not why hadn't he warned them?

'What are you giving him for it?' he asked then.

'Solpadeine.'

'That won't help.' He sighed. But it was what he had suggested.

He gave her a prescription over the telephone as well as
instructions as to how to take care of Eric. Then he said: 'It's
probably cancerous, you know?'

Sarah felt her stomach deflate like a punctured tyre. Blood drained
from her head and she was surprised by a huge wave of nausea. She
shook her head and clutched her stomach to prevent herself from
fainting. Luckily she was sitting down.

'I did not know that,' she said.

'Don't worry about it.' He spoke a little more kindly, a little more
slowly, than he had before.

'Well.' Sarah was not thinking at all now.

'Tell him to come and see me on Wednesday. He should keep rinsing in salt water every half-hour or so.'

'All right,' she said weakly. 'When will you know . . . what it is?'

'I don't know, in a week or so,' he said. 'Don't worry.'

The evening of her first date with Eric, Sarah dressed carefully in an outfit she believed would be appropriate for dinner with an older man. (At that stage, a startling amount of her intellectual time and energy revolved around clothes, and a startling proportion of her salary was spent on them.) A dark blue silk dress with a wide white collar, white shoes, a straw bag. Over it her loose, swinging white raincoat. She washed and brushed her hair till it gleamed like a copper pan, and applied her makeup with great care.

All these preparations took place in her bedroom, in her parents' house, where she still lived with her sister and mother and father. While she was undertaking them, Sarah concentrated on the work in hand. Any consideration of the end she had in mind she blocked out. Why was she doing this? What would happen next? When these questions, the image of Eric, tried to find a space in her head, she pushed them away so firmly that the gesture seemed almost physical. When the doubts came, they came not into her head alone, but into her stomach, or somewhere in the centre of her body. A tightening, a sickening, a coldening. And when she pushed them away, that knot of fear vanished as well. Her insides felt normal.

'How is David?' her mother asked, a bit suspiciously, when Sarah came downstairs much more glamorously got up than usual. 'I haven't seen him this long time.'

'He's fine,' Sarah replied.

'Tell him I was asking for him,' said her mother.

Sarah took the bus to the bottom of the street where Eric lived – a long winding road near the sea, in a suburb that seemed very far-flung to Sarah. She felt fine on the bus; it was a route she had seldom travelled on, and simply looking at the passing scene of unfamiliar houses, shops, gardens, preoccupied her.

When she got off the bus the trouble started.

It was a fine evening, but the road that ran along by the sea was windy and looked barren and cold. It was bordered on the sea side by a dank, disheartening marsh – a home for many sea birds, but Sarah did not know that. To her this sanctuary looked anything but nurturing. The sky above it was wide and pale, behind it was a forbidding, high sea wall, in front a grey road along which buses and trucks trundled, relentlessly churning out leaden smoke.

The road Eric lived on was narrow, long and winding. An architectural hodgepodge: new, hard-faced houses wedged on to lots between old crumbling houses like that of her parents; ancient huckster shops side by side with a brash red-painted pub. Vacant lots, car parks. Apartment complexes hidden behind high walls and big signs saying 'Residents Only'.

The sun was blocked out of the sea end of the street by the high houses. A sharp east wind pumped up the narrow road from the sea.

By the time Sarah had walked a hundred yards along this street, she was suffused with anxiety. Her stomach crumpled into a cold wet knuckle of fear. She could feel the skin on her face contract, her mouth pinch, her eyes stare crazily ahead.

Eric. Twenty years her senior. Grey-haired already, almost. His middle-aged masculine tweeds, his middle-aged male smells. His wife, divorced, somewhere out there. His daughter. How could she explain this to anyone? Her friends. Her mother. Her sister!

She stopped beside the granite wall of a garden, leaned against it, and looked back down the street.

There was the marsh, a car park, a tumbledown railway station. The hard grey stretch of Dublin Bay. The bus stop. Her mother's house. Her mother in the kitchen saying, 'Are you back already, alanna?' Her bedroom – shared with her sister. A divan with a sunray headboard, a set of plywood bookshelves. 'Has something happened between you and David?' Pity. Dead end. No escape.

She walked, nevertheless, back a few steps. Then she stopped again.

Eric waiting. Eric in the office on Monday, avoiding her eye. His sad face more disappointed than ever. 'It is quite understandable,' he might say, in his measured, rational tones. 'Let us say no more about it. All right?' And that would be that. She would never know what might have happened if she had simply shown up.

Shown up.

She breathed deeply.

When Eric opened the white door of his apartment – on an open sweep of lawn, sun-steeped – he took her in his arms without preamble.

She buried her face in his warm, tweedy, hairy shoulder.

He laughed, he smiled, he fondled her hair. 'Oh my darling!' he said. 'I had begun to be afraid that you were not going to come!'

Sarah exhaled a puff of surprised, amused air. Poof. Pooh pooh!

All the caution, the fear, the worry, she blew out in that puff of air. It was as if she emptied her lungs of all the preconceptions of her own past, and started out again.

Eric was so cheerful, so delighted, so happy that she was with him, that there was no question any more of turning away. His confidence that she was his became hers that she must be his. His what?

His wife. Within days, hours in fact, he was jumping this far ahead.

How could she have thought this man was sad, and cautious? He was like a child with a new toy. He could not get enough of her. He could not talk enough about her. He could not bear to be separated from her, even for a night.

She felt he was a man who had been missing love, female love, for decades, and who could now not believe his good fortune, that a woman was in his house and in his arms.

When she had regained her composure – in so far as she would ever regain it again, in so far as composure was a quality that mattered one way or the other to her – Sarah left the office and drove home, a long journey out past the old apartment where Eric had been living when she first met him, several miles out along the coast to the strange, mixed-up suburb where she lived.

At the chemist's she stopped and asked for the stuff that the doctor had prescribed – the prescription was written in her diary, on the page for 6 June the following year. The chemist, whom Sarah did not know very well, asked her how the patient was. Explaining, Sarah burst into tears. Right there in the middle of the shop, surrounded by the revolving racks of gift packs and lipsticks. She had to sit on a stool and be comforted and regain her composure all over again, under the care of the kind, compassionate chemist, who had much more time and care to spare than the doctor. Then she had to go home to nurse Eric.

Nursing Eric.

He is as cheerful and optimistic as ever, the man whom she had fallen in love with because she thought he was sad.

'I feel fine,' he says, all the time. 'Apart from this wound in my mouth. But I think it is getting better.'

'Che sarà sarà,' he says, blithely, absent-mindedly looking up from his book, when mention of the test, the test that will show whether he has it or not, is mentioned, tentatively, by Sarah. 'I must die sometime!' he says. 'That is something we all have to face.'

Sarah learns to laugh with him.

It is not as hard as you might think.

She finds that she loves being his nurse. Giving him medicine, providing water and salt, lemon juice, hot bottles. Mashing food in the food processor so that he can eat it. Making his bed, plumping his pillows, bringing up new books and music. While she is doing all this she is fulfilled, occupied, almost happy. Never has she felt more useful, to anyone. A man who is ill. Her husband who is ill. The man she loves who is ill. She is the one who should be looking after him, is what she feels, with her heart, her instinct. An old intellectual principle jogs her occasionally, asks her if she would enjoy this if it went on for a long time, if she would not get weary and resentful, running up and down the stairs, giving all her care and love to Eric.

Her legs grow tired quite soon. After four or five days. But she does not grow weary, or resentful. Her anxieties are centred on Eric, how he is feeling, what he is suffering (a bit, according to himself. He is either being heroically stoical – which is a distinct possibility –

or he is not suffering very much). Her fears are centred not on herself either, for once, but on him. She lies awake wondering, if he actually has it, will he suffer a lot of pain. What she could not bear is to see him suffer pain. She feels she would much rather undergo it herself, if it is to come. Or she would rather help Eric to end it, get out of it. She lies awake, angry that people are allowed to suffer, that there are laws against euthanasia. She lies awake composing letters to the paper, letters to politicians, diatribes against the injustice of the country and its oppressive, incompassionate legislation.

Eric has no worries at all on any of these scores.

She broaches the topic tentatively. His father died of cancer, long ago, in England.

'I don't think he had any pain,' Eric says. 'They can control that for people.'

'Do you think so?' Sarah wishes she knew more. She gets a book from the public library. *Cancer*. It has a blue cover, a well-organised layout, an optimistic attitude. Cancers of the oral cavity can be treated, usually. They are containable. There may be discomfort for the patient. (Dry mouth. Sarah can feel her own mouth dry up; this is what doctors call *discomfort*? Live with that! Try it!)

But no real pain, says the doctor.

Eric lies against his heap of white pillows, reading Agatha Christie and sipping lemon juice. The room is warm and cosy. The winter sea churns noisily against the cliff outside, the seagulls scatter above the telephone wires. A branch of Christmas candles is lit in the window, and the music of Mozart sweetens the air of the whole house.

David found out about Eric even before Sarah's mother or sister did (her father was a very Irish father – he was never going to get involved in the affairs of his children's hearts, or any of their other affairs either).

'You can't marry him.' He came around to Sarah's and asked her to go for a walk with him. 'He wants a nursemaid, not a wife.'

'Oh dear,' said Sarah.

They walked along the Victorian roads and squares in the area where they both lived. The gardens were fresh and bright with wallflowers, early roses, pansies. Everywhere, trees foamed and frothed great plump pillows of fresh foliage, softening the prim brick faces of the prim-windowed houses.

'If he was the same age as you I'd say fair do's. But he's not. He's taking advantage of you.'

Sarah should have declared stoutly 'But I love him!' However, she did not. She didn't say a single thing.

David had not said a word about the girl. The girl with the black hair she had seen him with a month or two earlier.

'Aren't you seeing someone else?' she ventured.

'What gave you that idea?'

They were moving towards the Grand Canal, at its best at this time of the year.

'I saw you with someone, a while ago.' He looked blank. 'She had black hair. A small girl.'

'Oh yeah.' He paused, and looked into the black water of the lock, which was filling up. 'That was nothing. Nothing.'

Sarah, who had been crazed by jealousy when she saw that girl, believed him. She believed him because he was crazed by jealousy now. Jealousy of her. What he had lost.

They crossed the grey hump of Baggot Street bridge and turned up the canal bank. The hawthorns were in flower, pink and white blossom billowing all along the deep, long-grassed bank like prayers to the summer skies, the dark, delicious canal water. Two swans glided along by the reeds, as always.

They sat on a bench under one of the hawthorns, and stared silently at the water.

David put his arm around her shoulder, and pulled her to him. Then she was lost, lost in a long long kiss, the kind of kiss they had enjoyed first when they were sixteen years old and had fumbled towards this moment, one as uncertain as the other if it would be reciprocated, if it were wise or possible or good. The first kiss they experienced again, in the painfully gentle spring twilight, with people behind them and people in front, going to the pictures, going to the pub, going to eat, going to work. Cars humming and the water lapping, green and black and cool. Kavanaghs' redemption.

Pouring not for them.

Because afterwards she went back to Eric.

For reasons that had something to do with pity, something to do with love, something to do with loyalty, reasons that were a rich, irresistible, mysterious cocktail of feelings she could never articulate, she went back to Eric and stayed with him.

David was young, handsome, clever. He would earn £30,000 before he was thirty, be a millionaire before he died. He would find someone else if he hadn't done so already (he had – the girl with the black hair). He would be all right.

That Eric would be all right, without her, as he apparently had been before, was not something she could believe for a second. Eric's life stretching emptily before him, the small flat near the lead-waved bay, the office, his daughter popping in at long intervals – she could not wish that life back on Eric, did not believe he deserved it or would be able to bear living it, and she could not bear to condemn him to it or to the danger of it. Somehow she knew that Eric might not try again, with some other woman. Somehow she believed that only she was approachable enough. That their eyes, their four sad eyes, locked in understanding on those grey mornings in the office, were the expression of a secret deep bond which held her and Eric together in some eternal supernatural mould, which had been there since the world began. She might find someone else – she could take back David, he was there, begging her to do it. But Eric. Who would Eric find, after her?

Was that arrogance? Or love?

Sometimes, in the afternoons, before the children have come in from school, she gets into bed beside him. The light fades early in the wide sky over the sea, darkness sinks into the water before their eyes. As night falls the candles on the window ledge gleam brighter and brighter against the deepening blues and blacks of the sky.

She and Eric are suffused with love.

It is like a golden mist, spun of honey and sorrow, spun from the passion of their two companionable hearts.

Every bone in his body is known to her. His long thin racehorse legs. His wide white chest, covered with black hairs, split by a scar like a zip fastener (made when he had a by-pass operation, the year Sheena was born. The day after Sheena was born – Eric had come by taxi from his hospital to hers, to see his new daughter). His fine sensitive hands, delicate as a sculptor's. The curve of his mouth, distorted by his swollen face, then by his sunken face.

Every bone, every inch of his skin. Every tone of his voice, every twinkle of his eye. Every thought in his rich, well-stocked mind. (He is always reading. Learning a new language. His general knowledge is vast and she has come to take it for granted, as they all do in the family. Ask Dad.) Every laugh. His old jokes.

They laugh a lot now, lying together on this bed, not speaking directly of what they both suspect. Maybe their fear, their nervousness about what is looming ahead makes them giddy, in spite of it all, lends an edge to the everyday? There is monotony, for Eric, confined to bed, having to rinse with salt water, sip lemon juice, take pills, every half-hour. There is drudgery for Sarah, washing and cleaning, endless tripping down to the sad kitchen, where it always strikes her that Eric – always a presence in the kitchen when he is well – is already moving out of the centre of their life together. Running back up with water and drinks and towels. But there is no boredom. Life is now illumined by a new star of knowledge. The knowledge of the end that lies before them, the knowledge of the life shared that lies behind them. Through thick and thin they have stayed together, weathering setbacks, despairs, betrayals by one another and by the world. Hundreds of dinners by candlelight, thousands of miles walked along the beach, along the pavements, dozens of holidays, thousands of car journeys, Eric beside her navigating as Sarah found her way around Ireland, around France and Italy and Spain. Thousands of lovemaking nights in this bed. Laughs, jokes, parties. It all spins together now, woven by that light on the horizon, and impresses both of them with its enormity.

'We are so lucky, aren't we?' Sarah asks.

To have this, she means. To have found one another. To have had so many years of happiness and so few times of real sadness. To have got through, and still be in love at the end.

'Yes,' Eric says. 'Yes, my darling. We have been lucky.'

It had taken a little time to persuade Sarah's mother that marrying Eric was a good idea.

'David was your own age.' She insisted on regarding David as the real suitor. He had, after all, spent many evenings at her fireside, eaten a lot of her serviceable, well-cooked meals.

'Yeah,' said Sarah. 'But he broke it off with me. How do I know he wouldn't do it again?'

This, too, was a genuine concern, or at least a rationale for the choice that was being made.

'He might have learned his lesson.' Her mother wore a red-flowered apron, dusted with flour. She was often baking – apple tarts, scones, brown soda bread. The typical smell of Sarah's family home was of baking bread. 'Eric is much older than you and he is divorced. That's two big problems, for a start.'

She did not object on religious principle to Eric being divorced, just as she did not object to his being a Protestant. Sarah's parents, like many Irish parents of that generation, had had to cope with great changes in attitude during their lives. They had moved from de Valera's Ireland – where every form of contraception was strictly illegal, where women were barred from most jobs, where families were large and poor and, it seemed, often cold and miserable, where life was a frugal vale of tears to be passed through *en route* to eternal bliss or damnation – to the liberal world of free love, no Mass on Sunday, unmarried mothers being supported by the state and openly parading their babies in the marketplace instead of being hidden away and punished, sometimes by a lifetime sentence, in convents that were prisons for fallen women. All change, no certainties, at least not as far as their children were concerned. She meant that if he had been divorced once, he might be again.

Not even knowing that, in Ireland, that would be out of the question.

In the end, everyone relented.

Except the Irish Department of Justice.

When Eric and Sarah presented themselves at the state registrar's office to get married, an anxious lady with blue hair and butterfly glasses glanced at their papers, and shook her head.

'You won't be able to get married here,' she said.

Sarah looked wildly at Eric.

'You're divorced,' the anxious lady said simply.

'Yes,' said Eric. He was a solicitor. He knew the law better than this lady. 'But it is a valid divorce according to Irish law.'

'It doesn't look valid to me,' she said.

This was not because of the terms and conditions of the divorce, but had to do with Eric's now living in Ireland.

'If I were not living in Ireland I suppose I would not be attempting to get married here,' he said, in exasperated tones. 'Would I?'

'No.' She was not unkind, merely a bungling, confused officer of the Irish Department of Justice. 'I suppose not.' She laughed nervously. 'Of course you could get married in England.'

'Are you quite sure?' Eric asked.

'Oh yes.'

'Very decent of you to allow me to do so,' he said. 'Since I am a citizen of that country anyway. But the fact is that I want to get married here.'

There was a legal tangle, a court case, a barrister arguing about angels on the head of a pin. Nothing about Eric's former wife, his daughter. Nothing about Sarah's or his wishes to marry. Countless letters and affidavits and affirmations and denials about where he was living ten years ago or five years ago or two years ago, where he planned to live in two years or five years or ten years. Divorce in Ireland was, then, all about where you lived. It concerned itself with nothing else at all.

'God help the poor buggers who have always lived in Ireland,' said

Eric, when they were finally getting married in the brown-panelled room on Kildare Street. The wedding was the culmination of a long-drawn-out legal battle of wits, costing thousands of pounds and buckets of nervous perspiration and tears. 'They can never get married at all!' Even Sarah's parents laughed. Everyone had become involved in the fight with the law and the government, the battle to get Sarah and Eric married. The wedding photos, taken in the rain on a cold December day, show a crowd of people who look as if they have arrived home from the Western Front, even if they have changed into some rather snazzy clothes and one or two are wearing funny hats. They all, from Julie to Paula, Eric's daughter, look as if they have recently won the Second World War, but are somewhat the worse for the wear. Even Eric's estranged wife, who was herself happily remarried in Edinburgh to a professor of medicine at the university there, had sent a card congratulating them and wishing them luck. Sarah had considered inviting her and her husband to the wedding reception, a glorious drunken bash, but at that Eric had drawn the line. One wife at a time was more than enough. 'They might come out and take you away if my former wife set foot on this hallowed land!' he said. It was part of his wedding speech.

They plan to go ahead and celebrate Christmas in the ordinary way. The ordinary way is that they have a big family party on Christmas Eve. Sarah's family – her sister is married now and has three children, and her father is dead – Paula and her family, Julie and her family, and a few others, come to lunch. They have a buffet, wine and beer, Christmas carols. Eric dresses up as Santa Claus and distributes presents to everyone.

'I haven't got presents for lots of them,' Sarah sighs.

'Get something simple.'

She went into town two days before Christmas Eve.

Their wedding anniversary, as it happened.

A tree two hundred metres high on the corner of Stephen's Green, festooned with so many silver and golden bows that you can hardly see the green needles. Fairy lights draped across Grafton Street and all the other streets. Harsh and sweet voices carolling, shaking money boxes. People thronging the streets, cramming into shops, buying buying buying, toys and ties and sweets and perfumes, paper and ribbons and candles and clothes.

Rubbish.

Sarah looks at it all and thinks, 'What rubbish!'

The whole business of frantic preparation. The commerce of the city, the things people do with their time. Rubbish.

She who has always been a fervent, serious shopper. Who has often admitted that there are few pleasures she enjoys as much as an afternoon roaming through the carpeted chambers of Grafton Street, eyeing and trying and buying.

So tawdry, so superficial, so pointless. So enervating, so irritating. All this nonsense going on while Eric lies in a dim warm room, pondering the end of his life. The weight of that and the lightness of this.

She goes to Waterstones and gets twenty book tokens, then adds another four just in case. She goes to a newsagent's and gets ten selection boxes.

After that, she takes a stroll along Nassau Street, then along Wicklow Street.

The carol singers are singing more softly now. It's 3.30. Darkness is falling into the streets, like a powder from above, floating down on to the streets, the people. The shoppers are, many of them, on their way home. The atmosphere is less frantic.

All this is still here, Sarah thinks. It is still here, while Eric lies in his room, while Eric lies in his grave. It is still here, for me, all this light and dark, this frivolity, this silliness of celebration. All this life.

Walking did it, probably. To every mystery its rational explanation. The endorphins in the blood stream as important as the carols floating along the streets like the music of the heavenly spheres. Cherubim and Seraphim. As important as the refreshing crunch of night frost on the air. As important as the fairy lights glowing, in all their brilliant colours, desperately cheerful, against the huge irrepressible backdrop of the falling darkness, like the wishes of children sending letters up the chimney to Santa Claus on Christmas Eve.

OLEANDER

The swimming pool has the brilliant turquoise sheen of all holiday swimming pools. It gleams in the afternoon sun with the promising glow of travel agents' brochures – the colour of childish, and childlike, hope. Surrounding it is a patio of old terracotta tiles, cracked and faded as ancient faces. Olive trees grow in the corners of the tiled area, flanked by shrubs of the startling pink flowers with long willowy leaves that grow everywhere in Italy. These flowers excite Brenda ten times a day, when they suddenly burst into stunning view, flouncy as kicking can-can dancers and graceful as ballerinas. But their name is still unknown to her. They remind her of the word frangipani. Their leaves are frangy aqueous fronds and their blossoms are voluptuously perfect, the rich pure pink of pink carnations. She knows she will find out, as soon as she feels like it, what they are called. The friendly, fair-haired receptionist who serves breakfast at the hotel would know, or the waiter, or the proprietor of the little hotel, who speaks good English and is the sort of man who knows everything. There he is now, bronze, virile, histrionically handsome, slouching like a muscular cupid in the centre of a frieze of slender olive-skinned girls.

There are many of these girls, scattered around the edges of the pool like otters, reclining on sunbeds or stretched flat on their backs on the russet tiles. There are even more young men, sunning themselves in a more active fashion, smoking and laughing as they do so. None of these young people are guests at the hotel, which contains only six rooms. They are people who have come for a swim during their lunch-hour break from work. Brenda has noticed them going up to the barman, in his little sparkling niche which is tucked between the restaurant and the pool, and giving him something, presumably the entrance fee. She herself comes into the pool area by another gate, the guests' gate, which is always on the latch.

Beyond the olive-skinned sunbathers and the olive trees is something even more stunning than the pink flowers: the city of Siena. There it lies, incredibly, a semicircle of ancient beauty above the pool, a raised curve of russet walls and houses and roofs, an arc of faded brownish-reddish brick. Brenda closes her eyes in the sun, opens them again, blinks at the amazing, rhapsody-inducing vista. Siena. Stacks of red roofs, flats of brick walls. Tiny black windows. The tower of the Palazzo, the dome of the Duomo, the big plain block of the basilica of Saint Dominic, soar from the regular reddish curve into the pale blue, bleached sky. Swallows swoop and dive in that sky – they are the only songbirds you ever see here, possibly because a lot of the others get shot and eaten, but what perfect birds they are, the arc of their bodies repeated in their forked tails. Some fly so high they are almost invisible. All you see are black specks far away. They are like negative images of stars.

It's never going to rain.

White clouds pass across the sky occasionally; they ramble aimlessly and slowly like delicate ladies in snowy blouses. Genteel and harmless.

It's never going to rain.

It's unimaginably lovely, Brenda thinks, closing her eyes, testing reality. When she opens her eyes will it be there, or will it vanish, this view of views, arranged like the background of some portrayal of the Madonna by Guido de Siena or Pintorucchio or Buoninsegna, local artists whose work she saw earlier in the National Gallery? The place is as carefully composed as a representation of Heaven. The pool, the flowers, the swallows. If you lived here it would be easy to believe in God – God the Artist. You could see his hand everywhere, selecting and drafting, composing, creating. A brick there and a flower there. A shutter here and a garden hidden in that corner. There I'll insert a window, opening from the narrow street on to the blue hills of Tuscany.

Perfetto. A man who had popped out from a door on one of the narrow streets this morning had proffered that word like a carrot. He explained that he was referring to the weather. Perfetto. He expanded and waved his hands about. Not too hot. Not too cold. He was really trying to find out if Brenda were alone. She had lied, saying she was meeting a friend in the Campo, as the piazza, the square, is called here. The information hadn't taken him aback in the slightest. If he'd been trying to pick her up he accepted defeat with far too much grace. Bella, he had said, smarmily. Molto bella. The friend had chosen well.

Brenda was flattered but afraid. It was a quiet street. There are plenty of them in the town. You turn off a street that teems with tourists and suddenly find yourself completely alone, on a long winding dim lane lined with ominous barred doors, shuttered windows. The man was middle-aged, fat, with black greasy hair, bulging eyes, buck teeth. She was wondering how she could possibly shake him off when, as abruptly as he had appeared, he said goodbye, turned and vanished into one of the cavernous portals, a plump rabbit disappearing into its burrow – which turned out to be the entrance to the public library. The city was like that, full of secret portals, hidden windows, secrets. Its architecture seemed designed to spring little shocks and surprises. So the greasy sleazy man was all right, after all. He was a man who read books. Maybe he was even a librarian, genteel and harmless as an Italian cloud.

She felt silly. If she had been a little less paranoid, a little more trusting, she could have made use of that bookish man. As it happened she was searching for a book, and so far this book had eluded her completely. It was a short novel she had written herself, years ago, soon after she had left college, in the days before she started to work in television, when she had planned to become an author – an ambition she has long since abandoned. The novel had been autobiographical, a portrait of the artist as a young woman, and had enjoyed the limited success of such works in Ireland, at that time, when anything written by a young woman was a rarity and a cause of celebration. The book is long forgotten. But recently it had enjoyed some sort of revival in Germany and Italy. Students had begun to analyse it and write undergraduate essays about it. The students telephoned her from time to time, and called to her house to interview her with their pocket tape recorders, asking many questions which Brenda found extremely difficult to answer. They wanted to know her views on postfeminism, postcolonialism, postmodernism, and post-Catholicism, concepts to which Brenda had given little consideration even before they had become 'post'. Two students had asked how many pages six thousand words would take, did she think? This was the sort of question she could answer. How many pages, and how much time it would take to read those words on radio (about an hour) or on television (about an hour and a half, allowing for facial gestures and commercial breaks).

One of these girls – they were usually girls; boys did not write about Brenda – had told her that her book had been translated into Italian and published there. But unfortunately this girl did not possess a copy of this translation, and neither Brenda nor Brenda's publisher, who had gone to the wall professionally but who still existed, teaching yoga in a cottage in Bray, had heard anything about that. Brenda had set herself the small, not unenjoyable task of hunting down this book while she was in Italy. It was clear to her by now that the shops in Siena did not have it, which didn't surprise her, even though she saw many familiar Irish names attached to unlikely Italian titles on the shelves. In fact she rather doubted that the book existed – young students could be wrong about so many things. But she hadn't tried the library yet.

It isn't the main reason for her visit to Siena, of course, merely a provocative distraction which will while away the time as she waits for the real holiday to start. The real business of her visit is passion. She is supposed to be enjoying this with a man called Robert O'Mahony. It's Monday now, and she has been in Italy since lunchtime on Saturday. So far, she has been swimming, walking, and reading stories by Richard Ford. There has been no passion, love, sex, or even ordinary conversation, in her days. But tomorrow all that will change because Robert will be here. He is due very late tonight in Rome, and tomorrow she will go to the railway station on the outskirts of Siena and meet him. They will have at least three, possibly four, days together in what will be their first holiday since they met, and the *tour de force* of their love affair. Brenda has high hopes.

Brenda has been separated for six years, and soon will be divorced. Robert is neither separated nor divorced, although his marriage has been over, in any sense that matters, for ages. In the legal sense, however, it has survived for fifteen years, and has produced three children, all still being educated. He works in television, writing scripts for a drama series which Brenda produces. In a sense she is his boss – but not in a sense that has much impact on their relationship, as far as she can see, either at work or out of it.

He started working on the series a year and a half ago. Brenda has been doing it for three years – it is time to move on and she would have asked for a change last year had it not been for Robert. But the series is convenient. It bestows a public blessing on their relationship. It means they can legitimately meet in public places and Brenda can telephone Robert, even at his home – she does this less and less, however, finding it unbearable even to hear the voice of his wife. First she did not like to hear it because she was guilty. Now the guilt has been replaced by jealousy, and fear of discovery. Brenda would prefer to forget that Robert's wife exists.

She got on well with Robert from the moment she met him. That was normal in her business. If you didn't get on well with all the writers and background team you were in trouble. As a producer, all your emotional resources – your patience and manipulative skills, your professional and instinctive ingenuity – had to be conserved for your dealings with the actors, who were invariably and perhaps inevitably more delicate and volatile and dangerous than anyone else involved in the show. Writers might have egos and problems but, since they worked in the background, three months ahead of schedule, and since you could always edit or rewrite their work, their power to disturb was minimal. In general, they had docile natures. If they also had a modicum of talent and reliability, Brenda was happy.

Robert had a little more: he had wit, and a capacity for creating and developing characters which was almost too good for television, where a lot of that work had to fall to the actor (if it didn't, the actor would subvert the script). He wasn't so hot at plotting, but there were others on the team who could do that. It had struck Brenda, early on, that his talents were those of a novelist rather than a screenwriter – he would be good, perhaps, at the kind of plotless, hopefully subtle, novel that she had tried to write herself, the kind that only worked when written by a writer of quiet tact, deep understanding, and outstanding natural skill – Chekhov, basically. Or possibly Richard Ford. Robert, Brenda thought, a slow psychological writer with some training in screenplay plotting, would be able to produce a good Irish Richard Ford-type novel – he could be the Irish Richard Ford, if he stopped writing soaps and film scripts and concentrated on words.

She hadn't told him any of this, though – not since the early days of their affair, when of course she told him everything that was flattering. Encouraging her writers to work in other genres would be counterproductive. It was hard enough to hold on to the best ones anyway. They were always tempted to abandon the derided world of popular drama for the prestigious world of literature – just as the real novelists were constantly making the move in the opposite direction, attracted by the promise of financial reward and mass audiences. The whole thing was an absurd seesaw, like so much else in life.

For Robert, Brenda had not felt, initially, anything more than the general feeling of attraction she felt for several men, and which at this stage in her life she interpreted as meaning nothing except that a man was a kindred spirit and a potential friend. Then one day, after many months of friendship, love had come like a speeding train around a bend in the railway in an E.M. Forster story, like a frangipani popping over the parapet of a city wall. They were sitting side by side in the canteen, drinking coffee at the time, with three or four other people. It was summer, like now, and Robert had just come back from a holiday in France. His arm was bare, and lay across the table. Although he was fair-haired, his forearm was covered with a thick mat of dark golden hair. It could have been any man's arm –

any hairy, muscular, masculine arm. Her own, hairless (thanks to the regular application of a depilatory) lay close to it. He twisted slightly, and she caught a glimpse of the skin of his underarm, pale and heartbreaking as the underside of a leaf. The skin of her arm was magnetised by his. She longed to feel his arm on hers, longed so much that she could barely restrain herself from reaching over and touching him right there and then, in the big noisy canteen, where everything except Robert's arm was hard and glaring – glass, chrome, shiny grey floor. Robert was utterly oblivious to her condition. He was just at that moment insisting that Bernie should shop her son Timmy to the police for the rape of a fourteen-year-old neighbour, even though she knew he had been set up and was mildly mentally retarded. (Almost everyone in the series had a name ending in ie, a homely, pet name.) 'It will be truly cathartic,' he was saying, in his warm round baritone. She wondered if he wore boxer shorts or the other kind of underpants. She wondered what the rest of his skin looked like, the skin on his chest, on his legs, on his bottom. He talked on relentlessly about storylines, in the excited manner writers adopted with producers when they had nothing much to say and tried to compensate for their lack of ideas with enthusiastic gestures and vibrant vocal tones. The cutlery clattered, the voices clashed around them. She gritted her teeth. After a while her desire subsided, as it does, eventually, if you are patient.

But a few weeks later Robert asked her to have lunch with him, alone – alone, that is, in that vast canteen packed with people they knew. On that occasion, over chips and burgers in onion sauce, they discussed their personal lives for the first time. He told her about his wife, his children, where he lived, and questioned her about herself – what defined her when she was not in the office or the studio. His eagerness for information, just then, astonished and thrilled her. He lapped up the trite details, his curiosity and the fact that he listened with interest gilding them again, making them not trite but significant. He honoured her ordinary uniqueness. She had lusted for his body and now he poured this grace over her, the grace of true interest. She fell in love, deeply and delightfully, slipping into the charmed benign pool as lightly as a teenager, but with considerably more appreciation.

He did too. It would have been nice to discover that the revelation of physical attraction had occurred simultaneously for the two of them, that as she sat drinking her coffee and hungering for his arm some message had been transmitted to his body, to his skin, from hers. Chemistry. But that had not happened. He had no memory of the day of the arm.

'I fancied you from the beginning,' he said, and she knew what he felt for her was always going to be subtly different from what she felt for him. 'You know? I just . . . didn't want to start any trouble.'

'But why start it now? You must have noticed something?' she prodded.

'Naw,' he shrugged. 'Maybe. And I wasn't starting anything really when I asked you to lunch. I just wanted to chat and find out how many episodes you were giving me next year.'

The affair started, however, and could not be stopped. It was conducted in a variety of places: in canteens, the quiet corners of pubs, Brenda's house – during the day, at the conjunction of time when her two daughters were at school and she and Robert were free from her work and his family responsibilities and his work – the tiny intersection of three, maybe four or five or ten depending on how you counted, sets of life. They didn't spend much time alone together, or in bed together. These Italian days were to be their first big break.

She reads deeper in her volume of Richard Ford as she lies by the pool. It's a collection of short stories, the long sort of short story that is becoming more common in the States and Canada nowadays, halfway between a novel and a short story, the kind that defies all the rules of short-story writing that Brenda in her young days lapped up carefully at workshops on creative writing. (Be concise. Keep your eye on the ball. Create epiphanies. Focus on the single moment of revelation. Cut out all superfluous words.) There were so many rules that she had stopped trying to write in that genre and instead produced her novel. Now the new long short stories seem to pay no attention to such regulations. They are as padded, as full, as novels, and they have their components: a bit of a plot, definite well-formed characters, often described physically. Brenda likes them much better than the other kind of short story, the precise poetic kind that's actually designed for a magazine or radio show demanding no more than two thousand words. Two thousand words is seldom a piece of fiction, that's the trouble. Two thousand words is fifteen minutes' air time or half a page of a newspaper. It's a prose poem, if it's good, an anecdote if it's bad. Richard Ford is having none of that. Richard Ford's short stories are a defiant thirty thousand words long. A few more days and he'd have made novels of them. And there's none of that obsession with the bare essentials either. These are stories with flesh on their bones, stories that linger over the coffee, take their time. This is a writer who takes one hundred and fifty thousand words to describe one weekend, after all. (How many hours of television is two hundred thousand words? Weeks, probably.)

The stories are set 'abroad', unlike his novels, which are emphatically concerned with at home. Disappointingly, he doesn't write about Italy. Brenda would have expected him to. So many have, of late. John Mortimer. Deborah Martin. Lorrie Moore. Deirdre Madden. And of early. Henry James and E.M. Forster. It's a country that was made for fiction. But Ford avoids Italy and sticks to Paris, where he mainly seems to spend his time having desultory relationships with cool Frenchwomen. The situations seem unlikely but the writing is so good they manage to read as autobiography. They meander like real life and the details ring true as bottled water. Close to the end of each a dramatic thing happens, however — a bad dramatic thing. A child is abducted. A woman dies. This is the E.M. Forster touch, the false sparkle that screams 'FICTION!' Children get abducted in real life, of course — Brenda quells her sudden alarm about her daughters, one of whom is at a summer camp in Galway; the other is on an exchange in La Rochelle. People die. Accidents happen. But not, perhaps, when you happen to be in Paris, conducting a liaison with a woman who is not your wife. Is that the coincidence that produces fiction? That produces a story? In a story, something really ought to happen, preferably something surprising and exciting that shakes the reader and teaches the writer a lesson. Life is not so generous with sensation and its lessons are often slow, sometimes abstruse. But then life isn't clapping itself between two shiny covers and selling itself to readers at ten pounds a go.

Brenda loves this book, however. She loves these stories. They are, she tells herself happily, as she reads in the sun and awaits her lover, the chianti classico of contemporary literature, its Siena, its *Birth of Venus*, its Sistine Chapel. Its Boccaccio, its Dante. Its Henry James – there's the model. The dense psychological detail of place and person and love.

Would he have all these women? Would anyone? Yes. Maybe someone like Richard Ford could. Brenda feels, reading the words of Richard Ford, that she could be in love with him herself, if she were not already so much in love with Robert. And there to help her on her way to love *is* Richard, a photo of him: you don't need to imagine what he looks like, the publishers help you out there. A full head-and-shoulders covering the entire back of the dust jacket: an ascetic-looking, balding head, eyes full of intelligence and wisdom. Those are eyes that would make any vulnerable, imaginative, reading woman feel a pang of longing. They are eyes that would send any woman running to buy the book.

In the evening Brenda abandons literature and the hotel. She is back in town, walking through the gate and along the narrow streets down to the centre, the Campo. The streets are alive with commotion. It is the week of something called the Palio – the famous horse race of Siena. Brenda didn't realise this event was on when she booked the trip and she might have gone elsewhere if she'd known about it. She hadn't planned to share Robert with a horse. But of course the festival is interesting in its own way. Many tourists come especially for it.

The Palio will last for a week. At the end of the week, sixteen horses mounted by bareback riders will race around the piazza in the centre of town, and one of them will carry off the banner of Our

Lady – the Palio. But before then, many elaborate rituals will be
played out, and these rituals have already started. The town is full of
excitement and celebration, expressing itself in thousands of silk
flags, and prancing horses and music and noise.

There are blue and yellow banners depicting shells and snails and
geese hanging from all the balconies along the medieval streets.
Crowds of men and boys dressed in satin shirts and pointy
court-jester shoes are marching, singing a rousing song, a song they
will sing about a thousand times before this week is over. Brenda
stands to watch for a little while, wondering how any mother can
persuade an adolescent boy to put on those pantomime shoes,
those ridiculous hats, and wear them in public. Then she ducks
down a lane and finds a quieter way to the centre.

It's a great pleasure to her, to stroll aimlessly along these streets,
simply enjoying the sensation of being on them. Outside, Siena is
open, a wide red–gold vista. Inside, it's a warren of grey stone – high
tight houses designed to keep the sun out. All the windows are little,
and most of them are shuttered. The fortressed feel of the town is
what appeals, the sense of mystery. What is happening behind those
stone walls, those shuttered windows?

She has already found one answer. Darting into the portico of the
University for Foreigners, she found herself in a shaded, terraced
garden, full of those pink flowers, of olives and fruit trees, giving on
to the countryside – the undulating red and green fields, the red
villas guarded by their sprightly dark cypresses. The impression given
by the street side of the buildings, that you were locked tight in the
heart of a dark city, was entirely false. A façade. Inside those walls
you could find anything.

She ate, last night, on one of the narrow streets, at a restaurant
recommended in the guide book. It would have been easier to eat at
the hotel, but she was impatient to taste the town, to experience it at
different times of day and night. The charm of it seems to her
miraculous. Lovely landscapes she can imagine living in, she can deal
with. But the beauty of southern towns is almost more than she can
grasp. It seems unreal. The winding grey streets, each leading on to

another as winding, as grey, as medieval, as the last, are like streets in a fairytale. In the great cities of the north you can have one or two of these streets – Gamla Staden, Temple Bar – preserved and dished up as special treats, like rich pieces of chocolate steeped in liqueurs after the mundane dinners of the wide boulevards of the eighteenth, nineteenth, twentieth centuries, the period when streets stopped being designed for people and began to cater for vehicles. To find a complete town, a city of sixty thousand people, dozens of streets, left alone, left alone and preserved on this human scale, is almost unbearable for someone trained in abstemiousness. It's not that it's Disneyland either. It is most emphatically real, and most emphatically beautiful. That's the combination that pulls her down the streets, early in the morning and late in the afternoon, that keeps her walking for hours and hours, from one side of the town to the other.

She bumps into Richard Ford again. There is a life-size poster of him in one of the tiny bookshop windows. The publishers stop at nothing. It's the same photo she already has on the back of the book, but with the rest of his body included. He's wearing jeans, you can now see, and is, as his face suggested, tall and lanky. Jeans and an open-necked shirt, his thin hair curling down the back of his neck, tendrils escaping to the front. He looks like an intellectual sexpot – it's remarkable that he can actually write at all. Usually men who look like that read the nine o'clock news – and nothing else. Or they market Coca-Cola. Richard Ford could model Armani T-shirts but he doesn't. He writes books. And not only is he a sexpot, he's a hippy sexpot. You can see from the clothes, the hair, that he was a teenager in the seventies. All middle-aged women, like Brenda, who still feel happiest in flowing skirts and Indian embroidered blouses, sandals on their feet, will warm to those denim jeans, that oh so gentle chambray shirt with its softly suggestive open neck.

She finds the restaurant she used last night on Cassato dei Sopra, and sits at an outside table, drinking chianti, the book opened on the table in front of her. She doesn't read. Her mind will not concentrate while she is drinking, observing those who pass – not many. It is a quiet, sombre street. Opposite the restaurant is a grocery store, and people trickle in and out with bags of food. It's only 7.30, so there are few other diners.

When she is eating her starter – scallopini, which she thought might be fish but turned out to be veal – she hears drumming. The beat of drums, the raising of baritones, that signal the Palio parade. Drat, Brenda thinks. You can't get away from it. The noise gets louder and louder, and soon the boys and men are passing, banging their drums and singing their song. The narrow street is filled with their yellow and brown costumes, their swelling music. A hundred or so march past, followed by crowds of girls, then older women, who are not dressed up but who wear coloured scarves around their necks to denote loyalty.

When the tumult passes, like a wave of celebration, one man is left, stranded, on the footpath at Brenda's table.

Siena seems to have an abundance of drifting men, floating in the crowds, who can land at the feet of a lonely woman at any moment of the day or night.

Does she mind if he sits at her table for a moment?

Brenda does not say yes. But she does not say no.

This flotsam of the parade is not the sleazy man of the morning, the librarian or reader. He is dry rather than greasy. But he is no Richard Ford. He wears a neat red blazer, a pale green shirt, pressed white trousers. His hair is short, pepper and salt, his face small and neat like a banker's or an accountant's, or a man of one of the drier professions. Glasses, unobtrusive ones, sit on his little rabbit nose. There is a big wart at the bottom of his left cheek, almost but not quite concealed by a neat beard, more black than grey. You can tell he's not a writer of psychological love stories, and has never been on the campus of an Ivy League university in his life.

The waitress – a cheerful, maternal woman, dressed in a pink nylon housecoat, who is so self-assured that she probably owns the restaurant – spots him immediately with her watchful motherly eye. She approaches the table with a questioning, concerned expression.

'All right?' she asks Brenda.

Brenda looks at the man. She shrugs and the waitress smiles, relieved.

He asks her if he can eat at the table. She considers for a second, then nods, planning to leave if he gets troublesome. He seems harmless, and also lonely, like an accountant who has lost his way in a library. And Brenda is getting lonely too. She has not spoken to anyone apart from waiters for two days.

With alacrity he orders his meal. Soon he is drinking wine and asking Brenda all about herself.

She tells him about Robert, claiming he is her husband. Rinaldo – for that is the man's name – says he is divorced, lives in a small apartment in the city. He is a schoolteacher, it seems, not an accountant. But it is not very clear what he teaches – she doesn't understand what it is in Italian, and he doesn't know the English for his own subject, oddly enough since he knows the English for quite a lot of other things. Brenda forms the impression that he teaches engineering, or computer studies, something like that. She forms this impression even though this man does not look like any teacher she knows. A teacher in Ireland would not wear a jacket of that colour, although it is quite a nice colour. Richard Ford would never wear that. He would wear grey, probably, or perhaps a bleached calico for summer, both enhancing, poignantly, the bleached paleness of his skin.

Rinaldo's English, like Brenda's Italian, is very good for about ten minutes; then it suddenly disintegrates entirely. It is as if after a short time speaking the foreign language they become exhausted and can't be bothered to remember even their narrow range of words. How else could one explain how so much was exchanged at first, and how little afterwards?

By the time this limit is reached, Brenda has finished her main course and is thoroughly bored with Rinaldo. She decides against dessert, and also decides to have coffee back at the hotel.

Rinaldo is not so easy to deflect, however.

He wants her to wait. He wants to abandon his dinner – just started – and take her back to the hotel himself. He wants her phone number.

With difficulty, she escapes while the waitress is serving his pasta.

She walks as quickly as she can away from him and the street, feeling eyes on her back, wondering how on earth she could have been so stupid.

There is a message from Robert at the hotel. 'Robert telephoned,' the receptionist said, not giving a surname. She thinks Robert is Brenda's husband and this cheers Brenda up. Robert had said he would ring back.

Brenda takes coffee on the terrace, and sits for a long time, looking at the sky turning lilac, then blue, then dark blue, then navy, over the walls of the town. When it's black she goes to bed.

Robert is not at the railway station the following day. She stands on the platform, examining every single person who steps off the train. She does this even though she knew he would not be there. That was why he was ringing her. He has not rung again because he could not. Something has happened at home that prevented it.

She takes a taxi back from the station to the hotel − passing through ordinary modern streets and suburbs. They exist, all around the walls, outside the town. You could live in a high-rise apartment block, the kind you could find anywhere in the world, and be Sienese. Probably only the lucky or the rich live within the walls.

She is able to think these thoughts while simultaneously feeling as if she has been struck by lightning, or attacked by some sort of psychological guillotine that has sliced her in half, like an apple, leaving her surface raw and absolutely vulnerable. She is able to feel like that, and simultaneously pay attention to the places she is passing through, to notice the sunshine falling through leaves on to the grey slabs of the wide ordinary suburban pavement, and the signs in front of the apartment blocks informing anyone who could read that they were approaching private property. She can notice that this part of town is several centuries away from the atmosphere inside the city walls.

She goes home, home to the hotel, and lies in the foetal position on the bed, curling her body together, in an attempt to restore it to some semblance of normality.

Robert is not going to come. Her sensible, logical mind tells her that there are practical reasons for his absence, practical reasons which might be overcome quickly enough. Maybe he will come on the next train, or the one after that. But her intuition – her pessimism, some dark sad part of her mind, of her stomach – tells her he will not. And it tells her too that he has voluntarily abandoned her, that his absence from the train, from the platform, from Siena, was no accident but a deliberate choice. He had loved her, he had needed her, but now that part of their affair is over. This was the first real test for him. The travel test. Will he follow me to the ends of the earth? Will he follow me to Italy for four days? It is the greatest test he has undergone in that tricky, complex subject: adulterous love. His love for Brenda he would have had to weigh against his fidelity to his wife, to his family. Well, the wife has won. Brenda knows it in the pit of her stomach. She knows it in the bleak orphanage that her heart has suddenly become.

After lying for a few hours in the darkened room of the hotel – always darkened to keep the impossible heat out – she gets up. There is a limit to the misery she can indulge in – it's real, but after a while it bores her. She tries ringing Robert on his mobile, but gets the message service, which she dislikes using in case his wife somehow listens in. Then she showers – she is always showering here – and goes off, walking, again.

The town is, of course, still there. Places don't go away just because your mood or situation changes. The faded red walls, the pencilbox tower of the Palazzo, are as relentlessly lovely as they were before, when Robert was coming. And to Brenda's surprise she does not resent that. On the contrary, it lifts her spirits to see that it's all still available, so immutably present. The thought, trite enough, that stones, things of beauty – art – could remain as faithful sources of comfort through the vicissitudes of human life strikes her. She is suffering. She is confused. But the sight of a stone wall can nevertheless give her pleasure.

She considers her situation rationally as she walks. She is not allowed to contact Robert. That has always been a slight problem, but now the enormity of it strikes her very forcibly. She is in love, deeply enmeshed in a relationship as profound as any she has ever had, with a man she could rarely telephone, to whose house she could not call, to whose address she could not send a personal letter. She can't even send him a private e-mail: people's machines, their personal mobile phones, their personal laptops, are not all that personal.

Why has she let this happen?

It was as if she had asked, why did she let the rain fall? She had control, of course. But it was as if she were asked, as if a beautiful woman were asked, why do you wear that fine dress? Why not get fat and spotty and ugly? It was as if a clever man were asked, why do you work so hard and achieve so much? Why not laze about and let the grass grow under your feet? When love presents itself, strong and powerful, passionate, who can turn their back on it? It does not come often. Brenda could not resist anything so precious, a golden bowl offered with open hands, the open arms of Robert. Spread across the table, offering themselves, spread across her body like a branch of peace. Perfection. If perfection of the human life exists, it does so when you are in love. That particular perfection you reject at your peril. Brenda was not the one to risk missing out on true love, although she was well aware of the risks it brought with it – risks of pain for others, and for herself.

She walks along the winding street that flows like a river down to the Campo. Along the street there are signs of new activity: long trestle tables covered with cloths are laid, waiting for some sort of party or banquet. And in the lanes leading from the Campo the parades of colourful men and boys are now headed by sprightly racehorses. While she was asleep the horses had been selected for the race and are now being led back to their stables, secreted in back yards, in sheds and stalls and outhouses deep in the heart of the town. Along the narrow lanes they trot, their polished legs prancing against the smooth grey concrete underfoot. In the town of people, always thronged with people, they look strange, like noble messengers from some exalted principality, divine almost in their highly bred naturalness. Of course a hundred years ago horses were everywhere on these streets, as ordinary as the tourists who stroll up and down all day long, from cathedral to Palazzo, from sanctuary to basilica, from morning to night. But now they look out of place. The prancing horse might be a tiger, so odd does it seem.

She finds her way back to the restaurant of last night – the motherly waitress had been kind, the food good. She will eat, to pass the time, and later there might be a message at the hotel. Anything. Walking increases her optimism. Anything indeed could happen. She might return and find Robert there, waiting for her. It is more than possible.

Thinking of this, she changes her mind about eating. She will go back now, and, if he is not there, she could eat on the terrace – a more open, gracious place anyway than the streetside bistro, if more lonely for a woman alone.

She is almost at the bistro when this thought occurs to her. She turns and walks down the hill – all the little streets seem to flow down into the central square, where red clay has been spread on the bricks to make a race track, the racks of seats installed for the races, and where at all times crowds of people gather to drink or eat, to watch the swallows overhead and the roofs, and the other people passing by.

She is halfway down, nearing the square, the Campo, when she feels a hand on her shoulder.

Rinaldo's hand.

He is all smiles. Smiling, it seemed, with genuine delight at meeting her.

'I am going back to the hotel,' she says, coldly.

'Always going back to the hotel,' he says, smiling, not unkindly. But he is not capable of smiling unkindly. His smile is automatic, insincere, ingratiating. He is a gigolo in nature if not by profession.

'I'm expecting a telephone call,' she says, as if she has to make excuses. He is standing in front of her, however, and there are few people about.

'I am going to have dinner. I thought I would have dinner here, at the bistro up here where I saw you last night. It is good.'

Brenda feels hungry. It is eight o'clock and she has had nothing since breakfast, she remembers. Crying makes you hungry. Her stomach aches for sustenance, and her legs feel tired. She has walked for miles. Every day she walks for miles and miles, from the hotel into the town, around the town, around and around. Back to the hotel.

Rinaldo smiles at her, not unkindly. Ingratiatingly. Longingly.

'You look tired,' he says, in a kind, human voice, and in her present mood she is vulnerable to kind human voices, irrespective of where they come from. 'Have an aperitif with me? Then you can go back to the hotel.'

She longs to sit down.

He brings her to a bar at the end of the street – miraculously open to the countryside. They have moved, in minutes, from a prison of grey stone to a vista of hills and villas, of trees and rivers. There on a terrace they drink a glass of cold white wine.

She sighs with relief as the cold liquid glides down and her eyes drink in the countryside. Behind them in the city the drums beat, celebratory, relentlessly. The song of the Palio rises on the air like a humming of great bees, its familiar tune resounding off the stones.

'What did you do today?' he asks.

She won't tell him. She says she walked about, shopped. She waits for the question about her husband but it does not come. Probably he believes that that was all a lie, a front, some sort of protection for herself.

He worked in the morning, perhaps at his teaching if he really were a teacher, which she increasingly doubts. When she asks him about school holidays, he seems not to understand the words 'school' or 'holidays' – and the latter, surely, is part of his stock in trade? In the afternoon he too had walked around. He praises the beauty of the town again. He tells her he comes from Cecina, another town, not so nice, not so nice. Now he lives alone in a small flat. It is expensive to have a flat in Siena but worth it, to live in such a nice town. He has a daughter, twenty.

His arm falls across the table, bare this evening. Brenda holds her breath, as she feels herself respond, in spite of everything, to the turn of the muscle and the mat of hair. Has it come to this, that she could be aroused by a sexual attribute, as men were supposed to be, even if it came attached to a person she did not particularly like?

Apparently it has come to this. She feels a mild pang of desire, for Rinaldo's arm, a desire that Rinaldo's face, with its wart, and Rinaldo's conversation, and Rinaldo's character, cannot quite destroy.

He seems to be unconscious of what is going on beside him. If he has any desire himself, it is probably of so bland and general a nature as to be invisible. His desire, what is it? To talk to a foreign woman? To have sex with her? What is he actually after, as he roams the streets, chatting with complete strangers? Normal men don't do that. But in Siena nothing is normal. The streets are a horse-race track. Teenage boys replace their jeans with doublets and hose and put court jesters' caps on their wet-look heads. Horses are led up the aisles of medieval churches to the altar rails, like brides.

'Now I will eat,' Rinaldo is saying. 'Are you sure you do not want to join me?'

Brenda decides to go. Easier to shake him off here, when he needs food, than later when he has nothing better to do than annoy her.

'I will go home,' she says. 'I am expecting a call.'

'All right.' He stands up. 'Then I will walk with you.'

She wishes, for the first time, that it were an ordinary town, with ordinary streets where buses and taxis ran. But it is a town of pedestrian streets. You never see a bus, and seldom a taxi. You could not quickly escape an unwanted escort unless you took to your heels and ran.

'It's OK.' She smiles. 'It really is. Thank you but I'd like to go alone.'

'No no, I go with you.' He is still being polite in his exaggerated, stupid fashion. He is close to her, his shoulder brushing hers, his arm dangling against her side, his hand reaching for her elbow, preparing to escort her down the hill.

'I want to go alone,' she says firmly, shaking him off and moving away from him. 'Goodbye now and thank you for the drink.'

She turns and walks, then runs, down the hill, towards the Campo.

But when she reaches it her legs feel weak and she has to sit down. She chooses a table at the edge of the big red square. Within minutes a waiter is at her side, brandishing the menu. Resigned, she takes it, orders a glass of wine, reads the thing quickly and orders the first thing on the list.

She sits back and sips her wine. She gazes at the square – red, slanting upwards slightly, a vast, crooked fan-shaped market place. The sky is a deepening purple overhead, the swallows are still circling. Young people, olive-skinned beautiful people, walk over and back. Ladies in white skirts and T-shirts, men with bronzed arms, snowy shirts, sit at the tables, laughing and drinking, eating their way through elaborate meals. Everyone is in a group, a couple. Everyone laughs and looks happy. The air is balmy as the night falls slowly on the town. Night is just another balmy layer to the day, a cooler, shadier version of the pleasurable time that has gone before. In a place like this, who would choose to sleep, if their companions were chosen, if they had friends or lovers?

She eats slowly, although she feels strange. It is a warm, friendly restaurant to look at, but no woman of her age, of any age, sits alone at a table in this very popular, public place. No. You need the protection of companions. And of course that is natural. Normal. It is not so normal to sit alone at a table in a crowded square, the week of a big festival. If you have not got a friend, you should be somewhere else, in some private, sequestered place. Few old people are here either. It is a festival for the young, the young in one another's arms, birds in the steeples. She is forty-three, single, abandoned, the mother of nubile daughters. She is the dying generation.

By the time she is eating her veal she feels so gloomy that she almost wishes that she had held on to Rinaldo. He would be better than nothing. With him at the other side of her table, she would fit into the jigsaw of summer and celebration, whereas alone she is an aberration.

Suddenly he appears in front of her, a genie out of an alley.

He is walking, jauntily, across the square. He catches her eye, approaches the table and says hello, not as coolly as you might have expected, given the circumstances, but coolly enough given his usual pattern of behaviour. The reason for the change of mood soon emerges. A few paces behind him walks a woman, about Brenda's age, wearing something longish and layered, some sultry colour, beige or dark purple, both perhaps. She has a straw hat on her head, or dangling from a string over her shoulders, and carries a shawl or stole draped over her arm. She gives Brenda a sidelong, surprised glance. Brenda is surprised too. Rinaldo really is a quick worker – it is half an hour, at most, since she sat with him on the terrace up the street. So he picked women up all the time, as a matter of course, as easily as men in Ireland might go for a pint, might go for a walk. Sly old Rinaldo! Brenda congratulates herself on having spotted him in time, on having been less foolish than that woman with the hat, walking now across the Campo with Rinaldo at her side.

And still that woman has something. She has what all the women in the town need at nightfall: a friend, a companion, someone to share a meal with, while Brenda is alone, looking like a freak, seated at a table for four on the precious Campo.

She watches Rinaldo and the lady with the hat walking, slightly apart – perhaps the woman is still making up her mind, although from the perspective of an outsider she could be his wife, his lover. They look fine together; nobody but the initiated would guess that five minutes ago he picked her up on a narrow street, probably at the very same restaurant where he had picked Brenda up last night. They make their way across the lopsided square and disappear, first Rinaldo, then the woman, into the darkness of one of the tunnel streets.

Brenda finishes her meal as quickly as she can and asks for the bill.

She reaches for her handbag to find some money. But her handbag is not where she had placed it while she was eating, on the ground by her feet.

She woke up at about five, when dawn came, and tossed and turned for a while before going back to sleep again. When she awoke for the second time, it was to the sound of a mechanical digger, working at a building site across the road from the hotel. Eight o'clock. She could have breakfast.

The kind receptionist came and said there had been another message. She had something written on a scrap of paper. 'Robert is in hospital.'

'He is your friend?' she asked, gently, understanding that Brenda was shocked.

Brenda nodded.

'Oh dear dear. Can I help you in some way?'

'I don't know,' Brenda said.

'Would you like some fruit? Some orange juice?' She glanced at the half-eaten roll. She must have noticed by now that Brenda never ate anything at breakfast.

'Thank you,' Brenda said, perfunctorily. In fact she was feeling quite calm. A sort of stoical endurance flooded her. Whereas yesterday, this morning, she had been a weakling, a sap in the wind, she now felt that she had iron in her blood and could begin to deal with the situation. 'I'll have some more coffee, thanks, that's all.'

She sat and looked out, planning what to do, now that she was without Robert, also without her passport, her credit cards, her return ticket to Dublin, now that she was alone, without man or handbag, in a foreign country. The great pink flowers bloomed in the corner of the car park. They were like patterns on upholstery, like chintzy, flowery curtains in a vast grand drawing room.

'Oleander'. Rinaldo had given her the name of the flowers.

The flowers had been growing in tubs in the wine bar where they had sat and had their wine last night. Brenda had realised that she could get this one thing from Rinaldo: the name of the flower that grew so profusely in this town.

'I don't know' had been his answer, however. But quick as a lizard he darted into the bar and emerged seconds later smiling broadly.

'Oleander!' He brandished the name like a banner, with the certainty of a lexicographer who brooked no ambiguity. He gave her the name of the flower, efficiently and graciously, with a happy smile, as he had given her the glass of wine. 'Oleander is their name!'

She telephoned her former husband, Frank. He was at his desk in the civil service. He was always at his desk in the civil service – that was probably why the marriage had ended. But reliability has advantages. Money was forwarded by Western Union. Brenda collected it, with more difficulty than the advertisements for that company suggest might occur, from a café in an obscure street outside the walls of the town, in the modern, boring part of Siena. Other calls had to be made, to the police, to the travel agent, to the Irish embassy. Most people were kind, some, like the embassy, exceptionally so. But she had a fraught, difficult day. By mid-afternoon she had dealt with all the problems. She checked out of the hotel and took the train to Rome.

On the train she replaced Richard Ford with Henry James. His long lyrical sentences poured into her soul like balm. That prose could calm her at such a time came as a surprise, the last surprise Siena had to give her.

She stayed in a small hotel on the banks of the Tiber, near the Castel Angelo. From her window she could see a jumble of roofs, all different levels, some flat and decked out as gardens or patios, others sloping steeply into their crumbling walls. Beyond that, there was a glimpse of the river, a dark mossy green between its white balustrades.

She could have asked her former husband to make enquiries about Robert, and he would have done so. But some instinct of delicacy had prevented her from going that far. She considered calling

Robert's home. She considered it in detail, deciding what she would say (that she was a colleague), what tone of voice she would use (brisk, matter-of-fact). She visualised the conversation. Robert's wife, pale and slight, as she knew her to be, with a thin, childish voice. She saw more than that. White walls, white flowers in glass vases splayed against the white walls. A clear sticky honey spinning itself in threads from the great bugles of the flowers all over the white house. A web of sticky threads – she would get caught in that web, like a pathetic frantic insect.

She phoned nevertheless.

'Hello. Linda speaking,' said Linda. Her voice was not thin, but rich and resonant.

'This is Brenda Costello,' said Brenda, feeling weak. 'From *The Murphys.*'

'Oh yes. Hi, Brenda!'

'Hello,' said Brenda, weakly. Her voice was the one that was thin and reedy. 'Could I speak to him, please? To Robert?'

There was a pause, slightly too long. Or did she imagine that?

'Robert isn't here at the moment,' Linda said, neutrally, even brightly. Not 'Robert is in hospital.'

'When will he be in?' Brenda asked, weakly, weakly.

'I'll tell him you called,' Linda said. Firmly. Was it firmly, neutrally, brightly? Triumphantly?

'All right,' said Brenda.

'Does he have your number?' she asked then. So she suspected nothing. And indeed there was not so much to be suspicious of, it now seemed.

'Yes, he does.' Brenda got bold. 'Tell him I'm out on location tomorrow, but I'll be in the office on Thursday.'

'OK,' said Linda cheerfully. 'Will do.'

Brenda could not bear to spend the long evening in her small, hot room, so she spent it walking around Rome, around the *centro storico,* its narrow streets reminiscent of Siena, and yet very different – so much bigger, more sophisticated, more urban, than that town, which seemed diminished by the contrast, its beauty suddenly minor and provincial, its atmosphere, which there had seemed sophisticated, now rendered simple and rural by contrast with Rome. She remembered, with a nostalgia that suggested she had been there long ago, not earlier today, Cassato dei Sopra, the bistro with the cheerful motherly owner dressed in a nylon housecoat, flat mules on her feet, her hair permed into a Marge Simpson frizz, her broad face. The parades of singing boys and men, the small-town gigolo, Rinaldo. The small-town crimes. Diminished, she immediately set foot on the Lungetevere Sangallo, walked along the Via Julia, which resembled the narrow medieval Sienese streets in its darkness, its narrowness, but was so much longer, just as the great porticos that turned their nailed and barricaded façades to the street were so much bigger. Behind them lurked, could lurk, palazzos, great villas. Isabel Archer's palazzo could have had such a gateway, concealing its vast elegant chambers, its exquisite, bitter secrets, from the passing throng. Outside one of these porticos a couple stood – a slight, dark-haired woman in a plain dark dress, a white-suited man. The woman smiled at Brenda, for some reason. One woman to another. Perhaps she recognised something, in her walk, in her face? Perhaps she wanted to reassure her, in her loneliness, alone on the dark stony street. The woman could have been a princess, if they still had them – there was an aristocratic turn to her chin, to the way she held herself, in the heavy gold jewellery that gleamed against her simple black dress. Brenda, empty now of all emotion, gave herself to idle wonder. Who were these people? What was their life? Where were they going?

A man and a woman, standing at a portico, waiting for a taxi. Smiling at passers-by. She could have stood at a door like this – or at least at the more public and ordinary door of the hotel – with Robert, openly waiting for a car to carry them to some dinner or party. In Rome she could have done that, but only because she was not Roman. In Dublin her life with him was the life of the subversive. They would never wait for a taxi together. They would never go to a party together. She had had with Robert her moments of greatest passion – the greatest passion her life had known. She had felt for him, he had felt for her, the deepest emotion possible for humankind. To reject that would have been madness. It would have been the greatest sin.

And still, she could not telephone Robert and talk to him. She could not go to the cinema with him or to a party. She could not find out, now, if he were dangerously ill, or faking, or if some other crisis had occurred. In her own crisis, she could not turn to him for help. He was the human being closest to her, in the world, but also the most out-of-bounds.

She wandered down from the river, her tourist map indicating that she was moving closer to the classical centre. A square opened before her, a vast square full of flower stalls, fruit stalls. All around the edges were the familiar tables, umbrellas, people eating and drinking. In the middle of the square were dancers, mime artists, portrait painters – a couple danced a tango, dressed in the vampish clothes of the twenties. A ballerina in a white tutu made pirouettes to the music of Tchaikovsky, her face a white, perfect mask framed in swan's-down. A magician, traditionally clad, with a handlebar moustache and a striped waistcoat, pulled doves from a black hat.

She clutched her new bag, paranoid now, conscious of too many people jostling her, aware that some of them were thieves. A histrionic place this was; an air of decadence, of mad pleasure-seeking, of frenetic gaiety, pervaded it. The quality of the sideshows was high – professional, slick. There was a pathos in watching such talent displaying itself in the marketplace. An air of the circus – poignant, wondrous – so much entertainment, in the warm dark air, the lights of the cafés shining, candles flickering on a thousand tables.

Bookshops. She walked into one, open now at nine or ten o'clock. There on a table lay her book, her name, the title translated, a new cover. It was the first thing that caught her eye when she walked in, although the cover was grey and black. She bought a copy and felt better, much better. A private pleasure, a private gratification. A comfort, a sop to her vanity, her deeply wounded vanity, or her pride.

Leaving the splendid gaiety of the square, she turned back into the narrow, deserted streets and followed one until she came to the

Palazzo Venezia, and, by a series of marble steps, to the Forum.

It was surrounded by a wire fence. Some sort of renovation work was being carried out, and the Forum lay deep in a bed of yellow clay, cranes and diggers and JCBS surrounding it like armed guards. But it was bathed in golden floodlights in the blue dark night. The great white columns rose from the rubble into the night, their familiar, ridged lines true and perfect. Perfetto.

For one delicious moment, she grasped with her mind and with her heart and with her blood the meaning of the word 'classic'. She felt the mysterious spread of centuries as they stretched beneath her, a vast tapestry of times laid on a marble floor. She understood the beauty of good art enduring in the rubble of human history, enduring it, transcending it, dependent upon it.

Below her lay the Roman Forum. Above, the canopy of stars.

THE BANANA BOAT

We'd been on holiday for a week, in a summer cottage in west Kerry. The weather had been glorious. Every day the sun shone, blessing the landscape. I had been sunbathing on golden strands, swimming in clear blue water with views on each side of moss-green hills rolling into the ocean, or walking along lanes lined with flower-studded ditches – purple self-heal, blue sheep's bit, everywhere the brilliant yellow of dandelion and buttercup. The typical outdoor sound had been the buzzing of bees. It had been a honeyed landscape and a honeyed holiday.

Our two teenage boys had not been enjoying it much, however. John was sixteen now, and Ruan fourteen. John was only happy when on the golf course. He would play thirty-six holes, on his own, staying away from morning until dinner time, coming home pale and exhausted under his tan. He refused to play with Ruan, claiming that his game was not good enough. Ruan denied this but in fact he had other fish to fry: computer games. All day he would spend close to the television set, controlling a hand-held pad and watching cartoon figures jerk around the screen to the sound of a monotonous tune. We had a constant struggle to get him away from the games, to encourage him to spend some time outdoors. The struggle dominated the holiday. He did not want to go for a walk, he did not want to go for a swim. We, of course, had bought the machine that seemed to control his life, but we blamed him for his addiction. How could we have foreseen that it would lead to this?

One thing was clear: this would be one of our last holidays as a family. Next year they would probably refuse to come with us.

After a week the weather forecast promised a break. We would have a showery day. Usually when the RTÉ meteorologists forecast a showery day it meant heavy rain where we were, out on the southernmost tip of the Dingle Peninsula. Mists were always rolling in from the Atlantic, hitting the hills of our parish and falling on us as rain, even when the rest of the country enjoyed sunshine or at least sunny spells. I suggested we go on an outing to Tralee, where the weather is often better than it is out here and where there is a big swimming centre, with pools and slides and all kinds of amusements. The response was not exactly enthusiastic, but eventually both boys agreed to come.

The weather forecast was wrong: next day dawned bright and sunny, just the kind of day we had grown used to. The swallows were fluttering around, chirping, high above the meadow in front of our house, and the island lay in a pale blue sea like a basking whale, complacent and enormous.

'It's a good day for golf,' John said sleepily, turning in his untidy bed. 'Do we have to go?' Yes. We have to go.

John insisted that he wouldn't go for a swim. I thought he might change his mind when we got to Tralee, and packed his swimming togs along with everyone else's. We piled into the car, lightly dressed, and set off, me driving as usual. At some stage in the past ten years this had become normal, although when I had married I did not know how to drive and Niall did.

There is bickering in the back of the car. John continues to insist that he won't go for a swim, and Ruan retaliates by saying that he won't go if John doesn't. 'OK OK!' I say, since there is nothing else to say. But this begs the question of why we are going to Tralee at all.

'We can go to the heritage centre,' I say. 'You haven't been there, Ruan, have you?'

'I hate heritage centres,' he says.

'It's got a little train that takes you on a trip through history,' I continue. 'Tralee through the ages.'

'For fuck's sake he's fourteen years old,' says John.

'Must you use that word?' Niall sighs deeply and switches on the radio.

Veteran of family holidays, I just switch off my ears and concentrate on the road.

I love driving along the narrow roads, with the fuschia branches dripping onto the sides of the car. There is a lovely, lustrous light falling on everything — hazy blue hills across Ventry Bay, olive green hills closer. It is so beautiful, in this sunshine, that you could hardly believe it was real. It surprises me, in a way, that the boys seem so uninfluenced by the surroundings. But as far as one could tell nature has absolutely no effect on their moods. If anything, it annoys them. They don't seem to see scenery in the way I do. So what are they seeing, as they stare out the windows, scowling?

'Did you turn off the oven?' Niall asks.

'Yes,' I say confidently. But of course how can I be sure? 'I think so anyway.'

Why should he ask? I remember then that two years ago we left the house — the same house — and came back two hours later to find the kitchen filled with thick black smoke and the oven on the point of bursting into flames. We managed to put it out and since then a new cooker has been installed.

'I don't think it would matter anyway,' I say. 'This one wouldn't go on fire even if it were left on. That old oven was filthy and covered with grease. Plus it always overheated — the thermostat didn't work.'

I believe this and I have absolutely no reason to suspect that I have left on the cooker or the oven. I'd been washing up — we have an optimistically planned washing-up roster and today is my day — and had been close to the oven for long after we'd finished cooking Ruan's breakfast fry. Still, the question makes me uneasy. And it opens up uneasinesses that are never far from my mind.

The holiday has been working fairly well, so far, but nevertheless I have often been assailed by worries. Niall believes this happens because I am a compulsive worrier, but I believe it happens because there is plenty to worry about. I worry about my job, back in

Dublin. I worry about what is going on in my absence, things I have forgotten to do, things I have done — this always happens on holidays, especially on holidays in Ireland where there is not enough going on to blot out the memories of work. The details of the worries vary from time to time but the anxiety remains the same. I worry about money, pensions, the future. I worry about my elderly mother. I worry about Niall, who is also elderly, or getting there, older than me. That he could become ill, that he could die, is always an idea conducive to a good old worry.

Sometimes I think that this must be the root of all the worries, and is the reason why I cannot be quite at peace. We are having a wonderful life together, just as we are having a wonderful holiday (when we forget that the boys are hating every minute of it). But I am somehow conscious of the threat of mortality putting an end to it all. Death hovers somewhere around, lurking in the corners like the mists that are always somewhere out there on the Atlantic, sweeping towards us on the wind. Maybe it is because of this that I am always afraid that the rug of my joy can be pulled from under me, that the whole delicate edifice of my domestic happiness will suddenly disappear. The structure of our secure, contented life seems to be held together by some magical charm. But I worry that at any moment that charm may lose its subtle, intangible power.

Maybe that is it. Or maybe it's much simpler. That I'm premenstrual, or premenopausal. I'm never quite sure if my worries are rational, or simply the result of some physical imbalance. Mind, body, reality: worries are thoughts but they are not like plain, unemotional thoughts. Emotional thoughts, they can have their origins in various places, or in more than one simultaneously. Stop worrying, men say. Niall says. The boys even say this. Nothing is going to happen. Everything is going to be all right. They do not believe in God, but they believe in the steadfastness of the spell that protects ordinary lives, whereas I believe in nothing. Or perhaps it is not that, but that as males they are naturally brave, naturally carefree, naturally insouciant. 'You have nothing to fear but fear itself' is one of Niall's mantras. 'The coward dies a thousand times, the brave man once' is another. These sayings always encourage me for a while, and then they lose their power.

Niall wants to buy a table for the bedroom, so that he or I can sit there, at the window, and write, while the children watch television in the living room. As we drive down from the Connor Pass I suggest that we turn off at Castlegregory, where there is a furniture store. Once, years ago, we bought a little suite of Dutch furniture there, big chunky wooden armchairs with wide squat armrests, covered with dull purple velvet. The memory of that suite of furniture does not attract me to the store, but I know that Niall will jump at the chance to visit it. I guess that his desire for the worktable will outweigh even his innate dislike of digression and changes of plan. And I'm right.

'What a good idea,' he says cheerfully, smiling across the gearbox.

'What?' snaps Ruan from the back of the car, more alert than one might imagine. 'We're turning off at Castlegregory?'

'Maybe we could go for a swim there later?' I suggest wildly. 'We could rent out boats and things at that water sports centre.'

'But I don't want to rent out boats and things,' says Ruan, not unpredictably.

'Me neither!' John chimes in automatically. At this stage his grumpiness has become lukewarm. His dismay at the way the day is developing is so immense that even his normal supply of negative energy has diminished.

A certain amount of half-hearted, uninformed complaining about the articles for hire at Castlegregory water sports centre goes on in the back seat, as we drive along the flat road between small fields and gardens overflowing with flowers: nasturtiums, geraniums, roses, tumbling abundantly over lawns and fences, a horticultural counterpoint to the abundant wild flowers of the landscape. Before I have actually turned off the main road for the village of Castlegregory, however, Ruan has performed one of those miraculous U-turns of which he is still capable, at fourteen. He has decided that he might like to go for a swim at Castlegregory. Probably he remembers previous swims during previous summers – the water around here, in the flat sandy stretches of the Maharees, tends to be considerably warmer than on the other, more rugged side of the peninsula. Maybe that is what has caused his change of mind, or maybe it is something else that he has remembered, or spotted on the roadside. One never knows but is grateful for even the slightest co-operation.

The village of Castlegregory is pretty in the way of Dingle, with pastel stuccoed houses and plenty of windowboxes on its three narrow winding streets. But the hordes of tourists who swarm up and down the streets of Dingle are lacking here. Two women wearing shorts and T-shirts, bronzed to the colour of toffee, stroll along the footpath dangling plastic bags of shopping. Otherwise the village seems as deserted as an off-beat Italian hill village at midday. You might assume, if you did not know otherwise, that the natives were all taking a siesta or a long leisurely lunch, and that come four o'clock the village would buzz with life.

We see a pub, painted pink, with a lot of geraniums dangling outside and a sign saying 'Seafood. Pub Grub'. It's called the Natterjack Inn. Inside, it is pleasantly furnished with pine and súgán, and the menu looks right. Like the village the pub is deserted.

We sit in a large conservatory, open on two sides to let plenty of air in, and furnished in a higgledy-piggledy way with old wooden tables, benches, some comfortable straw-seated súgán chairs. There are flowers and potted plants dotted around it in an odd assortment of tubs and skillets and pots. In one corner is a pool table. The boys' eyes light up when they see it. They get some coins. The balls crash out. They are happy for a while.

There are crab claws on the menu and Niall and I order them, while for the boys there are chicken nuggets and chips. I get a glass of white wine and Niall a beer. We sit and sip these drinks, the sun shining through the perspex roof. We talk about the natterjack toad. The barman tells us that yes, Castlegregory is one of its few remaining habitats in Ireland. If you walk down the lane opposite the pub until you come to a lake, you can hear the toads and even see them sometimes, at eleven o'clock at night. The barman has often done this. We wonder if it is worth coming back at eleven o'clock some evening just to hear the croaking of an endangered toad. As I sip the wine and feel extraordinarily happy, I think that it probably is. But I do not make a plan, knowing I might be forced to stick to it if I do. Even in my mildly inebriated state, I am not optimistic enough to hope that John and Ruan will put the natterjack toad high on their list of holiday priorities.

When the crabs come they are great: the biggest crab claws we have ever seen. They taste quite good too. Not perfect, but, given the sunshine, the flowers, the happy chatter of the boys, the wine, I am more willing than usual to pretend that they are perfect. For the price, which is low, it is a fantastically good lunch. We sit and munch and sip, and I feel that this is what a holiday should be: a family enjoying lunch in a sunny conservatory, with a colony of natterjack toads within walking distance and the wine cool and good.

At night, Niall and I go for walks sometimes, just to escape from the noise of the television, which tends to fill the house. Last night we walked down to the graveyard, which was cleaned up by some youth employment scheme a year ago. We recalled that when we had last been in it the long grass had been treated with some weedkiller, which had turned it straw-coloured and had created an eerie effect: long drooping hay draped over stones and walls and everything, like a surrealist vision of Golgotha. Morbid grass.

This year, all that is gone. The grass has grown back, and already it is long – apparently the employment scheme does not extend to ongoing maintenance. The old sign outside warning that the ground is uneven and that the graveyard contains ruins is still there. We went inside and looked at the first, most elaborate grave, which is that of Tomás Ó Criomthain, the Islandman. *Ní bheidh ár leithéid arís ann*, his most-quoted sentence, is engraved on the headstone, which stands sturdy and tall against the backdrop of the island where he lived, whose inhabitants he was referring to. Our like will not be found again. In the quiet of the graveyard the words regain some of their meaning, which have been diluted by overuse outside (you hear this saying everywhere, you read it on T-shirts in Dingle; if there is one sentence every Irish speaker knows, it is this one). There in the graveyard, however, I accept the truth of what he said, looking at the other, older, more poignant graves. Seán Ó Dálaigh OS. Died 1944. He was a writer who used the pseudonym Common Noun. His son was Niall's best friend in the parish. We often went out on Sunday nights with him and his wife Peig. Both of them are now dead. Almost all the natives of this parish are dead, although not in these graves. The valley is full of houses, but mainly they are summer houses, populated by people like us from Dublin or Cork, from Germany or America. The houses are busy for a few weeks, a few months, of the year. The rest of the time, empty. There must be more empty houses in this valley than anywhere else in Ireland — and still the sign SITE FOR SALE is ubiquitous; still the builders are busy making new white houses, the well-drillers steadily boring into the rock for water.

The graveyard has been improved. You can walk through all of it now, which you usen't be able to do. We passed the Islandman's grave, and Common Noun's, and turned the corner at the back — it is a tiny graveyard, containing only about thirty stones. Down at the back the ground is uneven, and pocked with holes. I looked into one of these — morbidly, wondering if indeed I would see what one might expect to see. And yes, I did. There were some sticks that might have been bones. I stepped back and got a better view. Then I saw the skull, framed by a V-shaped bit of stone — not stone, wood, the V-shape being the surviving bit of coffin. Everything else had rotted away, apart from a little cowl to shelter the head. Even most of the bones of this skeleton's body seemed to have disintegrated, or to have mingled with the dust that once covered him or her — there was no headstone so we didn't find out who it was.

Close to this grave is the grave of Bride Liath, with its sad, sentimental lines: 'Is anseo a luíonn Bride Liath, an cailín is gleoite agus is deise a mhair riamh ar an saol seo' — *Here lies the most beautiful, virtuous girl that ever walked the path of life.* A famine victim. There is a story about her, burying her three little children and then her husband, one after the other. Then dying herself, of starvation.

After lunch Niall and I leave the boys playing pool and walk to the furniture store. It is farther away than we think, since previously we have driven there. We get a good look at the village of Castlegregory, and wonder again at its beauty and its neglect by the tourist industry, which is capricious, unjust, and in a way not very intelligent – unless it is that everyone wants to be where the crowd is, which could well be the case. When we eventually reach the shop a sign informs us that it is, surprisingly, closed on Fridays. Today is a Friday.

We decide, more or less by a mutual consent possible thanks to the pleasures of the Natterjack Inn, that we won't bother going to Tralee, but simply have a swim here and then go home. We drive out to the beach, one of the flat, sandy beaches of this area, backed by dunes and caravan parks. It always seems very lighthearted and gay to me, and indeed it is the sort of place where families with small children come for a beach holiday: the sky is wide and blue, cotton clouds floating around airily over the pale green rushes and marram grass and clipped grass of the caravan parks, and places to park the car.

'It's nice, isn't it?' I ask.

'Yes, if it weren't for that strange building down on the beach,' says Niall. 'What on earth is it?'

That's where we're going. It's the water sports centre. It's not a building, it's a collection of paddle boats and surfboards, water bicycles and banana boats, canoes and bodyboards – all the sort of thing that makes my heart sing, maybe because I longed for such playthings during a childhood of summer holidays but only read about them in children's books. These things look attractive to me, and to Ruan and John, but I suppose if you did not know what they were they would constitute a blot on the landscape, and look like some sort of exceptionally offensive fish farm.

We park and go down to the beach. The tide is in and there is only a narrow stretch of sand, with plenty of people already sitting on it – plenty by Irish standards, that is, where having the whole beach to yourself is not unusual. We find a place close to the rocks and settle in. John says, 'I might go for a swim later.' Niall reads the newspaper. Ruan puts on his togs – which this year consist of shorts and a T-shirt, and look exactly the same as what he wears all the time anyway – and says, 'Give me some money. I want to rent out a surf bike.' I am delighted that he is interested enough to do this. I give him a few pounds and he runs off. I am pleased that he is old enough to take care himself of the transaction involved – he can make the enquiries, do the hiring, go off surfing. All I have to do is provide the cash and take it easy.

I put on my own swimsuit, and think about getting in. John doesn't change his clothes, but sits and stares moodily out to sea. A so-called banana boat is taking half a dozen children on a ride. They sit astride a longish banana-shaped tube, and are pulled by a motorboat which goes increasingly fast. When the boat makes a sudden turn all the children fall off the banana into the water; we can hear their screams of joy or whatever, their laughs as they scramble out of the water and try to regain their seats on the banana.

Where is Ruan?

'There he is!' I say. The part of the beach where the windsurfing and water biking goes on is separated from the part where we are by a string of buoys and a sign saying 'NO PLEASURE CRAFT BEYOND THIS POINT'. It is not too far away but much too far to distinguish an individual's face or even clothing. There are lots of pleasure craft bobbing around there – thirty or forty at least, it seems, several with children on them, peddling or paddling or surfing. I am pretty sure I can distinguish Ruan, however. I can tell the shape of his body, or perhaps it is the way he holds himself: rather stiffly and determinedly, his back straight and his head down. He is making a beeline for the horizon, which also figures – he probably thinks he is a bit old, at fourteen, to mingle with the smaller children who cycle up and down by the shoreline. Actually the bay curves out in a semicircle so that even as you go out to sea the shoreline is not too far away – I discovered this when Ruan did the same thing, i.e. went out too far, a year or two ago. I ran along that semicircle shouting at him to come back in. I feel he is old enough now to take care of himself. Anyway, there are lots of paddle boats and surfers around where he is. After a while he turns and makes back for the shore and then he goes out again towards the mouth of the bay, and back again.

I sunbathe for a while and then, having observed an older man (older than me, I mean) swimming with obvious pleasure, I go down to the sea. There is a fringe of brown seaweed on the edge of the tide, and I realise that there is no hope of getting John to come in. That brown fringe will deter him, if nothing else does. He is unafraid to die, but he is squeamish about squelchy substances. I wade through the soft obnoxious stuff, thinking, as I always do when I walk in seaweed, of a working holiday I spent on the Frisian Islands when I was a student. They are situated in a shallow, sandy zone (Erskine Childers wrote his novel *The Riddle of the Sands* about that area – I think I should try and read that novel sometime) and people walk on the flats in their bare feet for the sake of their health. *Wattlaufen*, the activity was called – something like that. The theory is that the oils or the vitamins from the seaweed sink into the soles of your feet and do you good. I suppose the seaweed baths at Ballybunion – which I experienced last year – are based on the same idea. Anyway these reflections take me through the brown mess which certainly looks rather unattractive, and into the clear greenish water.

It feels colder than I remember it, not any warmer than the sea at Ventry or Smerwick, where I have been swimming recently. Maybe this is related somehow to the tide. But it is not painfully cold, and this is the test for me now. If my feet don't ache from the cold I know the water temperature is reasonable. I plunge in immediately, and start swimming. It still surprises me that I am doing this. All my life I have been one of those swimmers who waits for a long time, walking around and paddling the water with my hands, before getting down to it. I was like this as a child and continued until now, when I am forty-five. I remember being amazed at John who, when he still went for swims, ran in and started swimming straight away, not making even a break between his run down the beach and his first strokes in the water. In fact I can see him running down this beach and doing just that, as I sat on the towel at the rocks where I can see him now, reading the newspaper. Niall seems to have fallen asleep. He is hardly visible because he is wearing green trousers and a beige and brown shirt. Camouflage. They are his favourite colours. He always blends in easily with nature, and there he is now, no more obtrusive than a clump of grass or a bramble bush. John in his turquoise shirt is easier to spot.

I get accustomed to the water very quickly and as usual I have a wonderful swim. The broad bay is rimmed with mountains – greeny lilac mountains, Binn Os Gaoith, Cathair Chon Roí, the Sliabh Mis range. I remember a poet telling some story about Mis at a conference I attended earlier in the year. Mis, some goddess or poetess, some mythical creature, lived in those mountains. I couldn't remember the story. I didn't like the name Mis, either. It sounded sneaky, and perhaps sexual, it sounded like an Irish word for some soft, secret enclave of the female body. Soft seaweed.

The water is clear as glass. I swim along, looking through the water ripples at the rippled sand beneath. Ripple, lap, plash, paddle. Back and forth I go, looking up occasionally at the rim of mountains, at the umbrella of blue and white sky, looking in at my husband and son on the beach, looking over to Ruan, still peddling furiously in and out, in and out, peddling away all the anger of the holiday and his teenagerhood.

I stay in for about a quarter of an hour or twenty minutes, then plod through the seaweed and back to the towels. I spread one out and lie down to dry in the sun.

Some women have taken the next spot. I can hear them talking as I lie there. What I catch is the end of a recipe, cooked recently for some party or celebration.

'I did a bake,' the voice says. 'You know, courgettes and peppers and everything with breadcrumbs and cheese on top.'

'Mm, sounds lovely,' another voice says.

I wonder what they had with it. The conversation fragments. 'That green top you had on looks lovely on you,' I hear. There is some discussion as to which green top is meant. 'I went home and watched a video for three hours last night, until three o'clock in the morning.' I wonder where. Was it one of those caravans back up behind the beach? Or a rented house? Or a summer house, like ours? 'That fellow from ER was in it.' George Clooney? John Carter, my favourite, young and noble-looking, standoffish?

There is a summer house on the coast visible from the window of our summer house. Even now if I stretch a little I can see it. Grey walls with a touch of blue – the woodwork, a lovely faded blue, the blue of the summer house in the garden in *A Passage to India*. A slated roof, sloping in four slopes over the house, rather than the usual two back and front. Hip-roofed, that is the term. It is a beautifully proportioned house, perching, as it seems, right on the edge of the coast, with nothing behind it but the sound and the hunk of the island. There are no other houses on that side of the road. You can't get planning permission to build there. But the bungalow – it is always called 'the bungalow', as the island is always called 'the island' – was built before that rule came in, perhaps before there was any such thing as planning legislation. It was the first summer house in the valley, which is now chock-a-block with them. Built in the twenties or the thirties, it is a reminder of more gracious times.

But although it looks perfect from a distance of about half a mile, the bungalow is really a ruin. The roof is beginning to cave in, every window is broken. Nobody has stayed in it for forty years.

Once it rang with laughter. Or quarrels. Or songs. Niall remembers visiting there in the 1950s on his first trip to the valley. He remembers a little girl – she now lives in America, and owns her own summer house in this valley – reciting 'The Owl and the Pussycat' in the middle of the kitchen. He remembers helping a local farmer to tie straw on to the seat of a chair, helping him to pull the rope taut. He thinks the house was beautiful inside, simple and rustic, with lots of books. It belonged to a professor of Irish and Greek, and his family and extended family spent long summers there long ago.

It is the oldest summer house. But it did not survive beyond a single generation – a long generation, it is true. Is this the fate of summer houses? People build their own, bring their children, come faithfully to their house for forty or fifty years – ours is already thirty years old. And what then?

The people of Long Island or Martha's Vineyard, of the Frisian Islands, of the Swedish archipelagos, could probably tell us. They have had a summer-house culture for hundreds of years. But I don't know. There is only one old summer house in our valley, and there it stands, a gracious ruin.

I look over at the pleasureboat enclosure. We've been here for about an hour. It's half past four. Niall stirs and asks if we will go home soon.

I look over at the boats. At first I can't see Ruan. Then I catch sight of him. He is moving out again. He seems to be cycling faster than previously and soon he is going out farther than he went before as well. He passes the last of the big paddle boats, and is out among the wind surfers. Then he passes them. He is beyond the mouth of the bay, well past the curve of the beach. He is out, alone in the sea, on his surf bike, still moving quite quickly.

'Look at him, he's heading for Tralee!' I say, a bit anxiously. I can see Fenit far away, miles across the water.

'Stupid eejit,' says John.

'Do you think he's all right?' I ask Niall. Niall can't see him at all. 'Of course he's all right,' he says. 'But it's time he came back. I want to go home.'

I keep my eye on Ruan – on what I think is Ruan. He gets smaller and smaller. Then he disappears – the banana boat is moored out there, about a kilometre out, a speck from here, and he seems to be behind that.

I give in to my anxiety and run to the lifeguard who is sitting in front of a hut close by.

'I think my child has got carried out to sea,' I shout at him. He seems unalarmed. But he asks me if I see him and I show him what

I think is Ruan – a far-off speck in the bay. It could be just an empty boat, or a lifebuoy, or any of the many objects that are bobbing about on the water. He looks through his binoculars and says, 'He's on the banana boat. You should go to Johnnie over there' – he indicates the sports centre hut – 'and ask him to do something. He could send out a boat.'

I run along the beach, passing the families sunning themselves, making sand castles, picnicking. When I get to Johnnie's I am quite alarmed. But the woman there is calm. 'There's a strong offshore,' she says. I am impressed by the professional abbreviation. 'Don't worry. The boat has already gone out to pick him up. There's a few of them out there. The offshore takes them out on days like this but we keep an eye on them.'

I see a small orange dinghy out at the banana boat. It takes a long time to do whatever it is doing – utterly invisible from where I am. But I feel relieved. Everything is being taken care of.

'What's his name?' the girl asks – she is a cheerful, competent-looking young woman with a kind face, and a mobile phone.

'Ruan,' I say. She repeats it and then asks someone on the phone if the boy in the boat is called Ruan.

'He's not?' I hear her saying.

I feel real fear then.

'What does he look like?' she asks me. I tell her. Blond. Blue eyes. Smallish. As I say these things I realise how useless they are as a description. The description could apply to almost every boy on this beach. What should I say. Nose a little flat and broad, like mine only smaller? Mischievous grin – no that wouldn't do. They all have that and he probably isn't grinning mischievously now anyway. Crooked teeth – I should get him to an orthodontist very soon.

If . . .

I realise right now that there are two ends to the story, two ends to the story of my day and the story of my life. I think of Mary Lavin's story about the widow's son, which I have recently seen told dramatically and well by a professional storyteller. In one version,

Packy is killed as he collides with a startled hen as he cycles home from school with the good news that he has won a scholarship (the equivalent of the lottery for bright children in those days. I remembered, even as I stood on the sunny beach wondering if my child were . . . all right, the day I got my own results from that scholarship exam). In the second version of the story, Packy is not killed but the hen is. Packy's mother nags him so much about the killing of that hen, which was her prize hen, or perhaps it was a prize cockerel, that he leaves home in anger and disgust a few weeks later and is never heard of again. The message of the story is that the loss you suffer through no fault of your own is much easier to bear than the one you bring about by your own actions.

But it's going to be more ambiguous than that.

I should perhaps have come over here with Ruan, booked his bike, warned him not to go out too far. I thought he was wise enough, at fourteen, to take care of himself. But I had misjudged him. I had misjudged the situation – the offshore wind, the vigilance of the water sports centre. I had misjudged everything.

'Where do you think he is?' the woman asks the man on the phone. I can see him nowhere. I think he is the boy on the banana boat, the boy who is now in the rescue boat. That is the boy I had my eye on, the stiff-backed, determined body that I think is my own body replicated, and also Niall's body. But if he is not Ruan, as they say, I have no idea where Ruan is. He could already be far out at sea. He could be at the bottom of the sea.

She talks to a young man who has suddenly appeared beside us. 'Tell him to find Ruan,' she is telling him urgently.

I am not shaking, I am suspended in a sort of jelly. The water is full of happy children and fathers (mostly it has to be said) paddling around, laughing and having a good time. The beach is golden, with its holiday-makers, its bronzed boys and girls, its bikini–clad mothers passing on recipes for vegetable bake, its toddlers making sand castles. Normal life. And I am part of it still, but only just. I am on the edge of a cliff. In a minute I could tumble off and fall into another kind of life altogether. A life of pain and tragedy. Loss and mourning.

Funeral arrangements. If . . . The long aftermath of life without Ruan. Unimaginable.

It happens.

On Friday a girl was drowned in a swimming pool in France. An Irish girl I mean. Aged fourteen.

Yesterday a man was drowned in Bray, near where we live in Dublin. On our beach in Dublin.

Peig Sayers lost several sons to the sea. Everyone on the island did. A commonplace tragedy then, not so commonplace now but it happens. It happens all the time.

One moment a family is cocooned in the happiness of normal life. The next it is elsewhere, in another land or another ocean. It happens in a few moments.

Those are the few moments I am in, the liminal time between ordinariness and tragedy (also of an ordinary kind; to others it will be so, ordinary and instantly forgettable. While for me it will be *the* tragedy – the raw edge of the unimaginably terrible. Parents never get over it. I have seen it. I have heard it. I know it).

'So who have you in the boat?' The young man is on the mobile phone. 'Well ask him, John. Ask him for Christ's sake. Ruan. Ruan. Ask him to tell you his name.'

There is a pause. In that pause I see in my mind's eye the small stiff determined figure making his way to the banana boat. In that second.

'His name is Ruan,' the young man exclaims. 'You gobshite, John!'

The young man turns to me. 'You're all right. He's in the boat. You should have called him some ordinary name like John or Michael for Christ's sake!'

I laugh and make a joke. I touch the young man's arm in gratitude (he doesn't like this; we are both practically naked but I hardly care).

I wait for a long time. What seems like a long time. Fifteen, twenty minutes, before the rescue boat comes to the shore. Ruan scrambles out, pale and cold-looking, and swims in the last bit of the way over the fringe of brown seaweed to the beach, which is stony down here and now looks sharp and sordid to me, with its rows of plastic machines, its pleasurecraft.

★ ★ ★

There is another story on my mind as I drive home. 'Miles City, Montana'. Alice Munro. A story about a near-drowning. The narrator's daughter Meg has a close shave in a swimming pool. She is rescued because her mother has an intuition as she walks towards a concession stand (what is a concession stand? some sort of kiosk, I suppose) to get cool drinks. '*Where are the children?*' flashes through her mind. Back she runs, just in time. Is it intuition or just a mother's natural, normal anxiety?

I think the point of the story is that a child who is looked after in the normal way, by parents who are protective, and normally anxious, tends to be safe and survive, while a child who is neglected . . . There is another, remembered boy in the tale, a boy who drowns. I could remember the description of his retrieved body, grotesque, with green weed in his nostrils. Usually in Kerry bodies are not retrieved, but perhaps that is not the case right here, Tralee Bay. It's more sheltered than the broad rough heartless ocean that stretches in front of our house, that beats eternally against the rocky shores of our parish. It's about that, as well as about the power of a mother's intuition.

I had no intuition. Just anxiety. I saw him. I saw him moving faster. I saw him being swept out. I admired him too, for getting off the bike and on to the banana boat, which was moored and big. The banana boat was exactly the right thing to head for. Of course I knew it was him, I recognised the way he carried his body. I recognised the way he cycled on a water cycle, as you know someone's way of walking. That's not intuition. It's familiarity. A mother's familiarity – Niall and John apparently did not recognise this at all. I knew it was Ruan, on the banana boat, in the rescue boat. Even as I was terrified to death, even when the friendly young woman's voice revealed alarm and said Ruan was not in the boat, but some other boy, I had a suspicion, in a deeply rational part of my mind, that the distant speck had the familiar shape of Ruan. The bits of the jigsaw that I had seen told me it was so.

He would have been saved anyway. The boat was on the way out before I reported the thing to the water sports centre. He was never in real danger.

That's what he said himself. In fact he insisted he was in no danger at all, that he had deliberately cycled out to the banana boat because he wanted to sit on it, that he could easily have cycled back. So why did he come back in the rescue boat? He had two answers to this. One was that the man in the boat offered him a lift. The other was that his 'go was up' (the bike was rented for an hour) and that the man wanted it back.

So maybe the man in the boat was a good psychologist? He was casual about the whole trauma, making little of it, to protect the macho feelings of the teenage boy. To protect his own feelings, as a businessman and owner of a water sports centre, competing with a strong offshore wind.

Ruan refused to talk at all about his experience, and was unusually cross and angry as we drove home.

Along the flat sunny roads of the plain, up to the alpine drama of the Connor Pass, down again to Dingle, and home. Home.

As we went along by Ventry Bay, I remembered the day we had found the kitchen full of smoke. Accidents. We could go back now and the house could be burnt to the ground, if I had in fact left the oven on – and I could have. I am increasingly absent-minded. I thought it unlikely that this would be the case. Just as I had, when the girl said 'It's not Ruan in the boat?', known that it was Ruan, because I knew that speck on the banana boat was a speck I recognised. Ruan. I felt that we still belonged to the lucky section of humanity that does not fall over the edge, usually. We still belonged to the charmed circle that may get an occasional premonition of disaster but does not actually experience it head-on.

And sure enough as we turn into the long grass of our field it's clear that the oven was not left on. The house is still standing at the end of its field, waiting for us to open the door and sleep there.

We are still safe. Alive and safe. We still belong to real life, the life that is uneventful, the life that does not get described in newspapers or even, now that the days of literary realism are coming to an end, in books. The protected ordinary uneventful life, which is the basis of civilisation and happiness and everything that is good: the desirable life. We still belong to the part of life that is protected from danger, by its own caution, by its own love, by its own rules, by its own belief in its own invulnerability. Usually.

But how reliable is that 'usually'? In a minute it can be swept away, on a freak wave, on an offshore wind, by a fast car or a momentary lapse of concentration. It is precarious and delicate, our dull and ordinary happiness, seeming sturdy as a well-built house but as fluttering and light as a butterfly on a waving clump of clover. As ephemeral as that; as beautiful and priceless.

Ruan's close shave happened on 16 July 1999. I thought about the event and wrote these thoughts down late that night and then fell asleep beside my husband in the wood-panelled bedroom we have shared, on holidays, for twenty years. In Fairfield, New Jersey, John Kennedy Junior, his wife and her sister were just taking off into the sunset in their Piper Saratoga 11 HP, on their way to a family wedding in Martha's Vineyard — the famous holiday resort five thousand miles from Dingle on the opposite shore of the Atlantic. An aviation expert, Mr Serge Roche, some days later described the Saratoga Piper as 'reliable'. By then, the newspapers were full of speculation about what had happened, and why John Kennedy Junior, his wife and her sister were at the bottom of the ocean.